"STRICTL...

Stacy, lost to ev... ...but
known it, he... ...
formidable tempers, raged at him. "You *can* speak
strictly, then? I had thought insolence was more
your line. But pray, continue," she added,
poisonously sweet, as she saw him open his
mouth. To explain, presumably. But what
explanation could mend this?

She no longer wanted her bed. She wanted to see
m'lord whoever-he-was groveling before her.
Nothing less would do.

Paula Marshall began her career in a large library and ended it as a senior academic in charge of history in a polytechnic institute. She has traveled widely, been a swimming coach, and appeared on *University Challenge* and *Mastermind*. She has always wanted to write, and likes her novels to be full of adventure and humor. She is married and the mother of three children.

DEAR LADY DISDAIN
PAULA MARSHALL

TORONTO • NEW YORK • LONDON
AMSTERDAM • PARIS • SYDNEY • HAMBURG
STOCKHOLM • ATHENS • TOKYO • MILAN • MADRID
PRAGUE • WARSAW • BUDAPEST • AUCKLAND

ISBN 0-373-51115-9

DEAR LADY DISDAIN

Visit us at www.eHarlequin.com

Printed in U.S.A.

Chapter One

'What! my dear Lady Disdain, are you yet living?'
Shakespeare

'So, Lord Axforde didn't suit?'

Miss Louisa Landen's question came out idly as she applied herself diligently to her canvaswork. It seemed almost to be an afterthought.

But was it? Stacy Blanchard, seated at her desk in the main office of Blanchard's Bank, situated in the heart of London's financial centre, raised her dark head suspiciously.

'Was that a question, Louisa—or a statement?'

'Whichever you please, my dear,' Louisa returned placidly, without taking her eyes from the peacock she was stitching. 'I must say that I wasn't surprised that you refused him—you have refused all offers made to you so far—but...' And she stopped, apparently lost in confusion over the important question as to whether the wool she now required was light or dark blue.

Stacy wrote down the date, October 24th, 1818, before

flinging down her quill pen, fortunately now empty of ink. 'But what, Louisa? Lately you seem to have developed the most distressing habit of not finishing your sentences.'

Louisa looked over the top of her work at her one-time pupil, now a handsome woman in her late twenties. Not pretty, or even conventionally beautiful perhaps, but something better. She possessed the oval ivory face of the Blanchards, their brilliant green eyes, and their dark, lightly curling hair, even if the curls were severely drawn back into a large knot at the nape of her neck—which merely served to enhance the pure lines of a classic profile.

'But, my dear, Lord Axforde is, after all, such a tulip of fashion, seems to possess a considerable understanding, and is so rich in his own right that one could hardly claim that he was marrying you merely to get at the wealth of Blanchard's Bank. All in all you could scarcely do better. A handsome, reasonably clever man, and a marchioness's coronet—what more could you ask?'

It was no more—and no less—than the answer Stacy had expected. Louisa had, indeed, made something of a litany of lamentation of it, repeating it, with variations, over Stacy's last six offers—except the one made by Beverley Fancourt, of course. Now *he* really had been an open fortune-hunter.

Louisa might be her oldest, indeed, if truth were told, her only friend, but that didn't give her the licence to choose Stacy's husband for her. She was perfectly capable of doing that for herself—if she wanted a husband, that was. She rose from the desk and crossed the beautiful room, more like a great house's salon than an office, a room which her late father had created and which she had left unchanged.

She stopped before the window to pull back deep green velvet curtains, the colour of the dress which she wore, and to stare at the dome of St Paul's, before saying a trifle satirically, 'Really, Louisa, really? D'you know I gained the distinct impression from the manner of Lord Axforde's proposal that it was to the Bank he was making it, and not to me as a woman?' She gave a short laugh, and continued to inspect St Paul's as though she had never seen it before.

'Do not exaggerate, my dear.' Louisa's reply was coolly judicious. 'I told you not to do that as long ago as the nursery. I am sure that Lord Axforde said everything that was proper.'

Stacy's lips thinned, and, unseen by Louisa, her fists clenched. 'Oh, quite proper, I assure you. A regular commercial transaction was taking place—no doubt about it. Why, I half expected that he would ask me whether the Bank's interest rate would continue to remain high if we married!' She shook her head at Louisa's pained expression. 'Worse, from his expression—that of a man taking medicine—I thought that he was prepared to pay any price to get at Blanchard's money to buy himself a dukedom— even if that price included marrying someone as undesirable as myself!'

'Oh, come!' Miss Landen at last looked up from her stitchery. 'You do not do yourself justice, my dear. You misunderstood him, I am sure. Few prospective brides are as handsome and as *comme il faut* as you are.'

'And few lack as much pedigree as I do,' retorted Stacy briskly, returning to her desk and sitting down again. The desk was another of her father's innovations; previously the office had been furnished with an old-fashioned lectern at which one stood.

She looked across at a row of oil-paintings on the opposite wall. The older ones were hack-work, done by travelling colourmen for a few shillings; the last two were fine things, one by a pupil of Gainsborough and the other by Romney.

'My great-grandfather began life as a Huguenot pedlar who turned himself into a prosperous back-alley moneylender.' She waved her hand at the oldest painting. 'My grandfather built up the business until he was able to found Blanchard's Bank, and my father transformed it into the richest bank in England.' Now she waved at the Romney. 'His father sent him to Harrow, and he had the manners and tastes of a gentleman and married a lady of aristocratic birth, but that does not make us gentry. And they do not really accept us, however much they and the nobility fawn on Blanchard's—when they need the Bank to lend them money to carry on their gambling and their follies.'

Opening a large red and gold ledger which stood on her desk, she said almost savagely, 'Would you like me to read to you the loans we have made to the flowers of English society—and tell you how many have reneged on them? No, I am merely the cit's daughter, who has the bad taste to behave as a young man might, and run Blanchard's—successfully, too.'

She closed the ledger again. 'Do you know what he said to me, Louisa, in the middle of his pretence of loving and admiring me? That he expected that once we were married I would give up the foolishness of running the Bank and put in a manager to do it for me, so that I could give my mind to being a wife fit for a person of his station.'

Miss Landen stitched for a moment in silence, before replying, 'Most husbands would expect you to do that, my dear.'

'Yes, I know that, Louisa, and that is why I promise never to marry. Father didn't train me to run Blanchard's in order to stop doing so once some handsome popinjay decides that he might like my money while consigning me permanently to the nursery or to talk nonsense to fine ladies.'

Louisa sighed, before saying gently, holding up her work to inspect it the better, 'I thought you told me not long ago that you would like to have children of your own, my dear. You are leaving it rather late to marry—you are already twenty-eight years old—and husbands do not grow on trees.' And she gave her one-time charge a sideways look.

So even Louisa was full of sententious piff-paff, it seemed, and she, Stacy, was condemned to live in a childless desert because in order to have children one must first have a husband. How much better if one were a plant, fertilised at a distance by a passing bee—with no idea where the pollen came from!

This ridiculous notion was enough to restore her good humour and bring a wry smile to her face. It was the kind of nonsensical idea which she could never share with kind Louisa but which would have amused her father. Tears pricked at the back of her eyes. Hardly a day passed but she missed him—her father, her tutor, her mentor, her friend, the parent with whom, improbably, she had shared her jokes.

It occurred to her that it was too long since she had made one, or heard one, and meantime Louisa deserved an answer. But she would not like it.

'Oh,' she said, the hint of unexpected laughter in her voice bringing Louisa's head up, 'never fear, my love. When one is as rich as the heiress who owns Blanchard's Bank, husbands forsake the trees and spring out of the ground! There will be no shortage of offers for the richest prize in England! The shortage lies, Louisa, in men whom I might wish to accept. And that is enough of that. I have work to do.' And she opened another ledger and began to write as briskly as she had spoken.

If Miss Landen was thinking sadly that her one-time charge was such a strong woman, both mentally and morally, that it would need a man of equal strength to contain and perhaps tame her, she did not say so. It was all her stupid father's fault, she thought ruefully as she watched Stacy's quill drive across the paper, bringing her up as he had done.

It had been the failure of Louis Blanchard's wife to give

him boy children who could survive birth which had done the damage. He had married Lady Rachel Beauchamp, of a poor and noble family, and he had loved her in his aloof fashion, but constant childbearing and miscarriages had made her sickly and ailing.

It had been a miracle that she had carried her one girl child to term—another miracle that the child had been born large and healthy—but the birth had killed her mother, and left her father, for a time, resentful of the child who had taken his wife from him.

And then, as she grew up, her bright intelligence had begun to impress him. The child was christened Anastasia, but he had early shortened her name to Stacy, not Anna, because Stacy sounded more like the boy he had wanted to continue the Blanchard dynasty. Louisa remembered the first time she had met Louis Blanchard and Stacy.

'I'm not hiring you as a governess,' he had told her bluntly in the rich study of his home in Piccadilly. 'I want her to have the manners and appearance of a fine lady, even if she has the brains and mental accomplishment of a clever man. I have hired male tutors to educate her. Why,' he boasted proudly, 'she can calculate a percentage and draw up a bill better than any of my clerks, and she still but a child.'

Louisa had risen from her chair, said severely, 'I do not wish to undertake this task, Mr Blanchard. You are doing the poor child no favour and I ought not to abet you.'

He had given her the smile which transformed his hard face, and which immediately won him Louisa Landen's heart.

'And that is exactly why I am hiring you,' he had told her warmly, 'to keep her still a woman, and a modest one, for all her accomplishments.' He had seen Louisa hesitate. 'I will send for her,' he had said, and had rung the bell, 'and you may see that I am not asking you to care for a hoyden or a female pedant.'

What Louisa had seen when a lady's maid brought Stacy in was a shy, dark little girl, the image of her handsome father, who, for all her shyness, was thoroughly in command of herself, and who took one look at Louisa Landen and thoroughly approved of what she saw.

'My dear,' her father had told her, as coolly as though he were addressing an equal, 'this is Miss Louisa Landen, who I hope will agree to become your companion and teach you the conduct and etiquette of a lady.'

Stacey had looked at the ladylike figure before her, and had seen through Miss Landen's modest exterior to the kind heart beneath it. She had made a short bow and said in a pretty voice, quite unlike anything which Miss Landen might have expected of the child prodigy whom her father had described, 'Oh, I do so hope, Miss Landen, that you will become my companion. I really do need someone to talk to and tell me exactly how a young lady should behave.'

Such composure in a ten-year-old Miss Landen had not met in her long career as a governess. She had bowed in her turn and murmured gently, 'And I shall be pleased to do just that, my dear,' and had begun her long association with Stacy and Louis Blanchard.

And if she had fallen a little in love with Louis Blanchard on the way, no one was ever to know. Occasionally she had remonstrated with him over his daughter's odd education, telling him in no uncertain terms that it was quite improper and that he was doing her no favour by insisting on it.

He had smiled at her and announced, 'I am not here to do her favours. I am here to secure for Blanchard's someone of that name who can run it when I am gone, and if that someone is a woman, then I must make do with what the Creator of us all has sent me!'

And that had been that. Louisa had never raised the matter again and here was the end of it, Louis Blanchard having died suddenly at a comparatively early age, leaving Stacy, still unmarried, to run the Bank, and waiting now for her right-hand man Ephraim Blount to come in to discuss the day's news and doings with her.

It grew increasingly likely, was Louisa's last sad thought, that Stacy would never marry now, and her unlikely situation was the cause of it!

Stacy didn't feel sad, however, and the arrival of Ephraim Blount, carrying a pile of papers and demanding some immediate decisions, served to invigorate rather than depress her.

He bowed to her, before he stood and presented each problem to her—he never consented to sit by her while they worked together, for Ephraim, although only in early middle age, was a man of the old school. Everything must be done exactly so, as Louis Blanchard had taught him, which was sometimes a disadvantage rather than an advantage, as Stacy had often found. Imagination was not his strong suit. He was often mournfully depressed, rather than happy, when some of her wilder innovations proved to be fruitful. 'So daring for a young woman,' he was given to murmuring to his own assistant, the young Thomas Telfer, who worshipped Stacy from afar, 'but I have to admit that up to the present Miss Blanchard's judgement has never let herself, or the Bank, down.'

Prim, starched, his thinning yellow hair brushed stiffly over his forehead, he was the perfect right-hand man. Now he was saying, his voice melancholy, as though announcing a death, 'Things are not going well at the York house, madam. All seems to be at sixes and sevens since Poxon was appointed. I fear that he is not up to snuff. Something needs to be done, or Blanchard's reputation will suffer. May I suggest that, given your agreement, of course, I myself go there to try to put matters straight?'

Stacy propped her chin in both hands—a gesture of her father's which always brought that formidable thruster to

Ephraim's mind. She looked steadily past him at the opposite wall, to where, before the blazing fire, Louisa was now gently sleeping. She no longer took her chaperonage of Stacy, when the latter was entertaining the Bank's employees—all male—seriously.

'D'you know, Ephraim, I have my doubts about the wisdom of that? I think that one of the things which may be wrong at York is that no Blanchard has visited there since my father died. I wish to remedy that. My aunt and uncle Beauchamp have asked me to spend Christmas with them at Bramham Castle, which is only a few miles from York. We have not met since Father's death, and to agree to their wishes would mean that I could combine business with pleasure—and leave you here in sole charge. You would like that, I think.'

If such a dry stick could be said to glow, Ephraim glowed. Stacy noted with amusement that he thought it politic to demur.

'Are you sure, madam? Think of the time of year. To travel to Yorkshire in mid-winter—is it wise?'

'Before the snows, I think,' Stacy murmured gravely. 'It is what my father would have done, I am sure.'

She had struck exactly the right note. Louis Blanchard had been Ephraim's god, and he bowed down before his very name. 'Oh, indeed, madam, yes, madam. Of all things the most suitable. You will take one of our senior clerks with you, I trust, to act as a secretary and aide?'

'Greaves, I thought,' murmured Stacy, happy to have got her own way so easily, 'unless you have any objections?'

'None at all, madam. The very man.' He was trying to contain his pleasure at the prospect of taking sole charge of Blanchard's for at least two months—something which he had longed to do since his late master's death. 'I will write at once and set all in train.' And he bustled importantly out of the room.

Stacy lay back in her chair and contemplated the prospect

of a few weeks' freedom from the daily grind of running Blanchard's. Lately she had begun to feel strangely restless, rewarding though her work was, and the power that came with it. A change of scene, the challenge of putting York straight would renew her spirits, she was sure. All that remained was to waken Louisa up and shock her with the news.

'God rest you merry, gentlemen,' she hummed to herself. Perhaps I may hear the waits singing in the northern snows, she thought, and perhaps...perhaps... I might meet someone more interesting, more to my taste, than Lord Axforde and his not so merry gentlemen-friends!

She walked across the room and bent to kiss Louisa gently on the cheek. She was sure that after her first shock was over Louisa would approve of what she was about to do—and would start to wonder what handsome and eligible young men, of whom her charge might approve, lived in and around York!

'Damn my father,' said Matthew Falconer violently to the lawyer who had been speaking of his parent's wish to be reconciled with his long-estranged son. 'I haven't crossed the Atlantic in order to please him—simply to end my associations here by disposing of all that I own, including this estate which my great-aunt has thought fit to leave me.'

'But, m'lord—' the lawyer began, in a feeble attempt to pacify the massive man who stood opposite him. Matthew Falconer was over six feet tall, and gave the appearance of being nearly as broad. His harshly handsome face, leonine beneath tawny hair, with matching golden eyes, bore the marks of his having worked in the open. His hands, Lawyer Grimes had already noticed, were those of a man who did much physical work with them. His nails were cut short, and there were calluses on his long fingers and on his palms. He was dressed like a farmer—plainly—with nothing of the man of fashion he had once been remaining to hint of his lineage, or of his newly acquired title.

Which he didn't want. He hadn't come to England to be called by his detested brother's name. He interrupted Grimes to say, 'I will not be addressed as Lord Radley— nor will you call me m'lord or sir,' he added as he saw the lawyer's mouth shaping to say it. 'You will address me as Matthew, Matt, Mr Falconer, or Falconer, as you please, or earn my instant displeasure.'

He saw Grimes close his eyes before he replied in a long-suffering voice, 'I will do as you ask, Mr Falconer, but that does not make you less the Viscount Radley, your father, the Earl Falconer's heir, now that your older brother has died so prematurely.'

The man standing by the window, staring sardonically at both Matt Falconer and the lawyer, gave a rolling chuckle before saying in a thick American accent, 'Y'all better learn soon, Mr Lawyer, sir, that what Matt Falconer wants Matt Falconer usually gets. That so, Matt?'

Matt noted with grim amusement the lawyer's wince away from them both, particularly from Jeb Priestly, who, in his determinedly Yankee garb of black and yellow checked trousers, tight at the knee, flaring at the ankle, his black frock-coat extravagantly cut, and his battered black top hat, which he had refused to remove in defiance of all English custom, stood for everything which Benjamin Grimes deplored. A mannerless rebel come to mock his late masters.

Worse, Matthew Falconer was allowing this creature, who was merely his valet-cum-secretary-cum-man-of-all-work, to address him as familiarly as though they were both of the same rank, and made no effort to check his rudeness to Grimes himself.

'I say again, Mr Falconer, before we even begin to dispose of your late great-aunt, Lady Emily Falconer's estate in Yorkshire, that you ought to consider the olive-branch which your father is holding out to you. You are, after all, his only remaining son…'

Matt found all this boring beyond belief. 'Why, sir, do you persist in telling me things I know? I am well aware of my position *vis-à-vis* both my father and Lady Emily. So far as the Earl is concerned you may tell him, with my compliments, *timeo Danaos et dona ferentis*. I am sure that he will know what I mean.' This last came out in a mocking drawl reminiscent of the young rattle-pate about town he had once been, so different from the large and sombre man he now was. He could see the lawyer registering shock again.

Priestley saw fit to put his oar in once more. 'Well, your pa might know what you mean by that gibberish, Matt, but, sure God, I don't. Try translating it into good American, would you?'

Matt knew that Priestley was, in his words, twisting the lawyer's tail. Uncouth he might look and sound, but his knowledge of the Classics equalled Matt's own, he being an alumnus of Harvard. Nevertheless, Matt decided to join in Jeb's game.

'It translates, Jeb, being said by a Trojan with whom the Greeks were fighting, into, "I fear the Greeks even when they bring gifts", or, in other words, It is dangerous to accept presents from an enemy.'

'Tro-jans,' drawled Priestley. 'An' which are you, Matt?'

'A Trojan, of course,' smiled Matt, 'ever since I was born to be my father's curse. Isn't that right, Mr Grimes? How many ultimatums had you the honour to face me with until the final one before I left England? No, don't answer; it would tax your memory to recall them all.'

Grimes' face flamed scarlet. He looked away at the shelves of law books on the wall behind his desk, and said in a low voice, 'I suppose it is useless to tell you how much I regretted m'lord's treatment of you, Mr Falconer, but I must also tell you that your father is a broken old man…'

'Only that, I suppose,' returned Matt, his eyes wicked, 'could bring him to wish to see me again—and Rollo's death, of course. That must have been the final facer.'

'You are pleased to be heartless...'

'My father cut my heart out long ago,' returned Matt carelessly. He was suddenly regretful of his baiting of the old man who had been the scourge of his childhood, youth and young manhood, until he had finally left England nearly twelve years ago, and added, a trifle stiffly, 'I am wrong to allow my dislike of my father to take the form of tormenting you. You were kind to me, I remember, when I was invalided out of the Navy after Trafalgar, and no one else was.'

'You brought your own doom on you,' Grimes could not help retorting, 'when you ran off with your brother's wife. My sympathy for you died on that day.' He saw Priestly's face change, and knew that here was something Matt Falconer's impertinent shadow had not known.

Matt Falconer was not nonplussed. He was no longer the eager boy who had yearned for his father's love and whom his father's lawyer could patronise.

'Leave that,' he ordered in his quarterdeck voice. 'It has nothing to do with you, or with the business I have come to settle.'

But Grimes must have thought he had found a chink in Matt's armour, although Matt was not conscious of possessing one, for he continued, although in a lower tone, 'And her death does not lie on your conscience, Mr Falconer?'

Oh, the old man did have weapons to fight with after all! Matt closed his eyes, only for a sad and beautiful long-dead face to swim before them. The memories that face recalled had him swinging away from both men. For the first time in the interview he was struggling for self-control.

'I lost my conscience with my heart,' he asserted stiffly. 'And if you refer to my late sister-in-law again, I shall leave this office and England within the day, and you, my inheritance from Lady Emily and my father may all go to the devil. Is that plain enough for you, sir?'

Matt was himself again—cold, strong and unshakeable, the man whom Jeb Priestley had always known, and whom the lawyer had never met. After that they returned to the business at hand, Grimes recognising that the man before him would never agree to any of his father's demands, and consequently now wishful to settle the matter of the inheritance as rapidly as possible.

Pontisford Hall, his late great-aunt's home on the borders of Nottinghamshire and Yorkshire, was the last reminder of Matt's childhood, and the only happy one. He had a sudden burning wish to see it. He remembered warmth and love, and a place where he, as well as his older brother, had been welcome. Before he had reached England, on the boat over, re-reading the letter which told him of his great-aunt's death and his inheritance, he had resolved to sell the Hall and its contents, to raise capital to enlarge his Virginia plantation, and partly rebuild and beautify the stark house which he called home.

But stepping ashore in England, travelling to London, seeing that great city's sights, smelling its unique smell, had reminded him agonisingly of his past, of his youth, before the world had fallen in on him. He had a sudden yearning to revisit the scenes of his childhood—if only to say goodbye to them before he parted from his homeland for the last time.

He said nothing of this to Grimes, merely, 'I shall travel to Yorkshire, sir, to pay my respects to Lady Emily's tomb in Pontisford church, and to visit the Hall for the last time. She was kind to me, and I must not let her go without a proper farewell. You will inform the staff there of my proposed arrival. I shall set out as soon as I have completed other urgent matters here.'

Matt could imagine Jeb's raised and mocking eyebrows

at this rare display of sentiment, and the silent cynicism of the old lawyer, but damn that for a tale. When he had reached his middle thirties a man had the right to say goodbye to his youth.

And so it was settled. Mr Grimes did not pry into his client's life. He assumed that Matthew Falconer had not married while in the United States, for there was no talk of a wife. He assumed that he had had some success as a plantation owner, but made no move to discover how much of a success. If the grim man before him wished him to know these things he would have told him. Once or twice he sighed for the carefree young man he had once known, who had faced life with a smile despite his father's displeasure, but it was plain that that man was long gone.

Business was done, and done quickly—after the fashion of Yankees, Grimes presumed. The old Matt Falconer had never been businesslike, or hard. Now he was both. He even kept his insolent man on a tight rein while he and the lawyer went through the necessary business of establishing identity, examining Lady Emily's will, and signing and witnessing the necessary documentation.

It was soon all over, and Matt and his man were in the street, holding their top hats on, braving the keen wind of early November, before Jeb spoke again.

'Well, there's a fine tale, Matt. Did you really run off with your brother's wife?'

'Yes, but not for the reason you might think.' For once he was short with Jeb. Revisiting England must have made his memories keen again. He thought he had been rid of that old pain long ago.

'Why, what other reason is there?'

Which, of course, was what everyone had said at the time. Matt replied, in what Jeb always thought of as his 'damn-your-eyes' aristocrat's voice, which he had rarely used in the good old United States, 'Nothing to do with you, Jeb. You may have the rest of the day to yourself. I shall meet you for supper at Brown's this evening. We shall set out for Yorkshire as soon as I can organise suitable travel arrangements.'

There was no brooking him in this mood. Jeb rearranged his face, pulled a servile forelock, bowed low, mumbled, 'Yes, massa, certainly, massa,' a ritual which usually drew an unwilling grin from Matt. But not today. Today he was unmoved, immovable, and his shadow, wondering where his master was going, would have been surprised to learn that he ended the afternoon in a church, before a marble memorial consisting of an urn held by a weeping Niobe whose inscription simply read, 'To the memory of Camilla Falconer, Lady Radley, 1785-1806, cut down in her youth... "Cometh forth like a flower".'

Naturally there were no pious words chiselled into the marble about loving wives or grieving husbands, and she was buried far from her home and friends, forgotten, probably, by everyone except the grieving man who had come to pay her his last respects too.

Chapter Two

Everything, but everything, had gone wrong from the moment they had left the confines of the Home Counties. Stacy thought that there must be a curse on the journey, her first of any length since her father had died.

And it had all gone so beautifully right at first—inevitably, with Ephraim and herself arranging things. She was to travel incognito; it would not do to let possible men of the road know that the enormously rich owner of Blanchard's Bank was travelling nearly the length of England in winter. Safety lay in anonymity. She was to be Miss Anna Berriman, to match the initials stamped on her luggage and entwined on the panels of her elegant travelling coach. Polly Clay, her personal maid, and the other servants had been carefully coached for the last fortnight before they set out to address her as, 'Yes, Miss Berriman', 'Indeed, Miss Berriman', 'As you wish, Miss Berriman', until Stacy had almost come to believe herself Miss Berriman in truth.

They were taking two coaches to accommodate Stacy, Miss Landen, Polly, James the footman, young Mr Greaves and his man, a coachman, and a spare footman, Hal, a big strong man, to act as yet another guardian to the party. It occurred to Stacy, as she watched the two post-chaises being loaded with luggage and impedimenta, that throughout her life she had rarely been alone, and for a moment she wondered what it would have been like truly to be not-so-rich Miss Berriman, who was no more and no less than an ordinary, unconsidered spinster. She decided that the uncomfortable truth was that on the whole she would not have liked it. She had grown used to being in command in exactly the same way as a man would have been.

It was while they were crossing from Lincolnshire into Nottinghamshire through heavy rain, after an unpleasant night in a dirty inn, that Greaves' cold, which had been merely an inconvenience to him, became much more than that. From her seat opposite him Stacy watched his complexion turn from yellow to grey to ashen, tinged with the scarlet of heavy inflammation round his eyes, nostrils and mouth. Her concern grew with each mile that they jolted forward, until she ordered the coach to stop when they reached Newark.

'Greaves,' she said, genuinely troubled, 'I do not think that we should go further today. You look very ill.'

Louisa nodded her head, agreeing with her, while Greaves muttered in a hoarse voice—his throat was badly affected—'I feel very ill, madam, but...'

'No buts...' Stacy was both brisk and firm. 'We shall stop at the first good inn in Newark, put you to bed and send for a physician. I do not think that you are in any condition to continue.'

He didn't argue with her, nor, a day later when the physician had said that his fever was a severe one and he must not rise from his bed, did he or Stacy argue that anything other was to be done than leave him at the inn, with sufficient funds, one of the coaches, his man and James, the senior of the two footmen, to follow after Stacy's party as soon as the physician pronounced him well enough to travel. 'Which will be some days yet, I fear,' he said.

So now the single coach toiled onwards towards York, through the East Midlands counties and beyond—land which Stacy had not seen since she was a small girl. Alas, the further north they went, the worse the weather grew. The rain turned into an unpleasant sleet, and even the stone hot-water bottles and travelling warming-pans, wrapped in woollen muffs and kept on all the travellers' knees, were hardly enough to keep them warm as the temperature continued to drop.

Ruefully Stacy privately conceded that Ephraim Blount had been right to worry about her going north in winter, until, at the beginning of the stage where they were due to pass from Nottinghamshire into Yorkshire, her party woke up to find a brilliant sun shining and the sky a cold blue. Everyone, including Stacy, felt happy again.

Everyone, that was, but Louisa Landen, who had endured a bad night and suspected that she had caught Greaves' cold, but, being stoical by nature and knowing that it was necessary to make up the time lost in caring for Greaves, decided to say nothing of it to Stacy. The cold might not grow worse—and besides, the day was fine.

Except that the landlord of the Gate Hangs Well had shaken his head at them, and before they set out had said gloomily to John Coachman and the postilion they were taking on to the next stage, 'Fine weather for snow, this, maister.' John Coachman, however, who wished to press on to make up for lost time, had decided that such country lore was not worth the breath given to offer it, and that he would ignore the warning.

It was a decision that he would come to regret.

Stacy was already regretting her ill-fated winter journey to York. She was to regret it even more as, towards noon, when they were still far from journey's end, the weather suddenly changed; the sun disappeared, it became cloudy, dark and cold, and the bottles and warming-pans grew cold too. Louisa began to cough, a dry, insistent cough, which had Stacy at last registering her companion's wan face, with a hectic spot on each cheekbone.

'Oh, Louisa, my dear!' she exclaimed, taking her companion's cold hand in hers. 'I have been so selfish, wishing to make good time and not thinking of anything but my own convenience. You have caught Greaves' cold, and we ought not to have journeyed on today. You should have told me.'

Louisa shook her head and croaked, 'My fault—I said nothing because we are not so far from our journey's end, and I knew you wished to make good time today since the weather seemed to have taken a turn for the better. I must confess I did not think that I would feel so ill so soon.' She had begun to shiver violently, and it was plain that she was in a state of extreme distress.

The shivering grew worse, almost in time with the snow which had begun to fall, turning into a regular blizzard. By the early afternoon they were making only slow progress into territory where it was plain that snow had fallen during the night, and only the fact that a few carriages had passed earlier, leaving ruts for them to drive in, kept them going at all.

John Coachman had consulted his roadbook, and had already told Stacy bluntly that they would be unlikely to find a suitable inn to stop at before Bawtry, which they had originally planned to make for. They were now, he said, in an area where hostelries with beds were few and far between. 'We'd best be on our way, madam, or night will fall or the road become impassable before we reach the inn.'

The prospect of being trapped by the snow and spending the night in the coach was not a pretty one. Polly's lip trembled, but the sight of Louisa lying silent in Stacy's arms kept her silent too.

Night fell early, and John Coachman was now gloomily aware that he must, in the dark among the snowdrifts, have taken a wrong turning, for he had no idea where they were, only that they were lost—something he didn't see fit to tell his mistress. He called for directions to the postilion who was riding the near horse, who shouted back, 'I'm as lost as you are, maister. Mayhap we're nigh to Pontisford,' which was no help at all, as there was no Pontisford in John's book.

Worse, the road was growing impassable, and only the sight of the lights of a big house, dim among trees, gave him some hope that he might be able to drive them all there safely—perhaps to find shelter for the night.

He had no sooner made this decision, and told the postilion of it, than the horses, tired by their long exertions, slithered into a ditch which had been masked by the drifting snow. The coach tilted and was dragged along for a few feet before toppling slowly on to its side.

Hal, the footman, who was riding outside, was thrown clear. John, less fortunate, was caught up in the reins, and before he could free himself completely one of the falling boxes of luggage which had been stowed on top of the coach struck him a shattering blow on the arm, fortunately not breaking it.

Somehow avoiding the plunging horses, he fell across poor Hal, who was trying to rise, winding him all over again. The postilion had also been thrown clear, only to strike his head on a tree-trunk and fall stunned into the freezing ditch-water. They were later to discover that one of the horses had been killed in the fall, breaking its neck instantly.

The three passengers inside were flung from their seats to land half on the floor, half across the door next to the ground. Stacy, when everything had subsided, found herself with Louisa still in her arms and Polly, on top of both of them, gasping and moaning, her wrist having been injured in the fall.

Stunned and bruised, but happy to be alive, Stacy could only register that their ill-fated odyssey was at an end, and that she was somewhere in North Nottinghamshire, but where she had no idea...

* * *

Matt Falconer was wishing himself anywhere but in North Nottinghamshire. He and Jeb had arrived at Pontisford Hall two days earlier, after a hard and uncomfortable journey in a hired post-chaise which had stunk vilely of tobacco and ale.

All the hard and jolting way to North Nottinghamshire he had sustained himself with the thought of the comfortable billet which was waiting for them at journey's end. The sardonic mode which ruled his life these days had told him later that if it were better to travel than to arrive then he might have guessed what he would find!

He had dismounted from the chaise in the dark of the November afternoon, the first snow of winter beginning to fall, to be greeted by an ill-clad bent old man whom Matt, with difficulty, had identified as Horrocks, the butler, whom he had last seen fifteen years ago as a man still hale and hearty.

'And who the devil may you be, sirs,' he had quavered at them, 'to stop at Pontisford? There are none here to entertain you since my mistress died—only a few of the old retainers who cared for her are still living at the Hall.'

Matt had blinked at him. 'Don't you recognise me, Horrocks? It's Matt Falconer. My aunt left me the Hall and I have come to claim my inheritance.'

The old man lifted the lantern he was carrying to inspect his face. He shook his head. 'Master Matt, is it? Lord, sir, I would never have known you. You've changed.'

'So have we all,' Matt told him gently. 'Are you going to let us in?' He pointed at Jeb and the shivering driver.

'Aye, but I warn you there's little to eat and little to warm yourselves with,' mourned Horrocks as he led them indoors. 'No money's come in since Lady Emily died, and we had little enough before that.'

Grimes had said nothing of this. Matt asked urgently, 'And Lady Emily's agent, where is he?'

'Gone, Mr Matt. With the money. He upped and left two

months ago, his pockets well-lined with all he'd stolen from the estate. But Lady Emily wouldn't hear a word against him. Wandering in her mind, she was. I wrote to Lawyer Grimes, but by chance the letter went astray.'

Matt could only suppose that it had. He didn't suspect Grimes of wrongdoing, only carelessness about matters taking place so far from London. He heard Jeb giving suppressed snorts of laughter as they entered the derelict house of which Matt had talked with such enthusiasm on the way north. It was plain that Lady Emily must have fallen into her dotage unable to control her life, for Horrocks' lantern showed the entrance hall to be dank and cold, the statuary and furniture covered in filthy dust-sheets, the chandeliers empty of candles, the smell of must and mould everywhere. And the whole house was the same. There was a scuttle of rats in the wainscoting of an unheated drawing-room which Matt remembered as full of warmth and light and love.

His aunt had died earlier in the year in her late seventies, and, by what Horrocks had said, having been pillaged by her agent. Her mind wandering, she had seen Pontisford as it had been, and not as it was.

'Turned nearly all the servants away, didn't he?' quavered Horrocks. 'Only left enough to keep m'lady fed and bedded. Short commons, we was on, while he lived in comfort in his cottage with his doxy—you remember miller's Nell, Master Matt?'

Yes, Master Matt remembered miller's Nell. She had educated him in the coarser arts of love the year he had reached fifteen, on the edge of the park not far from the ford in the Pont from which the Hall and village took its name. He shook his head, avoided Jeb's eye, and asked to go to the kitchen. Which was, as he had expected, the only warm room in the house.

The cook, a blowsy fat woman, stared coldly at him, bobbed an unwilling curtsy when told who he was, and grudgingly hung the big cauldron, which he remembered from his childhood visits, above the fire to make them tea. Bread was fetched from a cupboard, and a side of salt beef from which she carved coarse chunks of meat to fling at them on cracked plates. It was all as different from Matt's memories as anything could be.

A thin-faced serving-girl peered at them before being bade to 'Take the master's food into the drawing-room as was proper'.

Jeb finally broke at this point, spluttering with laughter, and said, 'By God, she'd better not do any such thing. I've no mind to freeze to death while sharing my meal with the rats.'

Matt would have joined in his laughter except for the agonised expression on Horrocks' face—he shamedly remembering other, better days.

'Right, Jeb, we'll eat before the fire. At least this room is warm.'

The kitchen door was flung open and a hard-faced woman bounced in. 'What's going on in here, Cook? Entertaining chance-met strangers, are we? Not in my house.'

It was Matt's turn to break. Bereft of his childhood's dreams, unknown in the house where he had been known and loved, he said as coldly as he could, 'Your house, madam? You are, then, Lady Emily Falconer?'

The woman drew herself up. 'I was the late Lady Emily's housekeeper, I'll have you know, and as such it is my duty to see that the servants here do their duty. I'll thank you to leave.'

Matt walked to the window to pull back the ragged curtain and reveal the snow falling relentlessly outside, 'No, madam. It is you who must leave. Were it not for the weather I should turn you out this instant, for it is all you deserve if you say that you are responsible for the state which the Hall is in. I am Matthew Falconer, Lord Radley, and my aunt has left me this house and her estate.'

He was aware of Jeb staring at him, jaw dropped, aware

that he had never sounded more like his stern and detested father, and that, for the first time, he had laid claim to the title which he had vowed he would never assume.

The woman before him clapped her hands to her mouth. 'M'lord, if I had known who you were…'

'You had no need to know,' Matt returned savagely. 'On such a night as this it was Lady Emily's habit to care for any lonely travellers who might need shelter. The fact that I am your master is neither here nor there. You will see, at once, that beds are prepared for Mr Priestley and myself, and a fire will be lit in the drawing-room and candles provided, and if there are any able-bodied men about they will begin to clear out the rats which have invaded the house. You will work until the weather allows you to leave, madam, taking your wages for the present quarter with you. See to it.'

He had turned his back on her as she'd run to do his bidding, but as he was saying now to Jeb, two days later, 'It is of no use. Cut off by the snow as we are, with only one half-witted boy besides Horrocks and the cook, and two young girls as maids, and little in the way of food and means to make fires and warm the place…' He shrugged. 'There is little that can be done to improve the condition of Pontisford Hall. It needs time and an army of workers, and I have no mind to organise it. Sell up and go back to Virginia, I say.'

The shivering Jeb nodded agreement. They were huddled over the drawing-room fire, with two small tallow candles to give them light, wax ones being unknown at Pontisford. Matt had insisted on using the room for part of the day, carrying wood and coals through himself to light the fire to ease the burden on Horrocks and the half-witted boy, Jake.

'We shall leave when the snowstorm stops, and I shall put the Runners on the track of that damned agent, and see him swing before I leave England.'

Jeb said, his teeth chattering, 'And then you can turn back into cheerful Matt Falconer again. I can't say I care much for Lord Radley.'

'Nor do I,' returned Matt. He walked restlessly to the window to look out at the grim scene. The snowstorm had abated and the moonlight showed a white and icy world. 'I'm sorry for anyone out on a night like this...' And then, 'What the devil's that?' For someone was beating a tattoo on the big front door and shouting above the noise of the gale.

He seized the second candle, said, 'I'll go. Poor old Horrocks will take an age to answer the door and the poor devils outside will be dead of cold before he gets there. You stay here and try to warm yourself.' He crossed the dim entrance hall, shouting, 'I'm coming, I'm coming,' as the knocking redoubled, and then as those outside found the bell it began pealing vigorously—as Horrocks said in the kitchen,

'Enough to wake the dead.'

Afterwards Stacy could hardly remember how her small party had made its way from the fallen coach to Pontisford Hall. One horse was dead, and another, which Hal and John released from its traces, escaped from their numbed hands and bolted into the distance.

They were more careful with the other two, and they and the recovered postilion put John and Louisa, now barely conscious, on the third horse, and Hall, with the injured Polly riding precariously sideways behind him, on the fourth. Stacy, oblivious to Polly's wails that it wasn't fitting for her to walk, helped the postilion to lead them along the lane and up the winding drive to the Hall, trying to avoid ditches and other obstacles, unseen because of the blanket of snow.

Fortunately the snowstorm was gradually abating and a wintry moon came out, which seemed to make the cold worse. None of the party was dressed to be outdoors in such cruel weather. John had put a horse-blanket around Louisa and had covered Stacy with the blanket from the box, which, even if it smelled dreadfully of horse, gave her a little warmth.

The one thing which kept Stacy on her feet and walking was what awaited her at journey's end. A warm house, a comfortable bed, food and succour, perhaps even some in-spiriting conversation after the trivialities of the past few days. The very notion made her blood course more rapidly, kept her head high and her spirits from flagging.

Hal slid off his horse as they reached the steps leading up to the entrance of the Hall, which the moon had already revealed to be a massive and brilliant structure, built in the Palladian style. It was a smaller version of the Duke of Devonshire's villa at Chiswick, although by now Stacy was incapable of registering such architectural niceties.

She followed Hal up the steps, leaving John still cradling poor Louisa in his arms and trying to keep her out of the wind. It seemed to take ages for the door to open, and when it did she eagerly walked forward to say to the butler who had answered it, 'My name is Miss Anna Berriman. The chaise taking us to York has broken down and we are in need of shelter and succour for the night, and men to rescue the chaise tomorrow morning, check the damage and ar-range for it to be repaired. Please inform your master of our arrival.'

All this came out in her usual coldly efficient manner, the manner which set everyone at her home and at Blan-chard's Bank scurrying about to do her bidding without argument. For a moment, however, the man before her did and said nothing. By the light of the dim candle he was holding she could merely see that he was very large, and only when the moon came from behind a cloud was she able to see him fully for the first time.

He was not wearing any sort of livery but a rough grey

country coat and a pair of black breeches. His cravat was a strange loose thing, black, not white, made of silk, with a silver pin in it. The only immaculate thing about him was his boots. A butler wearing boots! His whole aspect was leonine; tawny hair and eyes, a grim, snapping mouth—she was sure it was a snapping mouth. Who in the world would allow a servant to dress like this?

He seemed about to say something, and his mouth quivered, but he simply waved a hand and enunciated—there was no other word for it—curtly, 'Enter. We have little enough to help you with, but what we can do we will do.'

Well, on top of everything else he was certainly the most mannerless churl it had ever been her misfortune to meet! His harsh voice was as strange as the rest of him. There was an accent in it which she had never heard before. Now he was turning away, without so much as a by your leave to her, and motioning them in.

For a moment Stacy had a mind to reprimand him, but then she remembered poor Louisa. It was no time to be training servants.

'My poor companion has a bad fever,' she told the broad back before her, making her voice as commanding as she could—she was not used to being treated in such a cavalier fashion by anyone, let alone a servant—'and I think she ought to be put to bed in a warm room immediately.'

The butler turned around, to show her his leonine mask again. He really was the most extraordinary-looking creature, strangely handsome, almost. 'That may be a little difficult, *madam*.'

Was it her imagination, or had there been something unpleasantly sneering in the way in which he had said the last word? Stacy, followed by her small party, who were looking about them in astonishment at the decayed state of the entrance hall, continued to walk on until she said, 'I find it difficult to believe that your master would refuse warmth and shelter to forlorn travellers...' She stopped, indicating that she wished to know his name, and as he turned around just as they reached a large baize-covered door he apparently read her mind for he said, head bowed, almost in parody of a servant, 'Matt, madam. You may call me Matt.'

May I, indeed? was her inward angry thought, but, about to say something really sharp, she was stopped by Matt—could that really be his name?—checking his stride to say to John Coachman, who was carrying Louisa and was staggering with weariness, 'You're out on your feet, man; give me the lady,' and he lifted poor Louisa out of John's arms to carry her himself.

He waved at Hal to open the door. Hal was nearly as shocked as his mistress by this strange ménage and even stranger servant—as he was later to say to the assembled staff at Bramham Castle, when Stacy finally reached there, 'I were fairly gobsmacked by it all, and no mistake.'

At last, Stacy thought, comfort and succour. The whole party felt as though their life had been suddenly renewed—but what was this? They were in the kitchens, where, although they didn't know it, for the first time in years the great fireplace had been properly cleaned. Jeb had retreated to its comfortable warmth when Matt had left the drawing-room.

Behind her Stacy felt her party shuffle their feet and begin to hem and haw. The butler laid Louisa gently down on a settle in the corner of the huge, high-vaulted room, and, taking a blanket from a cupboard, put it over her. She surfaced for a moment to say blindly, 'Where are we?' before lasping back into semi-delirium again.

'You have brought us to the kitchens,' announced Stacy dramatically. 'Kindly inform your master of our arrival. I am sure he will order you to prepare somewhere more suitable for us.'

She was uncomfortably aware that not only were her feet frozen, but that her light boots were soaked as a result of her long trudge through wet snow. Approving of being

shown into the kitchens or not, she found herself holding
her skirts before the huge fire in an attempt to dry them.
She would wait to remove her boots until she finally
reached a comfortable bedroom. The rest of her party were
clustering round the fire, which was large enough to heat
even this most cavernous of kitchens. Steam was beginning
to rise from their wet clothes.

Jeb, who was finding life in the frozen wastes of northern
England even more amusing than he had anticipated, if not
exactly comfortable, gave a snort of laughter on hearing
Stacy's orders. Horrocks, whose wits seemed to decline
daily, began to speak, caught Matt's stern eye, and thought
better of it.

Matt Falconer offered the stone-faced termagant who
was speaking to him so brusquely his hardest stare. All the
pent-up anger created by this wretched visit to England,
compounded by what he had found at Pontisford Hall, was
making him behave in a manner totally unlike that of his
usual good-humoured self.

Oh, yes, he's Lord Radley to a T, thought Jeb gleefully,
guessing what was passing through Matt's mind as he was
addressed so peremptorily, and this icy-faced bitch had better watch her step. He's had a hard time lately, has our
Matt, and someone is going to pay for it.

Matt was thinking the same thing. What a shrew! She
hadn't even the decency to enter the house before she was
throwing orders about like confetti. She deserved a few
lessons in good manners, if not to say due humility. Never
mind if she had had to endure the storm and a wrecked
coach—that was no reason for her to carry on like a mixture
of the Queen of Sheba and Catherine the bloody Great
rolled into one.

'There are no warm rooms other than this one,' he announced, his voice as cold as the snow outside. 'We shall
all have to sleep down here tonight. By tomorrow some of
the bedrooms may be fit for habitation, and if so I shall

arrange for them to be made ready for you. Kate,' he told the little maid, who was helping Polly into a chair and exclaiming over her damaged wrist which Stacy had bound up with a length torn from the bottom of her petticoat, 'go and fetch Mrs Green from her room. And Cook, the soup left over from dinner can be heated up to stop these poor folk from dying of the cold.'

He stretched out a booted foot to kick one of the logs on the fire into a more useful position. 'And you, madam,' he added, drawing up a tall Windsor chair, 'may sit here— unless, that is, you care to make yourself useful. You seem to have come out of this accident more fortunately than the rest of your party. Instead of shouting the odds about what we are all to do, you would be better employed doing something yourself.'

Matt watched with a wicked delight as the shrew began to say something, then bit her tongue before the words could fly out. Stacy wanted to scream at him that she and the postilion, who was now on his knees before the fire with his frozen hands held out to it, had trudged more than a mile through the snow while the rest of the party had ridden, but her pride forbade it. She would not bandy words with servants; she would not.

If the half-conscious Louisa Landen had ever wondered how her wilful charge would fare when faced by someone with a will as strong as her own, and who did not give a damn for her name and fame, which he didn't know in any case, she was soon to find out.

Hal walked up to her, his face worried, to say in a low voice before she sat down, 'He should not speak to you as he does, mistress. Let me tell him who you are. That should silence his impudent tongue.'

'No, I forbid it,' Stacy whispered fiercely at him. 'On no account—and you may tell John Coachman and Polly the same. We shall not be here long, I trust, and I do not bandy words with servants.'

Hal was doubtful. 'As you wish, mistress.'

'I do wish, and now go and sit down. You have had a hard day.'

She sat down herself, in the chair which the butler had earlier offered her, and began to pull off her ruined boots, seeing that she was not going to be offered a decent room of her own in which to do so, only to discover that her stockings were as wet as they were. Which did not improve her temper, for she could see that there was no way which she could pull them off surrounded as she was by staring underlings, some of whom seemed to be taking a delight in her discomfort. She put her boots before the fire to dry after first helping Polly to remove hers; her damaged wrist was making life difficult for her.

The little maid had set out coarse pottery soup bowls and an odd assortment of servants' hall cutlery on the big scrubbed table, and presently the cook ladled out a thick vegetable soup for them all. Stacy's party set to work with a will, being hungry as well as tired. Even Stacy swallowed the greasy stuff, although it nearly choked her. Matt had left the kitchen for a short time, to return with blankets and pillows which he put to warm before the fire before making up an impromptu bed for Louisa.

Jeb had accompanied him, saying with a grin as he helped to collect bedlinen, 'Come on, Matt, put the poor bitch out of her misery and tell her who you are. She's in an agony about having to argue with a butler.'

'Not...likely,' Matt had sworn. 'She's just the kind of useless fine lady I thought that I'd left behind for good. Full of her own importance and fit for nothing but embroidery and spiteful gossip!'

He had said this with such venom that, not for the first time since he had heard of the scandal in which his master had been involved, Jeb had been curious about the details of it.

'You'll have to tell her some time—and soon,' he had argued.

'But not yet. Let the shrew sweat.'

Jeb had shrugged, and later he was a little surprised to discover that it was the fine lady herself who fed Louisa, whom the kitchen's warmth had restored to consciousness, sitting by her on her impromptu bed and spooning the soup gently into her unwilling mouth. 'Come on, my love. You won't help yourself by starving,' she coaxed, to be rewarded by a watery smile.

After that Stacy insisted on looking after Polly's wrist, rubbing goose-grease salve on it which the cook had grudgingly fetched from her store-cupboard. Matt watched her with a puzzled expression on his face—he had not expected so much practical compassion from such a proud piece— only for him to lose it when Stacy said curtly to him, 'I would like to speak to your master now. At once, if you please!'

What on earth was the matter with the man? This perfectly ordinary request produced such an answering spark in his golden eyes, and such a savage twist to his lips, that it almost had Stacy stepping back in fear. She was trying to imagine what kind of master would tolerate such a...wild animal...as a butler. A dilatory one, obviously, who in his idleness let his servants do just as they pleased, for after a second's hesitation this most unlikely butler came out with, 'Oh, I daren't disturb him just now, madam. More than my job's worth, I should say.'

For some reason, after he had offered her this piece of insolence, the uncouth and strangely dressed Jeb—and what was his position in this zoo, if not to say menagerie, which apparently comprised the Hall's staff?—saw fit to fall into a fit of the sniggers. He had previously been engaged in flattering Polly, who was simpering and grinning at him in the most unseemly fashion. Were her own servants becoming infected by this disorderly crew?

Not Hal, who said bluntly to the butler, who had turned
away to begin placing the used pots on the massive board
by the large stone sink preparatory to beginning to wash
them, 'Have a care how you speak to my mistress, man.
What your master requires of you is one thing. What she
deserves in respect from you is quite another.'

The butler turned to stare at Hal, who was belligerently
squaring up to him. Big though he was, he was by no means
a match in size for the butler who, now Stacy came to think
of it, resembled a prize-fighter rather than an indoors servant.

'Oh,' he came out with, a faint smile on his face, 'but
she doesn't pay my wages, does she?'

Which produced another snigger from Jeb, who, to stir
this delightful pot even more, added, 'I doubt whether she
could afford them.'

Hal turned on Jeb, enraged by his attentions to Polly, on
whom he was sweet himself. 'Oh, and who the devil are
you to tell me anything? And as for my mistress's ability
to pay this yokel...'

'Hal!' Stacy used her very best voice on him, not loud
but stern and compelling, the voice with which she had
dragooned the employees of Blanchard's Bank into realis-
ing that here was no girlish and innocent chit to be ignored,
but Louis Blanchard's true heir in person. 'Be quiet. I will
not have any brawling here on my account.'

'What a wise conclusion,' the yokel—and what a splendid description of him that was—drawled amiably, beginning to wash pots with what even Stacy could see was
exemplary speed and precision. 'Hal shouldn't begin on an
enterprise which he can't win.'

This had the desired effect on Hal, of starting him off
all over again. He had begun by defending his mistress
from discourtesy, but he was now defending his own prow-
ess. He advanced on the smiling butler with his fists raised.
'I'll have you know I work out at Jackson's gym. I've never

seen you there, and that's a fact. Put up your dukes—or shut up.'

The only things the butler raised were his wet and soapy hands, which didn't stop Hal. 'Any excuse to dodge a fight,' he sneered, and threw a punch in the butler's direction.

For a moment Stacy was frozen by the unlikely revelation that Hal was not only her loyal servant, but also saw himself as her champion. At all costs she must not allow him to fight with the butler. Desperately she threw herself between the two men to expostulate with them, to do anything which might stop the coming brawl.

All she stopped was Hal's fist. By good fortune she was struck only a glancing blow, but it was enough for her to see stars before she sat down, ignominiously and humiliatingly, on the kitchen floor. Through her swirling senses she heard Hal's cry of distress. 'Oh, mistress, God forgive me.'

She also heard the butler cursing under his breath, 'Oh, hell and damnation, what next?' as he put his soapy hands under her armpits and hauled her to her feet again.

Oh, God, what next, indeed? Would this dreadful evening never end? All that Stacy wanted was to be in her own comfortable bed, Polly in attendance, kind Louisa well and on her feet again, somewhere near by in loving attendance.

But what she got was something else entirely. The kitchen door opposite her opened abruptly to reveal to her dazed eyes a tall woman with a thin, hard face, decently dressed in black. The housekeeper presumably.

The woman took one comprehensive look at them all. At Stacy, white-faced and trembling. At Hal, now on his knees, agonised, begging forgiveness of her for his unintended blow. At Jeb, leaning against the wall, convulsed and chortling, 'Oh, Matt, boy, this is your finest turn ever. Better than a play.' At the assembled servants, both the Hall's and Stacy's, all either shocked or amused according to their preference, and lastly at the butler, a canvas apron round his waist, his soapy hands just releasing the now furious Stacy.

'And what,' the woman roared, happy to have a chance at getting back at the uncouth monster who had disrupted her easy life, and knowing that now she was under notice to leave she had nothing to lose by saucing him, 'is the meaning of this, m'lord? And why are you wearing Cook's apron and doing the washing-up?'

Chapter Three

Everything, but everything, went into a weird kind of paralysis, as though time itself had stopped. For a long moment no one moved and no one spoke.

M'lord? Thought Stacy and all her party. *M'lord*? She must mean the butler. She can't mean the butler, can she? Can she?

But she did.

Stacy turned to face him. M'lord. Of course, she should have known. Everything about him radiated authority—which she had mistaken for insolence. For whatever goddamned reason—and really, her internal language was growing more impossible by the minute—the coarse brute had chosen to lie to her from the first moment that he had spoken to her.

She did something which she had never expected to do, something which no lady should ever have done—but then, she told herself grimly afterwards, I am no lady, and for sure, for all his title, he is no gentleman! She slapped him across the face with all her strength.

Her blow broke the paralysis which had afflicted them all. Hubbub ensued. Hal rose slowly to his feet, staring at this unlikely lordship. Jeb gave a whistling roar into the silence which followed Stacy's blow, and then began to clap his hands slowly. 'Well struck, madam,' he called to her from his post by the wall.

For his part Matt Falconer held his flaming cheek, and slowly admitted to himself that he should never have allowed his hot temper, long reined in during his years in the United States, to take him over now that he was back in England again and incite him to taunt this headstrong shrew—however much she had deserved it. And now least said, soonest mended. He picked up a towel and began to dry his hands.

He didn't immediately address Stacy but said, almost mildly, to the triumphant woman who was defying him, 'I told you not to call me m'lord, and I meant it. I am Matt, Mr Matt, or Mr Falconer to you.'

Stacy, overwhelmed by her own unladylike behaviour, conscious only of poor, sick Louisa's reproachful stare, murmured hollowly to him, 'She called you m'lord. Was that another lie in this house of liars, which you, the biggest liar of them all, are supremely fit to head?'

Matt held on to his temper. A hard feat, since he could see that the cross-grained bitch in front of him now had the upper hand, the moral hand, and would use it to provoke him further. She had a tongue like a striking adder, and no mistake.

'Strictly speaking, madam...'

Stacy, lost to everything, resembling, had she but known it, her father in one of his rare and formidable tempers, raged at him. 'You *can* speak strictly, then? I had thought insolence was more your line. But pray continue,' she added, poisonously sweet, as she saw him open his mouth. To explain presumably. But what explanation could mend this?

She no longer wanted her bed. She wanted to see m'lord whoever-he-was grovelling before her. Nothing less would do.

Matt decided not to bandy words with her. They had an

audience, fascinated by the sight of their masters engaged in a ding-dong, knock-down quarrel in front of them, instead of it taking place decently in private. What a rare treat! And all the time in the world to enjoy it, since it was plain that they were all, except possibly the housekeeper, trapped in the kitchens for the night.

'Strictly speaking,' he said between his splendid teeth, his eyes still defying her whatever his tongue might say, 'I am Matthew Falconer, Lord Radley—Earl Falconer's heir. I prefer, however, to be known as Matt Falconer.'

'Oh, I thought your preference was to be known as the butler,' returned Stacy nastily, green eyes flashing, while inwardly she said to herself, Matt Falconer—now wasn't he involved in some massive scandal when I was barely out of childhood? And no wonder, carrying on as he does.

'Something wrong with butlers, is there?' gritted Matt, his own eyes shooting fire as he immediately forgot the resolution which he had just made, that he would be unfailingly polite to this icy hellcat—could hellcats be icy?— and giving her what his old nurse had used to call 'what for' again. 'Unconsidered serfs, are they? I had sooner be a good butler than a bad nobleman any day.'

'And, of course, being who you are,' Stacy shot back, all discretion, all decency gone, now completely the true descendant of the rampantly outrageous pedlar who had made the Blanchard fortune, '*you* know all about bad noblemen, I'm sure!'

Jeb, who was busy counting the score for each side as though he were the referee at a boxing-match, saw that red rage was overcoming his employer. He had experienced it rarely, but he knew the signs. And for once Mad Matt had met his match in a woman whose icy deadliness equalled his fiery temperament.

How he mastered himself Matt never knew. Each fresh insult she offered him had him wishing that he could teach her a lesson, put her across his knee... Added to his rage was his sudden shocked horror at the knowledge that, of all dreadful things, he was becoming sexually roused.

What he really wanted to do was to take her in his arms, bear her to the floor and show her who was master...

He shook his head to clear it, rebuked his misbehaving body, and ground out, 'No useful purpose is served by our being at odds in this situation, madam. I apologise to you for my deception.' Which, had he ended there, might have done the trick, but the sight of her small contemptuous smile had him adding, 'Although you must admit that you did come on too strong from the beginning.'

Behind them Jeb gave a groan, and Hal, forgetting his mistress's orders, grew angry with the arrogant swine all over again. Lord he might be, but his mistress was right. He was no gentleman.

Stacy was also ready to restart the battle. Just because he was a man, an aristocrat, was big and strong, and, it must be admitted, in an odd way handsome, that was no reason for him to think that he could speak to her as he pleased, but as she opened her mouth to deliver another broadside she was stopped by her companion.

Louisa Landen had watched the affray with growing horror, and total surprise at seeing Stacy, who was usually so cool and controlled, so completely and utterly lost to all ladylike as well as decent behaviour. At first she had felt too weak to intervene, but was now so shocked by the behaviour of both parties that she cried feebly, 'Stacy, oh, Stacy. I feel so ill! Do leave off wrangling, my love, I need you.'

This had the effect of Stacy exclaiming remorsefully, 'Oh, Louisa, forgive me! I had quite forgot how ill you are.'

While Matt Falconer remarked nastily, 'Stacy? I had thought that you had informed me that your name was Anna!'

Stacy dodged this question, which proved that he was

not the only liar in the kitchen, by running over to Louisa, putting a hand on her hot forehead and murmuring, 'Oh, dear, you have a strong fever.' She looked across at the housekeeper, who, amused by what she had provoked, was standing there mumchance, being, like the rest of the servants, content to leave her betters to their quarrel. 'Have you no willow-bark, madam, which we may infuse to break my companion's fever?'

A learned shrew, was Matt's grim inward comment as he turned his attention to the cooling water in the stone sink—to have the little maid twitter at him, 'Oh, you should not be doing that, sir. Allow me,' and try to push him to one side.

'Nor he should,' drawled Jeb. 'Even if you were the butler, Matt, you wouldn't be washing up. Most remiss of you. Should have given you away immediately—if everyone was in their right mind, that is.'

Taking this remark as a reflection on herself, Stacy, her language deteriorating further, pronounced in her most deadly manner, calculated to bring idle clerks to heel, 'And who the devil may you be, to speak to both me and Lord Radley so impudently?'

Before Matt could answer Jeb executed a low bow. 'Matt's man, ma'am, right hand and factotum. Adviser, too, as you may have gathered.'

'Your man, m'lord!' Stacy was all indignation. 'And you allow him to speak to you so insolently? Did you learn your manners from him, or he from you? No matter,' she added hastily, as Matt flung down his washcloth and began to advance on her. 'Pray do not disturb yourself; you will never finish the washing-up at this rate!'

Only Louisa Landen, throwing a conniption fit—Jeb's words—at this point, stopped both Matt and Stacy from prolonging their slanging-match into the night's watches.

As Stacy, remorseful again, bent over Louisa, that good lady hissed at her, 'For shame, Stacy, and use your common sense if it hasn't quite flown away. You do no good bandying words with him. He has an answer for everything.'

'And so do I, madam,' retorted Stacy between her excellent teeth, 'so do I.'

'Quite so, and that is what I complain of. He is a dangerous man, and, for him, you appear to be a dangerous woman. A quiet, ladylike refusal to join in his games would end all.'

His games! Was he playing with her? Perhaps so. He had returned to his duties, to fling over his shoulder at her, 'I am late from the United States, Miss Stacy, or whatever your name is, and we have no masters and servants there, only equals working together.'

Forgetting all her resolutions and Louisa's wise advice, Stacy shot back at him, 'Which country, sir, since you are no gentleman, must be an eminently suitable place for you to live. I recommend that you return there.'

'And by the same token, madam, since you are no lady, you should surely accompany me. Except that in the States your haughty manners would soon earn you a reprimand from everyone unfortunate enough to meet you.'

Behind her, Stacy heard Louisa wail her name, and how she refrained from answering him back she never knew. She knew only that her common sense, which seemed to have taken flight from the moment she had set foot in this accursed place, told her that she must consider poor, stricken Louisa, and try not to disgrace herself before her own people, who, apart from Hal, were staring openmouthed at her. Who would have thought that their cool and haughty, if kind mistress could behave so wildly?

Astonishingly, bending over Louisa again, Stacy found tears pricking at her eyes. No, I will not cry, she told herself. This vile bully, who, as I recall, is no better than he should be, shall not make me cry. I will see him in hell first! And what on earth was happening to her that she should think such dreadful thoughts, use such language?

She straightened up, turned towards her tormentor, and said in a more normal voice, 'You have said that we must sleep here tonight, sir. Are you sure that you have no rooms in this vast house sufficiently warm for us to sleep in them?'

That's more like it, madam, thought Matt grimly. A little due humility works wonders. He forgot that he hadn't been humble either. But he replied more gently, 'I arrived here only two days ago, and no one has lived in most of the Hall's rooms for the past fifteen years, nor, I fear, have they been heated during that time. We also face a shortage of fuel, so I am afraid that we are all doomed to spend the night in the kitchen—where it is at least warm—or die of cold in one of the bedrooms. I have already moved the servants from their attic bedrooms—I wouldn't stable beasts in them.'

Jeb was nodding agreement, as well as old Horrocks, who, by what was being said among the servants, really was a butler. But what a butler! Physically frail and in his dotage, he was nearly as unsuitable in his way as Matt Falconer had been in his.

That gentleman was now asking Hal to accompany him and Jeb into the linen-store, which was kept upstairs, to fetch down sheets, more blankets, pillows and pillow-cases, and air them before the fire, which he kept going by fetching logs from a store in a lean-to against the kitchen's outer wall. It was plain that 'm'lord' he might be, but he was performing menial tasks to the manner born.

It wasn't only the logs which were almost in the open, but also the very necessaries of life. And, since the earth closet used by the servants had become frozen, Stacy was soon to discover that relief was only to be obtained by using the buckets and pails in a small storeroom with a door which didn't shut properly and a broken window through which the keen wind whistled.

Trying to keep her voice reasonable, a difficult task,

Stacy returned indoors after she had visited it to address
Matt Falconer, who was now using blankets to rig up impromptu partitions to separate the women from the men
during the hours of sleep. 'I would like to wash myself,
and Louisa would probably benefit from being sponged.
Where shall I do so...please?'

To Matt's grim amusement he saw that it almost choked
the haughty bitch to be polite to him. And well might she
ask. 'The kitchen pump,' he told her agreeably, 'will supply
you with cold water. Use the big iron cauldron which stands
by the fire to heat it. Cook will help you.' And then, seeing
that Cook was already engaged in making up beds on the
floor, he added, 'No, allow me to assist you.'

Never in her life had Stacy ever contemplated having to
do any such thing as haul buckets and pails about, or to
wash herself in the full view of Cook, the little maid and
Polly, whose right wrist Jeb had placed in a makeshift sling.
It was quite plain that anything she needed she would have
to supply herself! And the beast knew that, and was waiting
to see her throw a tantrum at the prospect of having to be
her own servant, as it were. Well, damn him, and his ready
sneer too. If Stacy Blanchard couldn't learn how to do the
simple menial tasks which so far others had performed for
her, she wasn't worth the signature she wrote on the
cheques and accounts of Blanchard's Bank.

'Very well,' she replied crisply, avoiding his satiric eye,
and walked across to the cauldron, which she lifted with
some difficulty before placing it beneath the pump which
stood by the sink. Not only was Jeb watching her, but also
her servants, their jaws dropped at the sight of madam being so meek and obliging.

But, alas, when she came to try to lift the cauldron with
water in it it was too heavy for her, and presently, as she
struggled, she found a large hand pushing her own smaller
one to one side, and Matt Falconer was lifting it with ease
to hang it from the great hook above the fire.

His hands, Stacy noted, were long and shapely, but the strange thing about them was that they were the hands of a workman, not a gentleman. They were brown and scarred, with calluses on them, like Clem's, her gardener, and his nails were cut short, quite unlike those of the men who had danced attendance on her since her first season, begging her to marry them.

Matt saw her eyes on them, smiled wryly, but said nothing. Later he ladled warm water for her into a bowl, and she retired behind one of the screens to give Louisa and herself what passed for a wash.

'Oh, my dear, you shouldn't be having to do all this,' murmured Louisa ruefully, after Stacy had draped blankets round her and helped her outside to what they all referred to as the conveniences, although John Coachman forgot himself once by asking loudly before all the company, 'Where are the jakes?'

'Well,' replied Stacy incontrovertibly, 'Cook can't do everything, the maid is useless, Polly's wrist prevents her from assisting us, all the able-bodied men have gone outside to shovel the snow away from the fuel-store and the path to the conveniences—such as they are—so who else can help us, I should like to know?'

Louisa patted her hand. 'You are a brave girl, my dear. Try not to mind too much the pickle we have found ourselves in. After all, we might be freezing to death in a ditch, or killed or maimed for life in the accident. And I am beginning to feel so much better after your ministrations.'

Which was no lie. The willow-bark had broken Louisa's fever, and presently Stacy tucked her up for the night before going back into the main part of the kitchen to find the men all sitting round the scrubbed table drinking good ale. The other women were already in their beds behind the hanging blanket.

Jeb waved a hand holding a pewter pot at her.

'Ah, Miss Berriman, what can we do for you?'

There was bread and cheese on the table, she saw long-ingly, and from somewhere Horrocks had found bottles of port as well as the ale. Matt, who was seated at the head of the table, stared coolly at her and said, 'There's food here if you want it.'

Did she want it? Of course she wanted it. She had been too strung up to eat much earlier, but she had done a lot of unaccustomed physical work during the day, and hunger gnawed at her. Pride as well as etiquette said, No, it is not possible for you to sit here, the lone woman among a pack of men, all but one your social inferiors, and tope with *him* and Hal and the rest; it wouldn't be proper. They had al-ready unwillingly dragged themselves to their feet on her arrival.

'Sit, sit,' she said imperiously, meaning to tell them that no, of course she wanted nothing.

Then *he* said mockingly, 'I think that the fare here is too coarse for m'lady, perhaps.'

Was it, indeed? And was she to starve because she was too finicking to sit down with them on the worst night of the year, and please *him* by starving herself?

'No, indeed,' she shot back. 'I find myself ravenous, and ale and bread and cheese, after a day spent in the snow, seem just the thing!' She sat down by the amused Jeb and stretched out a hand for the loaf and cheese, to cut herself a good share of them and place them on one of the pewter plates which Matt had set out.

And if that broke up their damned masculine drinking-party, so much the better. They would have clearer heads in the morning, when, with luck, the storm would have abated, the coach and their possessions would be rescued from the ditch, and she could be on her way again.

A pewter pot of ale was pushed in front of her by Jeb, who, she could see, now that she was close to him, was quite a personable man despite his strange accent and even stranger clothes. She took a defiant swig from the pot and said, as though she were conversing at dinner with Lord Melbourne himself, or perhaps the Duke of Wellington, with both of whom she was on terms of friendship, 'Pray tell me, sir, how do you find England after the United States?'

Jeb nearly choked into his ale at the sound of such ineffable condescension. He surfaced to say, 'Cold, ma'am, damned cold. Nigh as bad as a Virginia winter, eh, Matt?'

Matt drawled, his lion's eyes hard on her, 'Oh, I don't think that Miss Berriman really wishes to know about the States, Jeb. She is merely making dinner-party small talk, to put you at your ease.'

His man—or whatever he was—considered this unlikely possibility solemnly. Since Jeb was always at ease, whatever the company, high or low, the notion of a spinster lady putting him there seemed rather odd. He was about to reply, but was unable to do so, for Stacy put down her pot of ale with a defiant bang and threw loudly down the table in Matt's direction, 'When did you take up mind-reading, sir? Recently, I hope, if your present failure to perform it correctly is any guide. I am most intensely interested in... Jeb's...impressions of his ancestors' country.'

'So there', would have been a nice ending to that piece of defiance, but Louisa had long cured her of that trick. Now let him trump that ace, if he could!

But of course he could. He threw back his head and laughed, and damn him, why did he have to look exactly as she had imagined the dashing hero of every delightful Minerva Press novel which she had ever read, when she disliked him so? 'Tell her why your ancestors found themselves in Virginia, Jeb, and then Miss Berriman will understand why your impressions of the old country are hardly likely to be favourable ones!'

Ever willing to oblige, and putting on his best smile, Jeb offered a trifle tentatively—for, while he was not ashamed of his ancestors' behaviour, he was not exactly proud of it either—'Why, Great-granfer Priestley was transported to Virginia as a convict, ma'am, having taken part in the Monmouth Rising, when his sentence of hanging was transmuted to penal service in the colonies.'

Stacy, overcome by what she had provoked, and angry with herself as well as with Matt, said as firmly as she could, 'Well, Mr Priestley—' for she now knew his name '—a man is not to blame for what his ancestors did. I own that if I had to answer for my own great-grandfather's actions I should be hard put to it to excuse them. And Mr Falconer should not have compelled you to answer me thus, but that doesn't surprise me, since he obviously gave up the pretence of being a gentleman long ago.'

Matt, who was a little surprised by this generous offering to Jeb from someone whom he had thought was steeped in pride of birth, still could not prevent himself from asking, 'And what, pray, Miss Berriman, did your ancestor do which was so scurvy? Entertain us, please.'

She had entertained them enough, Stacy thought. She had behaved like a vicious termagant in the stews or in an alehouse, and in front of her own servants too! What Louisa would have thought of her sitting at a kitchen table with a gang of men swilling drink she couldn't imagine. At least she had avoided the port, of which Louisa always spoke in shuddering horror as the corrupter of men. But she had drunk heavily from the pot which Jeb had mischievously refilled several times, and the effects of the ale, tiredness, and the increasing warmth of the kitchen were beginning to overcome her.

'Certainly not,' she told him firmly. 'I will now retire.' And she stood up, to find the room going around her. Her face paled, and Matt Falconer, moved by an impulse he refused to recognise, swore to himself and as swiftly as he could ran round the table to catch her and prevent her from falling. Cold bitch she might be, but she had had a hell of a day, and behind the autocratic and imperious manner was a woman with a lot of guts—he had to grant her that. She had cared for the welfare of all her people before she had so much as sat down herself.

He picked her up, to find her strangely light for such a tall female, said softly, 'Allow me, madam. I think that you are not accustomed to drinking strong ale,' and carried her, unprotesting and already half asleep, to her bed, which was made up between those of the sleeping Polly and Louisa.

Stacy, unaware of anything but that she was in someone's strong arms, was back in her childhood again, being carried to bed by her father. Without thinking, eyes closed, she kissed the man carrying her, on the cheek which she had earlier struck, murmuring drowsily, 'Goodnight, Papa,' and by the time the surprised Matt had lowered her to the bed she was soundly and sweetly asleep.

Chapter Four

Stacy started awake as a dim early light began to steal into the kitchen. She had been dreaming that she was on a wide plain, quite alone, no friend or companion with her. There was a brilliant sun overhead, and on the far horizon there was a stand of strange trees, quite unlike anything which she had seen before.

On impulse she looked down at herself, to discover that she was most oddly dressed—or rather undressed, since she was wearing nothing but a short garment made of skin, which left her arms and her legs bare. Her hair streamed, long and unruly, down her back.

Where can I be, and whatever am I doing here? she thought rather than said, looking around for help and succour. But there was no one in sight. A strange terror seized her, which deepened when from out of the stand of trees a male lion emerged, his back rippling as he moved slowly towards her, his mask inscrutable, his golden eyes blazing.

Paralysed with fear, Stacy could neither run nor speak, but stood there, staring back at him, waiting to be eaten, she supposed.

Only…only…something weird happened. The nearer the lion drew, the more he began to change, his shape shimmering, so that when he reached her it was not a lion who stood before her but a man, dressed in skins like herself; his tawny hair, like hers, flowed down his back, his strong jaw was bearded like the lion's, and his eyes, a golden-brown, were lion's eyes...

The lion-man gave her a brilliant smile, revealing his splendid white teeth, his eyes flashed, and, before she could register anything, whether fear or desire, she was in his arms, his mouth was on hers, his hands about her body... And she was sitting up in bed awake, panting, sweating. An ecstatic sensation which she had never before experienced was sweeping through her body, its passing leaving her weak and shuddering, as though she had run a race.

A fever! I must have caught Louisa's fever! she thought. But when the shudderings had subsided they left no sensations of illness behind, only those of shock. It was *him* she had been dreaming of, and in her sleep she had allowed him to begin to make love to her.

She must be going mad. Or had gone mad the night before, for she was wearing all her clothes except her shoes, and she had no memory of how she had reached her bed. And what a bed! Memories of the previous day came flooding back, all of them unpleasant.

The kitchen was quiet except for the occasional groan, cough or snoring of the humans who occupied it. She had a strong desire to relieve herself—all the ale she had drunk, doubtless—but she had to drive herself to visit the outhouse, only dire necessity compelling her to do so. She must try not to wake the sleepers on her way there and back.

Stacy found her shoes on the floor beside the bed—who had taken them from her feet and placed them there? Was it...*him*? Her memory failed her again, but as she picked her way cautiously out of the kitchen it came back. Yes, *he* had carried her to bed, and had stopped short of stripping her of everything, had merely removed her shoes.

It had begun to snow again, and the wind had risen dur-

ing the night, so that using the inadequate convenience was
even more of a pennance than she had feared, but needs
must. She pulled the blanket she had thrown about her
shoulders more tightly around them before making her way
back. With luck she would be in her bed again before anyone was up and stirring.

But the kitchen door opened even as she put a hand out
to open it, and, of course, it was *he* who was up and about.
He would be. Matt closed the door carefully behind him
before he saw that she was there, and for a heart-stopping
moment they stared at one another in silence.

She was right: he *had* been the lion-man. He was carrying a heavy greatcoat and his perfect boots, the only dan-
dified thing about him. Otherwise he was, all things considered, lightly dressed, wearing only his shirt, unbuttoned
almost to the waist, to show a tawny pelt extending from
his neck to his middle, and his black breeches, with his legs
and feet in black silk socks. If anything, he looked even
larger and more massive than he did when he was fully
dressed. And she had been right about him looking like a
prize-fighter: he was fully as muscular as she had imagined
him to be.

His firm jaw showed a light, tawny stubble, and a pang
shot through her. She had a dreadful, insane desire to run
her fingers along the strong line, to feel his growing beard's
roughness. His eyes, the most compelling thing about him,
were on her, as avidly as hers were on him. Yes, this place
was driving her mad to make her think such thoughts.

Matt Falconer, for his part, saw a transformed woman.
The softness of sleep was written on Stacy's face; all the
stern lines, together with the strong set of her mouth, were
quite gone. She looked like a woman ready to entertain her
lover. Did she know, or was she quite unconscious of what
she looked like when she wasn't playing Lady Disdain?
Her black hair had come loose during the night so that it
was no longer strained away from her face, sharpening it,

but tumbled in soft, curling waves almost to her waist, adding to the impression of soft abandon which the rest of her gave.

The stasis which held them both paralysed passed. Stacy said in a whisper, 'You are out and about early, sir.'

Matt shrugged, replied prosaically, 'Someone must look after and feed the horses.'

The horses! She had quite forgotten about the horses in worrying about everyone and everything else. Matt was now sitting down on a low stool which stood by the door and was beginning to pull his boots on. *He* was going to feed the horses. How odd. Why not Jeb, or one of the other menservants—Hal or John Coachman, for instance, or even the postilion? She could not think of one of the many men who had passed through her life, offering for her hand— no, for the Bank—who would have gone to the trouble of caring for and feeding the horses when there was a kitchen full of menservants who could be ordered to do so.

The wind struck her keenly and she began to shiver, with cold this time. 'I ought to help you,' she offered.

Matt, now booted, stood up and began to pull on his heavy many-caped coat. 'No,' he told her curtly. 'Not that I couldn't do with your assistance, but you are not properly dressed for the task. If it becomes too much for me I shall fetch that tall footman of yours, the one who is so keen to defend you, to help me. He will probably be awake by then. Now go indoors before you die of cold, and if you really want to be useful make up the fire and put water on to boil for the breakfast porridge.'

His coat was on and fully buttoned, and without further ado, and certainly without any of the usual empty politenesses with which gentlemen usually favoured ladies, he was gone, struggling through the driving snow to the stables. What a strange creature he was! One moment insulting her by talking so of Hal, the next off to save Hal and the others trouble, after speaking to her as though she were a servant!

Anger flooded Stacy as she made her way to the big kitchen fire, to find Cook there, already beginning to work, but grateful to the fine lady who insisted on helping. In the daylight she could see how large the kitchen was, and also that, over the years, it had been allowed to deteriorate. The walls were black, the copper pans were dull, overgrown with verdigris, and the tables looked as though they had not been scrubbed since the Domesday Book had been written.

Which was probably due, thought Stacy disgustedly, to Matt Falconer's easy way with servants. No wonder he orders me about as though I were a kitchen maid if he is so willing to do the menial work himself—but how can he bear to live in such a pig-sty? This was a puzzle which occupied her until the next time she crossed swords with him.

Matt Falconer, feeding the horses, throwing extra blankets over them, was occupied in trying to solve another problem—that of Miss Anna Berriman, known to her companion and servants, when they weren't thinking of what they were saying, as Miss Stacy.

He had met many women in the United States who carried themselves with a frankness usually reserved for men, and who often, out in the fields of Virginia in the poorer plantations, did the work of men. But Miss Berriman was another thing altogether. It was plain that all her people were, if not frightened of her, ever-ready to jump to her orders. She had an unconscious arrogance, giving her orders as though it were the only thing in life she existed to do. But she was, he was coming to see, much more than your usual domineering fine lady, who took her rank as *carte blanche* to be as unpleasant as she could to all around her while doing nothing herself.

She organised her affairs in a wholly practical way. There was nothing frivolous about her. And she was ready to do things herself. She had helped to feed Louisa and had bound up Polly's wrist, and although she had bridled and tossed her head at his orders she had carried them out once she saw that her assistance was necessary if they were going to get through the night without undue distress.

And Hal, the young footman, once the ale had begun to work on him the night before, had roared belligerently at Jeb, who had said something deliberately provocative about Miss Anna Berriman, calling her 'your typical idle fine lady', and suggesting that she was more decorative than useful. 'You just watch your manners, sithee. Miss Stacy ain't no useless fine lady. Why, tonight she not only took the lead in getting us all out of the pickle we were in when the coach overturned, but she walked more than a mile through the snow herself, helping the postilion so that poor Polly, who was injured, could ride pillion with John Coachman, when by rights *she* ought to have been sitting there with him.'

Well, now, that was a surprise. Eager to discover more about this odd young woman, who annoyed him every time they met—and partly, he acknowledged, by not conforming to any of the expectations he had of women—Matt had commented sardonically, 'And is that her sole claim to not being a fine lady? If so, it's little enough.'

Hal had just been about to retort hotly, Well, she runs Blanchard's Bank as well as any man, when he had belatedly remembered Miss Stacy's injunction that no one was to reveal who she was until they reached York.

So he had consoled himself by sulking until Matt, still pushing at him, had asked, apparently inconsequentially, 'And what is her real name, Hal? She says she is Miss Anna, and you and the rest sometimes call her that and sometimes Miss Stacy. Which is it?'

Hal had muttered sullenly into his ale, 'Her pa used to

call her Miss Stacy, and it stuck. Something to do with her ma, I think.'

'Oh, and who and what was her pa when he was at home?' asked Jeb, who, like Matt, found Miss Berriman intriguing as well as annoying.

'A gentleman.' Hal had enough sense left to be evasive. 'His pa left him money, they say.'

One of the *nouveaux riches* created by the late wars, then, thought Matt. Which might explain the hauteur as a form of defence, in a society which tolerated rather than approved of them, although the explanation seemed thin. He wanted to ask, How much money? but he thought that any more questions and Hal would be waving his fists at him again, and the last thing he wanted, with the women sleeping at the other end of the kitchen, was a brawl.

Just before they finally retired for the night Jeb came up to him and muttered, so that the others couldn't hear what they were saying, 'Hot for her, are you?'

Matt drew back, almost assuming the aristocrat again. He stopped abruptly. He didn't like the effect being back in England had on him. The very air breathed social difference and unwanted deference. He was used to being a man among men, not a demi-god among men.

'Now what should make you think that? I don't even like the woman, as you must see.'

Jeb shrugged. 'Liking has nothing to do with it, as well you know. Wanting to wipe that don't-touch-me expression off her face by having her on her back was more what you were thinking of by your own expression, I should say.'

There was such a grain of truth in this that Matt turned away, saying irritably, 'For God's sake, Jeb, have you nothing better to do than try to talk me into bed with a noisy termagant? And now off to your own bed before I lose patience with you.'

Well, he hadn't convinced Jeb that he didn't want Miss Anna Berriman, if that was her name, beneath him, that was for sure, if the knowing expression on his face when he crawled into his makeshift bed was any guide.

And what did he think of her? Nothing, of course, only that she was someone chance-met and now in his house, and he wanted her out of it.

Which, he now recognised wearily, wasn't going to be soon. If the worsening weather was any guide, they might be penned in the Hall for days. The sooner they could warm up some of the bedrooms so that they were all spared her dictatorial presence the better.

Later on in the day he found that trying to heat some of the many bedrooms was a mammoth task, and no mistake. Matt, Jeb and all the able-bodied men lent a hand, including the postilion, who, when he moaned that this was no business of his and he wasn't paid to lug coals and logs about for free, was rapidly informed by Matt that to do so was some part of his payment for his board and lodging.

On his second trip upstairs Matt found Lady Disdain, as he was coming to think of her, toiling along the landing with a full scuttle of coal.

'Come, madam,' he told her roughly, 'allow me to take this from you. Carrying coals is men's work. What are you trying to prove?'

Stacy looked him firmly in his blazing amber eyes. Her eyebrows rose, and she evaded his reaching hand, swinging the scuttle away from him. 'Men's work, you say? How many maidservants have carried scuttles full of coal up and down these stairs, do you think? That poor child in the kitchen can barely lift a pan on to the fire, and Horrocks was commanding her to see that this was taken up to the master. You mean, I think, that ladies don't carry coal. But you have already informed me that I am no lady, so have done, I pray you.'

There was no telling her anything.

Stacy saw that she had scored a hit, a palpable hit.

He shrugged. 'As you will, but remember that the servants are trained to do this work, and you are not.'

'Then I collect that I must learn, m'lord,' was her smart riposte to him, and she swept by him, a slow and laboured sweep, she thought afterwards ruefully, for it was true that her whole body was beginning to protest at the back-breaking work she had been doing since she had arrived at Pontisford Hall.

The coals were for her bedroom, one of the smaller and less well-appointed ones, since its size would make it easier to warm up quickly. The fire was alight, but there was more smoke than flames rising from it, and Jeb was poking at it in an uninformed way, she saw. Doubtless he was more used to squatting half-naked in a wigwam and nursing a few sticks to life, was her acid inward commentary.

'Allow me,' she said briskly and, wrenching the poker from his astonished hands, she stirred the fire vigorously, producing a blazing flame which she presently fed with a few coals, before standing back to look at her room.

And what a room. No lady's bower, this. The dust-sheets had been ripped from the bed and the furniture and were lying discarded in the corner. Grey fluff and cobwebs were everywhere. Clean linen, ready for the bed, and a great quilt had been placed on a chest under a window whose only view was of snow, and yet more snow.

'I can't sleep in this,' she told Jeb. 'The room needs a thorough cleaning before it is habitable.'

'So it does.' Jeb's grin was sly and he lifted his shoulders in a massive shrug. 'Poor Polly's wrist is worse than ever this morning, the cook isn't paid to clean bedrooms and the little maid has woken up with a fever. So, who's to do it?' He was being particularly insolent because he wanted to see how far the woman opposite him would go if provoked. A long way, it seemed.

'If there is no one else able to clean this room, and the one which is being prepared for Miss Landen,' Stacy told him, wondering how long she could keep up her iron determination to show him, and his impossible master, that there was nothing, but nothing this fine lady would not do to prove herself as willing as any high-nosed man, 'then I shall clean them myself.'

Jeb bowed to her, and whether he meant the bow to be one of admiration or derision he wasn't sure. 'Ma'am, I think that you may be ill-prepared for such a task.'

Up went Stacy's eyebrows again. 'Oh, you are an expert on housewifery, Mr Priestley? It seems to me that nothing but diligence, common sense and a strong back are needed to carry out most of the duties I see done around me. But if I fail in the doing, be sure that I shall come to you for advice.' And this time she did sweep out, a real sweep, not an arthritic one, since she had no bucket of coal to discommode her.

'Oh, Miss Landen,' wailed Polly, later in the day, 'I wondered what Miss Stacy was doing, running in and out all the time, and now Jeb tells me that with the maid's help she has been scrubbing, cleaning and dusting the bedrooms which are being warmed for us. On her knees, Miss Landen. It cannot be proper. She should not be doing that. What would her late pa have said to such goings-on?

'And he,' she added, nodding at Matt, who was falling asleep after a hard morning moving furniture, feeding horses, hauling logs and coal and ashes up and downstairs, and trying to keep a pathway cleared to the back door, 'he don't make no effort to stop her. "Do her good to do a bit of hard work," he said to Jeb and me.'

'Good God, Polly,' murmured Louisa faintly, 'you cannot be telling me the truth.'

'As God's my witness, Miss Landen, I would not lie to you. And he's as bad,' she moaned, waving a hand at the semi-conscious Matt. 'He does more work than his man or his butler. He's the strangest lord I ever met.'

And Miss Stacy's the strangest mistress, was her unspoken gloss.

Stacy, her colour high, her back aching, her hands like coarse crêpe from being constantly immersed in water, entered, carrying a bucket and a scrubbing-brush in time to prove the truth of Polly's unlikely tale. Louisa sat up in bed, and, using the voice which had brought the childish Stacy to heel, called to her, 'Anastasia! Whatever do you think that you are doing?'

Her first word was so loud and shrill that it woke the dozing Matt in time to hear the rest of the sentence.

Stacy sat down plump on one of the Windsor chairs to rest her protesting body and replied as cheerfully as she could, 'I don't *think* that I'm doing anything, Louisa. I have been making our rooms habitable. But, of course, if you would prefer to remain in the kitchen until the weather changes, then I will stop.'

'It is not fitting, it is not proper,' the agitated Louisa wailed. She turned to Matt, a useless ally, she was to find. 'Tell her m'lord, tell her that it is neither fit nor proper for a young lady of her great position to be carrying out menial tasks.'

'Oh, no,' returned Matt placidly, sinking even further into his chair and putting his booted feet up on to a bench. 'I shall tell her nothing, for she never takes the slightest heed of anything I say—or of anything anyone else says, for that matter.'

Jeb gave another of his snorts of laughter, and Hal, aware that his mistress was being criticised again, sat up straighter, ready to do battle on her behalf.

Stacy, rising and carrying the bucket to the sink to empty it, to wring dry the swab she had been using and to clean the scrubbing-brush, merely said over her shoulder in the general direction of everybody, 'I shall always listen to anything of sense which is proposed to me, Louisa, as you well know. But I take no note of nonsense, however great the station of the person who offers it to me. Lord Radley would do well to keep his opinions to himself—the neglected state of his home is no testimonial to the soundness of his judgement or of his organisational abilities.'

Louisa, by now deprived of any ally, told herself miserably that she might have known that if Stacy was uncontrollable in her own home and at the Bank, then it was not to be wondered at that, given the circumstances at which they had arrived, she should be uncontrollable here too. Only the prospect of a comfortable room where she might be ill in private could console her for Stacy's total abandonment of all the decencies which made up a genteel female's life.

'And when,' Stacy queried briskly, drying her poor damaged hands on a coarse towel, 'will luncheon be ready? All this hard work is making me feel uncommon hungry.'

Cook looked up from the fire to announce that if madam cared to bring over one of the crockery soup plates she might have a couple of ladlefuls of vegetable broth. As for the bread, butter and cheese, that was laid out on the table, and she could help herself to them.

This was so unlike her normal life, where a deferential butler served her exquisite and delicate food in fine porcelain on a damask tablecloth, offering her a noble French wine to go with it, that Stacy almost laughed aloud. Instead, she said, without thinking, 'You see, Louisa, you always said that I worked too hard, but I assure you that a morning spent in cleaning is harder than a week spent in figuring. Never reproach me again. But, as you only live to reproach me, I fear that that is probably a vain hope.'

And she carried over Louisa's bowl to hand to her before fetching her own share of the soup and sitting down at the table with Hal and the rest to eat it.

Figuring? A week spent in figuring? Now, whatever could be meant by that? was the thought which crawled like a maggot through the brains of both Matt Falconer and

Jeb Priestley. What figuring could Miss Anna Berriman possibly be doing? And what did Louisa Landen mean by Miss Anna—or Anastasia—Berriman being a lady of great station? Who and what was her family? Berriman was not a name which sprang to Matt Falconer's mind as carrying a great weight in Society!

Only too well aware that she had made a slip of the tongue, Stacy decided to say nothing further, but instead to eat her luncheon as quietly as she could, avoiding the sardonic gaze of Matt Falconer and his shadow.

Later, going over to take Louisa's empty soup bowl from her, she said quietly and reproachfully to her, 'You must understand, Louisa, that without my active help we are both condemned to live here in public until we leave. May I also remind you that your comfortable life with me is built upon the daily work which I do at Blanchard's and which brings us our profits? I don't think that you quite understand that Papa left Blanchard's to me to run because he didn't believe that, faithful though they may be, either Ephraim Blount or any of his associates possess either the skill or the foresight to steer Blanchard's Bank in the direction in which he thought it ought to go. That is my last word on the matter, Louisa. You may advise me, but you will not issue orders to me. Now I will give *you* an order. Rest a little, I beg of you, before we carry you upstairs to your room.'

She had never spoken so to Louisa before, although occasionally she had spoken even more sternly to members of the Bank's staff who had failed to carry out her orders efficiently. It was not a tone which Louisa approved of or liked, but it was one which she had heard before—when Louis Blanchard was alive. She was truly her father's daughter, thought Louisa sadly, and as she had loved the father, for all his faults, so she loved the daughter. But from now on she knew that their relationship would have changed. Stacy had cast off the last bonds of her childhood.

She wondered what Matt Falconer would have made of Stacy's little speech if he had heard it. That gentleman was now fully awake, eating his luncheon, and directing a quizzical stare at his most unwanted guests as he did so. He was wiping his mouth with a much darned napkin which Horrocks, who was trying to carry out what his poor old brain hazily told him were the duties of a good butler, had given him a few moments earlier.

His meal finished, he walked over to Louisa and said in a kind voice, 'My dear Miss Landen, I trust that you will be delighted to learn that in a short time we shall be able to carry you to a warm bedroom, where you may recover from your malaise in peace and comfort.'

He finished this pretty speech with a short bow, bringing a blush of pleasure to Louisa's wasted cheek, and also bringing a sardonic curl to Stacy's lips. But she said nothing—safer so.

Nor did she speak again to any of the company while the arrangements to move herself and Louisa to their new rooms went ahead, but contented herself with sitting comfortably before the fire, falling into a doze which eased her aching back and legs. It might be true that the hard menial work of servants was not difficult, but oh, it was exhausting.

Jeb watched her with amusement, whispering to Matt, 'Looks a proper gentle fine lady when she sleeps, don't she? Nice and quiet! Pity she don't sleep all the time!' To which Matt said nothing. He too had come to the conclusion that least said was soonest mended.

Stacy's sleep was a happy one. She was dreaming again of the lion-man, although this time it was not bright day but dark night, with a big moon and stars overhead, and the lion-man was sitting opposite her, tending a fire. A bird was calling somewhere, and she was lying on skins.

The lion-man was looking at her, the firelight making his amber eyes glow, and presently he rose in one lithe movement and walked over to her, to sit beside her. She knew that he was going to embrace her, and delight shuddered through her.

Alas, as before, even as he touched her she was sliding awake, a smile on her face—to hear Matt Falconer's taunting voice in her ear. 'At least, madam, I see that you are happy in your dreams—if nowhere else.'

Stacy looked up at him, and knew at once that he was the lion-man of her dreams—indeed, momentarily she didn't know whether or not she was awake, or whether she was still lost in her dreams.

She was now awake, that was for sure, and why should she dream of *him*? Simply to think of her dream caused a hot and betraying colour to flood her face. Jumping to her feet and turning away from him to avoid his mocking amber gaze, she muttered in a stifled voice, 'The warmth made me sleepy, I fear. Does it still snow?'

By asking the last innocent question—anything to take her mind off what her dreams might be telling her—Stacy hoped to turn the conversation into channels which would neither embarrass her nor cause him to attack her. This ploy seemed to work, for he told her mildly, 'Yes, I'm afraid that the storm shows little signs of abating as yet. Jeb and I have carried Miss Landen upstairs to the room we prepared for her earlier, and where Polly will be able to look after her during the day—if that is agreeable to you?'

'Of course. And my room—is that ready too?'

Matt nodded gravely. 'Jeb and I are agreed that it is sufficiently warm for you to retire there as soon as you wish. Supper will be served at six of the clock. Cook is making tea for us all, and you might like to share a cup with us before you go—if you don't object to being without either your companion or your maid, that is.'

Was he offering her an olive-branch by speaking to her so steadily and calmly? If so, she must try to respond in kind, and accept the offered tea before she took herself out of his disturbing presence. She seemed to have taken leave of her senses since she met him, and as for dreaming of him in such a dreadful fashion… She was only too happy that dreams could not be shared. Who knew what might happen if he knew that he walked so intimately through hers?

For in the last dream he had been stripped to the waist, and how could such an innocent maiden lady as herself know that the rough pelt of tawny hair which covered his chest would arrow down into his stomach? It must be the Greek statuary which Papa had purchased for the gallery in their country home outside London which had produced such immodest thoughts!

'A cup of tea would be most welcome,' was her even reply, eyes downcast so that she could avoid looking at him, and she took from him the porcelain cup and saucer, two fine and delicate pieces, which Matt told her had been rescued from a glass case in the ante-room off the dining-hall.

For a moment Stacy considered asking him how he could have allowed such a splendid place as Pontisford Hall must have been to fall into neglect and ruin, but prudence said, Do nothing to provoke him, and after she had drunk her tea in silence she allowed Matt to take her arm and escort her upstairs. And that was worse than ever, for his very touch seemed to scorch and burn her skin as the lion-man's had done in her dreams. But no matter; she must control herself. They walked upstairs as decorously as though all the fierce words they had so recently hurled at one another had never been uttered. On the way to her bedroom they passed through what had once been a noble gallery hung with portraits, now hidden in canvas bags, and in which statuary of all periods stood, also hidden away under dust-sheets.

Matt felt her arm stiffen beneath his hand and, because touching her was affecting him almost as strongly as his touch was affecting her, with the difference that Matt Falconer knew what the spark which was being lit between them meant and was determined to stifle it, remarked coolly, 'You are strangely quiet, madam.' He couldn't be attracted to such a strong-minded, strong-willed termagant; he couldn't. She was everything which he most disliked in women, so he made his tone as cold as possible to demonstrate that he tolerated her only—which was a damned lie if ever there was one! Every moment he spent with her only served to magnify his growing and unnatural desire to have her in his arms, or in his bed.

His tone undid Stacy's resolution not to provoke him. She replied, her voice sharp, 'You have given me the distinct impression that you prefer my silence to my speech, so I was duly obliging you. If, on the other hand, you wish me to say what I think without fear of offending you, then I will cease to keep my thoughts to myself.'

They were by now at her bedroom door. Matt threw it open with an elaborate gesture. 'Your bower, madam. I regret that I cannot deck it about with the nettles which your mode of speech deserves.'

Stacy walked by him into the room, turned, and hurled at him, 'And I regret that I have to be in this benighted hole at all. You will forgive me if I don't come down to supper. I would rather not eat at all than owe my bread to someone whose only wish appears to be to insult me.'

That's better, madam, was Matt's unholy thought. Nag at me like that and I shall soon lose all desire to teach you what men and women can do together besides talk! But again he was lying, for he was beginning, unwillingly, to understand that what attracted him was not only her fiery spirit but the wit and intellect which fuelled it. She was gradually destroying all his easy expectations of women and their behaviour. He had always told himself that he was attracted only to women like poor Camilla had been—

small, delicate, shy and—yes, admit it, Matt—innocently worshipful of any man they might love.

There was nothing of any of that about Miss Anastasia Berriman. She was certainly not ready to worship any man! He almost resented her for it, for she was beginning to tell him something about himself which he was not sure that he wished to know. That he had changed fundamentally over the years since Camilla's death. He pushed the thought away from him, to say curtly to his tormentor, 'I cannot allow that. The cold is such that you must eat, madam. I have no desire to nurse you on a sickbed. If you are as demanding as this in rude health, I can scarce imagine what you would be like when ailing.'

Stacy turned. 'I shall not,' she blazed at him, 'come down if I do not wish to.'

'Madam, if I have to carry you down by main force to compel you to eat, I shall do so. Do not provoke me to act thus, I beg of you. It is for your own good, I assure you.'

They were face to face now, like two duellists. Stacy knew that he meant it. That he would do as he said. The lion's eyes told her so. His whole demeanour told her so. A strange excitement coursed through her. She would defy him! And then, dismally, she asked herself, Is that what I want? For him to manhandle me, lift me up, carry me down, while I try to stop him? Does the notion excite me?

Dreadfully, only the thought of what the servants downstairs would think if she were to allow any such thing stopped her from trying Matt Falconer to the point where he would physically overcome her.

'You leave me no alternative,' she muttered. 'I will come down at six, but under duress, mind. It is not my wish.'

'With or without duress, it is all the same to me, so long as you do as I wish,' he told her arrogantly. And if, thought Stacy after he had gone, he sees me as Kate in *The Taming of the Shrew*, then, damn him, he's as cross-grained as Petruchio!

She sank on to the bed, clutching her hot cheeks. How can I think such things, for how did Kate and Petruchio end? In one another's arms, and she agog to please him. I must be going mad. I'll be damned before I let the unnatural circumstances in which I find myself lead me to believe that I could ever have developed so strong a *tendre* for such a damned domineering oaf as to wish myself in his arms.

On his way downstairs Matt was thinking similar thoughts. But the play of Shakespeare's which he appeared to be trapped in was *Much Ado About Nothing*. My damned Lady Disdain, was his fiery thought, and then, But by God I'll not be Benedick, for he ended in his lady's arms, and I'll see her in hell before I give way to such a ridiculous impulse. She's just another woman, after all.

But he knew that he lied.

Chapter Five

'No sign of a thaw, my poor Louisa,' announced Stacy on the fourth morning of their stay, looking out of the window at the featureless white world which was Pontisford Hall's park. 'But even if there had been I do not think that we ought to have attempted to continue our journey to-day—you still look a trifle wan.'

'For all that,' returned her companion, pleased to see Stacy more like her usual equable self, 'I shall rise from my bed today. My fever seems to have broken during the night.'

'But you must promise me not to overdo things. We shall leave Pontisford instanter the thaw does begin and the coach is rescued. Even if it proves to be too damaged for us to continue in it, I shall arrange either for Mr Falconer to allow us to borrow his, or send to the nearest inn for a post-chaise to speed us on our way. I have quite taken this place in disgust. I find Mr Falconer and his impudent servant to be intolerable beyond belief.'

Louisa held her tongue. She thought that Stacy's behaviour had also not been beyond reproach. But Stacy had also made it plain that she was not in Louisa's charge any more, so caution in speech must be the rule.

Polly came in while Stacy was helping Louisa to dress

to tell them that breakfast was ready—did Miss Stacy wish to eat it in the kitchen, or should she bring it to her room?

Louisa said briskly, before Stacy could reply, 'I should prefer to eat in the kitchen. I must recover my sea-legs and my strength.'

Stacy would have preferred to remain where she was. Her room was now sufficiently aired and warm for Matt Falconer to be unable to demand her presence in the kitchen, and to go there might now look like conceding him some right to dictate what she did. But Polly's wrist was still painful, and she couldn't have her carrying trays several hundred yards through all the long corridors and up the great winding staircase of Pontisford Hall.

'I shall eat in the kitchen too,' she announced. 'Come, Louisa, give me your arm. We must not keep the company waiting.'

But, of course, when they reached the kitchen no one had waited for their arrival and breakfast was in full swing—Matt Falconer, indeed, had already finished, and was shrugging himself into his big coat preparatory to taking buckets of mash to the horses.

'Good morning, madam. You have condescended to breakfast with us, I see.'

Trust him to come out with some disparaging remark. Well, she had a suitable answer for that. 'Good morning, sir. I had hoped that a night's sleep might improve your manners, but I see that I was wrong!'

Louisa closed her eyes at this. Stacy, head high, having reproved insolence, picked up two pottery bowls and went over to the cauldron of porridge hanging over the fire and ladled the steaming oats into them. Carrying them back to the table, she looked for milk to put in her tea and over the porridge but found none. Matt Falconer, who had ignored her cutting response to his curt welcome, remarked drily from the door, 'We have run out of milk, I fear, but there is plenty of honey, Cook says, so you may use that instead.'

No milk. Well, she could not reprimand him for that. In all fairness, it was the sudden arrival of Stacy and her party which had depleted Pontisford's supplies so rapidly. Jeb had told her the day before that most of their store of fresh food came from the home farm from which they were now cut off.

She spooned honey over the oatmeal and began to eat it. She was so hungry that the coarse stuff tasted good, and she said so.

Jeb, who sat astride a bench mending tack, said brightly, 'Well, that's a good thing, madam, seeing that we have run out of bread, butter and smoked bacon too, and shall be reduced to eating oatmeal and vegetable soup at alternate meals.'

'Better that than nothing,' she riposted. Louisa gave a faint groan, porridge not being her favourite food. Jeb offered Stacy his impudent smile as a reward for her stoicism—never say the haughty bitch had other than a gallant spirit. If Mad Matt hadn't set his heart on having her—for Jeb had no doubt that he had, even if he refused to acknowledge it—he might have tried to give madam the time of day himself. Such spirit augured well for her performance in bed.

Something of this showed on his face, so Stacy gave him her most haughty and repressive stare before she carried the bowls over to the sink. Jeb put his tack down and followed her there. 'My dear Miss Berriman,' he murmured, 'pray do not be over-hard on Matt. We had a difficult journey here from Virginia, unwelcome news for him when we reached London, and another long haul before we arrived at Pontisford. Now, as to the Hall's condition...'

'I should worry about your condition, Jeb, if you choose to gossip about my affairs,' Matt Falconer's hard voice ground out. He had returned earlier than expected from his task, having taken Hal and John Coachman with him to finish examining the horses to see how they were bearing up under the cold.

Jeb turned an unrepentant face on his master and friend. 'Why, Matt, I but thought to put Miss Berriman wise about our reason for being here...'

Matt said harshly, throwing down his wet greatcoat before the fire, 'I shouldn't trouble yourself overmuch. I doubt whether Miss Berriman thinks that anyone could put her wise about anything.'

'Oh!' Stacy rose to her feet to excoriate him. 'Enough, sir. I shall retire to my room at once, where I may read in peace.' Yesterday she had found and explored the dusty library, and had discovered there Sir William Blackstone's great treatise *Commentaries on the Laws of England*. Just the right corrective, she thought grimly, to the lax goings-on at Pontisford Hall. In any case, the owner of Blanchard's would do well to be *au fait* with her country's legal system.

'As you wish,' was Matt's curt answer, while Louisa closed her eyes again. Her eyelids were going up and down like a shop's awning on a showery day, but what could be wrong with Stacy? It was not like her to be so cross-grained and downright rude. Why, she'd even flounced like a reprimanded parlour-maid when she'd walked out of the kitchen.

Blackstone, Stacy found, might be useful, but was hardly riveting. She visited the kitchen again for luncheon: soup without bread. Cook had unearthed some withered potatoes and had roasted them in the front of the fire, and Stacy found herself eating them as though they were manna, trying to avoid Matt Falconer's satiric eye while she did so. Later, after several more stunningly dull, if instructive, pages of Blackstone, she found herself supping off porridge, with more honey than seemed advisable.

Her ill-temper, something which she had never known that she possessed before she had arrived at Pontisford Hall, was not improved by having read Sir William's pompous dismissal of the Rights of Women, who were, he wrote, fit only to be the handmaidens of men, and who, once they were married, were dead to law and lost all the rights which they had possessed as single women!

Worst of all, Blackstone solemnly asserted that this proved how favourably the law regarded women! At this point Stacy had closed the book with a bang, sending dust flying about her room and making her sneeze. 'The man is a fool,' she had announced in ringing tones to no one at all, 'if he can believe anything as stupid as that.'

After enduring Sir William Blackstone's vapourings it was the outside of enough to watch Matt Falconer striding about the kitchen, giving orders to all and sundry and doubtless regarding her as a member of an inferior species. Papa had not brought her up to be the instrument of fools. No, she would never marry—to be the appendage of a husband, no more than his tail...

This unlikely thought brought on a fit of the giggles, so that she almost choked over her porridge. Louisa clapped her on her back and the whole table, masters and servants, admired her scarlet face. Matt Falconer seemed particularly to enjoy her discomfiture. For some reason this enraged Stacy so strongly that a red mist rose before her eyes, a response out of all proportion to the offence. Later she dismally conceded that it had been reading Blackstone which was responsible for her anger, but, whatever the cause, she was lost to everything.

'Laugh on, sir,' she threw at him furiously. 'It becomes you, who, I collect, have little care or respect for women so to enjoy a woman's discomfiture. I seem to remember that Society cast you off for your disgraceful conduct. It has seldom made a better judgement. You had done better to remain in the savage country you chose to settle in, where you might exploit women as you pleased, rather than return to these more civilised shores.'

The silence which followed this public denunciation could almost be felt. Matt's face became truly a lion's mask of fury, as Stacy's was a Medusa's, all hateful condemnation. Then Louisa gave a wailing cry. 'Oh, Stacy, Stacy, you forget yourself.'

'On the contrary, madam, I have never remembered myself more. I bid you all goodnight.' And for the second time that day she flounced out of the kitchen.

Jeb read the signs on his master's face. He had risen, stood with his hands flat before him on the table, his expression a rictus of anger. Oh, madam had tried him beyond endurance—and what delightful consequences might flow from this to entertain a man of sense! Which Matt Falconer at that moment plainly was not. He was all Lord Radley, with a vengeance. And vengeance was what he wanted.

He snarled at Jeb, 'See to the horses for me, man,' and strode out of the kitchen after the shrew who had at last succeeded in smashing his fine control. 'I shall be down presently.'

The door banged shut behind him; the company all let out its collective breath, and began to talk frantically about anything but the conduct of their betters—although later, when Louisa and Polly had gone to their beds, speculation and sly amusement ran rife among the men—except for poor Hal.

Stacy reached her room, shaking at the enormity of her behaviour. Louisa was right. Of course she was right; never more so. What would Papa have thought of her? She had always been, until she had reached Pontisford Hall and met Matt Falconer, absolutely in command of herself—icy cool, reserved, correct at every point of her behaviour, almost a joke in the eyes of Society for her determined rectitude. And where had it all gone? And how could she have behaved so dreadfully? Whatever would the servants think of her? What did *he* think of her?

She was soon to find out. The door to her room flew open, and he stood there, either an avenging archangel or a demon come from hell to devour her, whichever version of him you preferred.

He kicked the door to behind him and advanced on her, the amber eyes shooting sparks at her. Stacy almost expected to see a lion's fangs appear when at last he spoke. She found herself retreating before him, until the wall stopped her from retreating further.

'Damn you, madam, who gave you leave to speak to me thus so publicly? You are exactly the kind of high-nosed bitch I most detest.'

Shivering and shaking at the sound of him, Stacy said through her teeth, all her recent remorse flown away in the face of his insults, 'And you, sir, are the most boorish oaf it has been my misfortune to meet.'

'Then it seems, madam, that in terms of dislike we are quits.'

'Quits, sir, quits? Indeed not,' she flashed back at him. 'We can never be quits, nor do I wish to be so. You are beneath my consideration, sir. I beg leave to continue disliking you more intensely than you dislike me.'

'On the contrary. I shall make it my good fortune to be the winner in this contest.'

They were eye to furious eye now. Stacy, who was standing on tiptoe in an effort to be level with him, was trembling, and so, she saw, with fascination and trepidation equally mixed, was he.

Matt's jaw was clenched, the muscles standing out on it. His eyes devoured her, as a lion by doing so might hypnotise its prey before sinking its jaws in it. The whole room was warmed by their wrath. He began to speak again, hissing at her through his clenched teeth, causing Stacy to walk sideways along the wall to try to escape him as he stalked her, step by ruthless step. 'What unkind God sent you here to plague me? A woman lacking in all the womanly arts which give your sex grace. A disputatious, loud and un-lovely shrew. By God—' and he raised his hands '—I have a good mind to give you a lesson in decent submission, a lesson which your father should have given you long ago.'

Stacy found herself, improbably and to her complete astonishment, to be in a condition of intense and quivering excitement. Her whole body hummed and throbbed, and, far from fear at the sight of Matt's ferocious mask so near to her own, a mask which resembled the face of the battered Hercules which she had seen in the gallery, she felt a strange exhilaration.

She felt more alive than she had ever felt before. His anger and fury, added to her own, had broken the icy shell in which she had been living since her father had made her his aide and his confidante at Blanchard's.

'Touch me, sir,' she panted, 'and I promise you that you will live to regret it sorely.'

'Touch you? Why should I touch you, other than to chas-tise you? What man in his senses would wish to touch you?' But he continued his slow pacing alongside her, and now Stacy had reached the wardrobe and could move no further—other than towards him.

From eye to eye they were breast to breast. Green eyes met golden-brown ones, flashing an equal fire. The whole world had shrunk down to the pair of them. Matt stood back a little and Stacy slipped by him, only to have him catch her by the shoulders and turn her, so that now she was trapped against the bed curtains, and to retreat further was impossible—unless she wished to take him with her on to the top of the bed.

Excitement made her reckless—she felt that she lived only to provoke him. To do what...? She put up her hands against his chest to push him away from her. Immediately the strong and rapid beat of his heart, matching his breathing, assaulted her. Her touch, light though it was, served only to excite him. His heart beat more rapidly still, his breathing grew shorter, the very pupils of his lion's eyes dilated.

'You challenge me with your body, madam, after challenging me with your tongue. Is that it? Is this what you have wanted all along, the cause of your provocation? To be beneath me, in my arms? If so, I accept the challenge!'

So saying, he grasped her wrists to pull her to him so that she could feel the power of him, to feel—for Stacy was not so ignorant that she was unaware of what a roused man might feel like—the hard evidence of it stark against her stomach.

Stacy gave a tiny sob, quite unaware that her own face betrayed to her enemy, who was rapidly becoming her lover, the strength of the arousal which their mental and physical struggles had created in her.

His mouth was hard on hers, his hands clasped her head, and now that she was free to fight him off Stacy made no attempt to do so. Rather, she clutched him to her, and was returning his kiss with interest, finding his mouth again when for a second he raised his away from hers for very breathing's sake.

They stood like this for a long moment before he whispered into her ear, 'And this too, madam, this too,' and he was lifting her on to the bed before joining her there, where her hands became as purposeful as his as they continued their busy work about her body.

He was unbuttoning the bodice of her dress, to find her breasts fashionably unbound, to release them, to stroke them, to take them in his mouth, while she moaned and whimpered in his arms, before imitating him by unbuttoning his shirt and stroking the tawny pelt which she had seen before only in her dreams. It was as though her body, quiescent and dormant for so long, had been released from a long sleep. Each touch of his lips, hands and body stoked the fire of passion which was rising within her.

She was on her back, her arms around his neck; his

mouth was now on hers again, his tongue found its teasing way inside, and they were touching there too as her tongue learned what to do from his. The acute pleasure this created in them both had Stacy half lifting herself off the bed and Matt pulling away to groan fiercely, 'And this, madam, and this?' and his hands were inside her skirts and were stroking her inner thighs. Oh, God, such sweet delight!

And where, in all this maelstrom of lust, was icy Miss Anastasia Blanchard? Disappeared quite in the gasping maenad on the bed. And when, finally, Matt lifted his body above hers, it was her hands and body which helped him, rather than repelled him, on towards the final act of love.

Above him, for a fleeting second, Stacy registered the grimy and cracked plasterwork of the ceiling, before her eyes closed, to seal the sensation of being apart from her body; Stacy Blanchard had disappeared from the moment she had surrendered her will and her reason in her desire to be one with the man who was rapidly fulfilling that wish.

He was pulling up her skirts and she was unbuttoning his breeches' flap to stroke him—or was it the other way round, and she was taking the lead...? Her principles seemed to have disappeared with her clothing and his—she was too busy enjoying the new sensations which coursed through her to trouble about them. Afterwards she was to ask herself how in God's name they could have changed from blistering hate to an equally blistering passion in the blinking of an eye. So blistering that the only thing which mattered was their ultimate union, as though all their life had simply been a preparation for what was happening upon the bed...

In this, in passion, as in all else between them, they were equals. In no way afterwards could Stacy excuse herself, call what had happened between them rape. She had connived at her seduction—nay, asked for it, by provoking him until he had lost his self-control. Afterwards she was to ask herself from what depths of womanly knowledge, untaught, never before plumbed, she had fished up the skills which had enabled her to pleasure him as he pleasured her.

Strangest of all, although they had begun by making love with the same ferocity with which they had warred, gradually, as they lay naked together, tenderness followed, and although desire never slackened it became channelled into softer kisses, gentler stroking, so that when, with a groan, Matt entered her, there was nothing violent in his actions. The only pain which Stacy felt was the momentary tearing pang which told of virginity gone.

And if for a moment Matt hesitated at the enormity of what he had done, was doing, it was lost in Stacy's cries as she clutched him to her, tighter than ever, until the ecstasy took them both higher and higher, to deposit them, satisfied, on the further shores of love, where they lay quiet in one another's arms.

Downstairs, as time passed and Matt did not return, Jeb began to whistle thoughtfully. Hal sprang to his feet, shouting, 'I shall go upstairs to protect the mistress' but Louisa pulled him down, saying gently,

'I think that Miss Stacy can protect herself.' But what she really thought was, I dare do and say nothing, for if I do she might cast me off, with a pension, no doubt, and I shall die alone and friendless, which I do not want—and nor, I think, does she. She has made her bed and she must lie on it, which, I fear, is exactly what she is doing.

She looked around at the assembled company and defied them to say anything as the clock ticked on and they were all left masterless…and mistressless.

Chapter Six

The inhabitants of Pontisford Hall slept on until the dawn. Jeb, imitating his master, though unable to sleep with the woman he had—against all the odds—begun to admire, contented himself with Polly in his bed instead.

Louisa passed Stacy's closed bedroom door, wondering whether she and Matt Falconer were still together, before resignedly shrugging and retiring to her own empty bed—to enjoy the first peaceful night since she had arrived semiconscious at Pontisford. Stacy had declared her independence of all restraint, and she must live with that decision.

Inside Stacy's bedroom the strong man and the strong woman slept in one another's arms. Shortly after their first coupling, while Stacy had lain temporarily replete, in the dim light from the dying fire, Matt had slipped from her bed to renew it. She had watched him walk naked through the shadows, a Greek statue come to life, and instead of feeling shame or regret had felt only admiration of the superb body which had so recently pleasured her.

His return had found her slipping her arms and body around him to warm him, so that presently they were making love again, slowly this time, Stacy exploring sensation while Matt explored Stacy.

After that sleep had claimed them. They had defied winter by celebrating the renewal of life, and outside a steady dripping sound told them, had they been inclined to listen, that winter had been temporarily routed and the Blanchard party's forced occupation of Pontisford Hall would shortly be at an end.

Matt woke first. Momentarily he wondered where he was and whose head it was which lay so confidingly on his broad chest. Memory revived, to have him sitting up, his heart hammering again, but not with passion. In the cold light of early dawn the euphoria of bliss which he had shared with Stacy was dissolved, and all that he was left with was a strong and strange sensation of shame.

What in God's name had he done? And why had he done it? To put it bluntly and brutally, in the plainest terms, he had lost his temper to such a degree that he had set upon and ravished a maiden lady of mature years. He was at last worthy of all the reproaches and insults which had been heaped upon him at the time of poor Camilla's death. If he had been innocent then, he was assuredly guilty now.

He looked down at Stacy's sleeping face. It was soft in the harsh light; all the lines of strain, of hauteur, which he had seen upon it since he had first met her, had vanished. Peace surrounded her like a halo.

This almost made matters worse, not better. He remembered the passion with which she had so freely offered herself to him throughout the long night, and closed his eyes at the memory of it. He wanted to deny what he had done, what their loving meant. He wanted to deny that he had been strongly attracted to her, for he had long told himself that after Camilla he could give himself to no woman other than as a temporary lover.

He put out a hand to stroke her into life—then drew it back. Shortly, when she awoke, she would remember too, and, being what she was, she could only do so with the deepest regret for what she had done. She would hate him for being the cause of her ruin, her surrender of virginity, honour and chastity, all things which a virtuous woman would hold most dear. He put his head in his hands; what to do?

He could ask her to marry him—but what would that mean to her? She didn't even like him, and he certainly didn't want to lose his freedom, or so he told himself. No, the best way was for him to leave her bed, and by his actions help her to pretend that last night had never happened. That she was still untouched icy Miss Anna Berriman, who would leave Pontisford Hall as chaste as she had been when she had arrived.

But the servants must know what had passed, surely? He hadn't returned, and Jeb at least would be aware that Matt Falconer had not slept in his own bed that night. No, they could not *know*, they could only suspect. Let him return to his room, to be found there later, and there could be no certainty attached to their suspicions.

So thinking, he gave his sleeping love one last gentle kiss, pulled on his shirt and breeches, picked up his other clothes and walked to his bedroom. To find Jeb already there.

The two men stared at one another. Matt said violently, as he saw Jeb begin to speak, 'Not a word, you understand. Not a word. I spent the night in this room, and you must bear me out. Whatever happened last night was my fault, no one else's, and no one else must pay the price.'

'If you say so, although I find difficulty in believing that whatever you got up to was not most vigorously consented to by the lady in question. I am certain that she knew her own mind, and exactly what she was doing.'

Matt flung his clothes on the bed. 'Damn you, Jeb, be silent. I gave you an order. Obey it. She deserves your consideration as well as mine.'

'And shall surely have it. I take it, then, that officially nothing happened? Is that what she wants?'

'How the hell do I know?' groaned Matt. 'I left her sleeping. And why am I discussing this with you? I said silence, and I meant it.'

'Ah, but can you guarantee her silence? No, don't strike me—' as Matt raised his fist '—it is surely a consideration. Is she likely to come after you, through a relative, with a pistol, to redeem her honour—or does she want a permanent mate, not a fly-by-night?'

There was no silencing him. 'You are not my conscience,' snapped Matt. 'Look to your own. Whose bed did you spend last night in?'

'Oh, "a hit, a very palpable hit"!' quoted Jeb. 'But I have never claimed to possess a sense of honour—you do. What made you lose it?'

Matt closed his eyes, turned his back on Jeb who had, strangely and uncharacteristically, apparently constituted himself Miss Anna Berriman's defender.

'Go and join Hal,' he said as he pulled off his shirt to change into a fresh one. 'The pair of you are lost in the wrong century. Chivalry is not dead while you and Hal still live!' After which unkind remark he refused to speak again. But he thought a great deal, and none of his thoughts was pleasant, and all of them reproached him.

Stacy awoke, her right hand questing to find Matt's. Unlike him she had no doubts about where she was, or with whom she had shared her bed and spent the night. Nor had she any regrets—as yet. The first of them surfaced when she found him—and all his clothing—gone.

It was only when she sat up and full consciousness had returned that the full enormity of what she had done struck her. Her hands rose to clutch her flaming cheeks. How could I? No, I must have dreamed it, she thought. But the hard evidence of a night spent in loving was all about her: her swollen mouth, her face reddened where his beard had caught it as they had kissed and clutched at one another.

Her nipples were sore and tingling, and the very thought of what he had done to them brought them erect again.

She had been shameless, quite shameless, and whatever would he think of her? Simply, of course, that she was as loose as any whore, not even offering him a token resistance. When he had come to his full senses he must have been disgusted by her, and that was why he had crept away without so much as a kind word or a last caress.

It had never happened. Yes, that was it. If she thought and said so, then it must be so. Had not Bishop Berkeley, whom her father had admired, said that nothing existed except in the mind of the beholder? If so, then all that she had to do was wipe last night's madness from her mind until it no longer existed. There was no beholder. He was only a part of her mind, not she of his.

The boldness of this notion brought a sad smile to Stacy's lips. And if he tried to pretend that something had happened, then she would deny it, firmly and truthfully, since such an unlikely happening as Stacy Blanchard taking a man to her bed was, of course, unimaginable.

But it had happened. Worse, not only had she enjoyed it, but she had found inside herself a cauldron of passion like the one which boiled and bubbled above Cook's fire. Which reminded her that she was hungry, and she must go downstairs and face the assembled servants, persuading them by her iron control that nothing, absolutely nothing had happened and that she was indifferent to him.

But inside herself, as she was dressing, something shrieked and wailed, Oh, but I am not indifferent to him, and I want him back in my bed and in my life, and without him I am but of a barren stock, and always will be!

A timid knock came on her door. She called, 'Come in,' as she brushed her hair back into its most severe mode, having smoothed down as best as she could the deep green woollen travelling-dress in which she had been living since the coach had broken down five nights ago.

It was Louisa, looking better, but also looking timid, bleating anxiously, 'I trust I see you quite well this morning, my dear?'

Her brush still battering her curls into smoothness, Stacy lied boldly back, 'Of course, Louisa. Why should I not be?'

'I thought Mr Falconer seemed rather annoyed by what you said to him last night, Stacy. I feared that he might reproach you.'

'Oh, he did, Louisa, he did. But you know me, I trust. I gave as good as I got.' Which was the literal unspeakable truth, was it not?

'I fear that you are too bold with him. He is not one of your bank clerks, my love, nor does he take kindly to strong-minded women. Most men don't.'

She couldn't resist speaking out after all, only to have Stacy reply briskly, 'Which doesn't worry me in the slightest, seeing that I have no interest in what any man, let alone most men, think of me. They must take me as I am.'

Which he had last night, even if he apparently regretted it afterwards. But it had been lovely while it lasted.

'All the same—' began Louise.

'All the same, Louisa? Nothing has been the same since we arrived at Pontisford.' And that is telling the truth with a vengeance, she added silently.

She swept downstairs in what Louisa was dismayed to see was her haughtiest mode. She made Jeb a languid bow as he emerged from the drawing-room, also on his way to breakfast; she wondered what he had been doing there. She missed the admiring glint in his eye as he watched madam brazenly throw open the kitchen door to sweep in and equally brazenly carol, 'Good morning all,' as though she were the town crier wishing everyone well.

Sure God, Matt had pleasured madam last night to the top of his and her bent—she was on even higher ropes than usual. It was to be hoped that she didn't fall off them.

Louisa was thinking the same thing in slightly different terms.

All the servants gave her a slightly stunned, 'Good morning, madam,' including Hal, who was relieved to see that his lady, far from looking subdued and downtrodden after a rating from that unpleasant bastard Matt Falconer, or Lord Whoever-he-was, was, on the contrary, more pleased with life and herself than he had ever seen her. Unlike Jeb, he and the rest of her servants did not draw the correct conclusion from this.

The cauldron supplied her and Louisa with porridge. Ten minutes of time supplied her with Matt Falconer, who entered the kitchen after having overseen the horses, feeling that he was either about to be beheaded or would behead. He wasn't sure which.

All his expectations were confounded when his late bed-mate looked up from her porridge to announce briskly, 'Good morning, sir. I trust that you spent a pleasant night? It was my first comfortable one since arriving at Pontisford, and I do believe that a thaw is setting in, which will be a great relief to all of us.'

So that was to be the way of it. Nothing had happened. She had made the same decision as himself, so all would be well, and all manner of things would be well.

So why was it that, far from being happy, his own spirits took a nosedive? Could madam dismiss him so easily, then? Why, had he not pleasured her as few women had been pleasured, and had she not screamed beneath him in ecstasy, not once but several times? It almost demeaned a man that his doxy could be so airily non-committal after such a night of bliss.

'Middling,' he growled back at her, 'middling. I have known better.' And there, that should hold you, madam, if nothing else does.

Jeb was enduring another fit of the chokes, a real one this time, as the late lovers' double-edged conversation flew above his and everybody else's head. Stacy pounded his back vigorously. She had begun to have her suspicions of Jeb, and if she couldn't strike his conniving master, who had loved her and left her, why, then, she would strike his man—hard.

She took Matt's dismissive comment in her stride. 'I am sorry to hear it, sir. Such hard work as you indulge in deserves a better reward. You will, I am sure, be relieved to find that the weather has changed. I trust that as soon as possible labourers may be fetched to lift our coach from the ditch into which it has fallen, and, if it prove unroadworthy, that we may hire—or borrow—a post-chaise so that we may soon be on our way? You may rest a little easier then.'

The bitch, the magnificent bitch! She was taunting him before them all. What a nonpareil she was, to lose what no woman should lose before marriage and then to dismiss so casually the man who had done it, and defy him, publicly, to say or do anything which might betray both him and her. He was in no doubt that it was her behaviour which had caused, and was still causing, Jeb's splutterings.

Stacy rose, to recommend sweetly that Jeb consult a physician. 'You have these spasms far too often for your own good,' she informed him, and said to Matt, 'I'm sure that I need hardly remind you to act with all speed to arrange our departure. ''Welcome the coming, speed the parting guest'' is a maxim that I can recommend to you. It is one which I have always followed.' And this time she didn't flounce out of the kitchen, but moved like a Spanish galleon, carrying all before it in state and majesty. My dear Lady Disdain in person. Nothing, but nothing, anyone could do would ever be able to overset her.

Even Louisa was openmouthed. Jeb was having convulsions again. Matt Falconer looked at them and the smirking servants with exasperation. 'For God's sake,' he bawled in their direction, not being able to vent his anger on

Stacy, 'rattle your hocks. The sooner Pontisford is rid of you all, the happier I shall be.'

Which was just about the most curmudgeonly thing that he could think of to say, when all that he really wanted to do was to pelt after madam and have her on her back again, welcoming him, but where in the world that would lead to scarcely bore thinking of!

What *did* bear thinking of was the rapid thaw, and the arrangements for Pontisford Hall's unexpected guests to leave. Matt, Jeb, Hal, John Coachman, the postilion and the dull boy, the last two having watched all the goings-on openmouthed and uncomprehending, trudged through the slush to rescue the luggage from the coach. They were watched by Stacy from the window of her room. She had resolved to remain there until they left. She would have nothing to do with him ever again. Nothing! He was a vile seducer, that was all.

Louisa had come to her, later in the day, when it was decided that Matt would lend them his post-chaise to take them on the final stages of their journey to York, their coach being beyond immediate repair. Louisa's face was grave. 'I believe that we may be able to leave tomorrow, my dear, or so Mr Falconer seems to think.'

Stacy looked up from reading Blackstone to say coldly, 'He has not the good manners, then, to come to tell me himself?'

Louisa hesitated, and said placatingly, because she had rarely seen Stacy's face set in such uncompromising lines, 'I think that he will, my dear, when all the arrangements are made and it appears that the present milder weather will hold.' She hesitated again. 'I have remembered a little about what the scandal in which our host was involved consisted of. Your own remarks to him, in the circumstances, could scarcely be more unfortunate.'

'Indeed. And am I to be allowed to know?'

No, Louisa had never known her so icy, so withdrawn. 'I think that you ought. You will then be able to guard your tongue a little.'

The cauldron inside Stacy almost boiled over. Somehow she controlled herself, said, 'Continue, pray. I am agog.'

Louisa sighed. 'It seems that when he was a very young man he fell in love with and ran away with his brother Rollo, Lord Radley's wife. She died shortly afterwards, while quite young. The details of what happened were hushed up.'

'And that's it?' Stacy's voice was stifled. She had tried to keep it level, but could not.

'Isn't that enough? To run off with his brother's wife? He was cast off by his family, as you may imagine, and fled England to farm, his man Priestley tells me, in the Virginias on some land settled on him by his mother—her mother was an American. He worked alongside his men, I collect, which perhaps explains his strange behaviour here, working alongside the servants...'

'And expecting me to do so. Thank you, Louisa; I wish that you had told me the details of the scandal before.'

Louisa nodded. 'It was remiss of me, I own. But I thought... I don't know what I thought... That it would not be helpful. I was wrong.'

Stacy sat on the bed. 'Leave me, I beg of you. I wish to make ready for the journey.'

Which was a monstrous thundering lie. She wanted to face the fact that she was not the first woman he had ever seduced—as though she had ever thought that she was. But worst of all was that he had dishonoured his brother.

And I? Stacy suddenly thought, springing to her feet to put her hands to hot cheeks. Suppose I have been left pregnant? And what has possessed me that I should never think of such a possibility, either before, during or after what we did? Yes, I have truly run mad ever since I set foot in Pontisford Hall. God help me, but I must leave as soon as possible, and also trust in God that I may not pay a price for what I have done. What could I have been thinking of or, rather, not thinking of? How could my wits have gone so far astray?

And he? Should he not have considered what might be the inevitable end of…last night? And I was a virgin, too. Oh, yes, after our night together nothing was left of any maidenly modesty I might once have possessed.

Stacy's whole body was burning and shivering as though a fever afflicted it. The knock on the door in the middle of her torment had to be repeated before she pulled herself together and called, 'Come in!'

It was Matt Falconer. He had the effrontery to look and speak as though nothing untoward had passed between them. He bowed, said, 'Madam, I am come to inform you that with luck, and the thaw holding, you and your party should be on your way by first light tomorrow morning. Your luggage has been brought from your coach. Hal will be carrying your boxes up so that you may change for the journey should you wish to do so.'

Stacy inclined her head graciously, looking away from him as though the sight of him hurt her. 'I thank you, sir, for your consideration and the hospitality which you have shown to me and mine.'

Matt could not help himself; he started forward, said impetuously, 'Do not look at me so, madam. I do not know how to express my regrets for what occurred here last night—'

Her smile was frozen. 'A little late, wouldn't you say, sir?' And then putting up her hands as if to ward him off, 'No, do not say anything further, sir. Your departure this morning, without a word, tells all. I do not wish to dwell on what should never have happened. I pray that we do not meet again.' And she gave him her back.

'Miss Berriman,' Matt found himself saying hoarsely to that forbidding sight, 'I can only ask your forgiveness, and ask you to marry me. That is the least a man can do who behaved as I did.'

So, 'the least a man could do' was all that he had to offer her! And why not, pray, the most? Had he, then, felt nothing of the burning passion which had overwhelmed her, allied to the feeling afterwards, as she'd lain in his arms, that she had come home, had found the lost half of herself?

Apparently not, so coolly had his proposal been made. A proposal plainly made to salve his conscience rather than because he had felt anything but a passing lust for the woman he had bedded so casually. Desolation, followed by rage, overcame her.

'Marry you, sir? Marry you? I had as lief marry one of the apes from the zoo at the Tower. Or lead them in hell, as our forefathers said spinsters did! Marry a man, chancemet and chance-bedded? Indeed not. Take your proposal away, to offer it to someone less discriminating than I!'

Face on fire, he was almost on her again. Mastering himself, he stopped without touching her. 'That was not what you felt last night, madam, when you sighed and moaned in my arms. Where was your discrimination then?'

'Lost, with my wits,' she hurled at him, near to tears, near to breaking down, to clutching at him and howling, Say that you care for me a little. That what we felt in our transports was more than mere pleasure, was an identity shared.

Pride forbade it. And he, conscious of the enormity of what he had done, and that, excuse himself as he might, he deserved no more of her than the scorn which she was pouring over him, could not believe other than that was all that she felt for him.

She was splendid in her anger, splendid in her straight-backed independence, which offered neither him or any man quarter.

'Think again, madam. I have a title to offer you, if that

might please you. And a good name, even if I have done little to cover it with glory…'

'I would not have you,' lied Stacy, 'if you offered me the Crown of England.' But oh, if you offered me your love, I would have you though you had not a penny, and I not a sou to my name, and we walked ragged through England.

No, he was not about to offer her that. He was backing away, saying as he reached the door, 'You will not reconsider?'

'You have had my answer, sir. I am accustomed to my yea being accepted as my yea, and my nay as my nay. Nay it is. You should have considered what you were doing when you set upon me.'

For the second time in two days she had broken through his usually iron control.

'Oh, madam, do but you consider. I may have begun our bout of love but, by God, you joined in it so lustily that you had my breeches off before I had your skirts up!'

She should have fainted, died away, at having anything so gross thrown at her, but dreadfully Stacy had only one impulse overcome…and that was to laugh. She was hard put to it to stifle her giggles at the picture this conjured up, which was unfortunate, because had she laughed things between them might have been mended immediately, they being so equal in all that mattered between a man and a woman—in humour as in everything else.

Instead, she lifted her hands primly before her face and said in a fainting voice, 'Oh, for shame, sir, for shame! I did not know what I was doing I was in such shock.'

'But I think you did, madam, I think you did—to succeed in your objective when so stricken! But no matter I will leave you with my apologies, and with my offer. It stands, madam, it stands. Remember that.'

She shook her head at him, and he was fain to take her in his arms, to say, For God's sake, woman, for no reason on earth you attract me, sharp-tongued though you are, as no woman has ever done, not even my poor Camilla. We should deal well together, you and I, so let us deal well for life.

But, like Stacy, life had made him fearful of expressing himself, of betraying his emotions. If she distrusted men because all that they had ever wanted of her was Blanchard's Bank, then he distrusted not women, but the wretchedness which loving one woman had caused him. Better not to love them but simply to enjoy them. What distressed him over his treatment of Miss Anna Berriman was that he had taken her into his bed at first without her consent, even if by her conduct she had freely given it to him afterwards.

Stacy turned away from him. The word 'remember' rang in her head. She would always remember him, but she dared not trust him. Besides, duty and Blanchard's called, York awaited her, and she would not exchange her free life to be a man's slave, not for all the love he might have offered her but hadn't, and certainly not for his title—which he apparently didn't value anyway.

It was over. Useless to continue. He said, 'Remember,' again, and stalked out of the room, having bowed to her. Nothing was left to her but to open her boxes, change into clothes which she had not spent five days a-wearing, and leave for York. To resume her character as the passionless owner and ruler of Blanchard's Bank, her father's true daughter.

Matt walked downstairs, and only later, when the chaise was being driven through the slush of the drive on its journey to York, did he think to rebuke himself for not taking madam in his arms and convincing her that, chance-met or not, he and she could make a pair to withstand the world.

But by then it was too late.

Chapter Seven

'Thank goodness it's behind us,' sighed Stacy dramatically as the turning road, which for a fleeting moment had offered them one last glimpse of Pontisford Hall, took it away from them.

She had to admit, inwardly—not outwardly, that in the distance, beneath the clear blue of the November sky, Pontisford Hall, set in a landscape which was rapidly changing from an engraving in black and white to a dramatic oil-painting, looked singularly lovely. Its severe classical façade gave no hint of the horrors within.

Louisa nodded. 'So neglected,' she sighed, 'I wonder at Lord Radley allowing it to fall into such decay, I really do.'

Polly, sitting opposite them, not sure whether she had been using her common sense in allowing Jeb Priestley into her bed with her two nights ago, interrupted her betters pertly.

'Not Mr Falconer—I mean Lord Radley's fault,' she announced knowingly. 'He and Jeb—I mean Mr Priestley—only arrived there a few days before we did. Inherited it from his great-aunty, Lord Radley did, who was too old to care what condition she lived in. They were as shocked as we were by what they found.'

Which only goes to show, thought Stacy resignedly, that

the servants often know more than we do. And, of course, Jeb was trying to tell me so that time when Matt came in and stopped him. She wriggled a little—she had misjudged him over that at least, but it was his own fault that she had done so. But I won't think about him, I won't. With luck I shall never see him again, she told herself.

Then why did she give an odd little shiver at the very idea that he had passed out of her life for good? She shook her head to clear it, and remarked briskly to Louisa, 'It is to be hoped that we reach York without further delay. They will be wondering what has detained us—unless, of course, they shared our bad weather.'

As if to make up for the disasters inflicted on them in the earlier part of their odyssey, Stacy's party reached York without further trouble, to find that the rooms taken for them in a house in the shadow of the great Minster were as warm and comfortable and as unlike Pontisford's filthy splendour as rooms could be.

The landlady welcomed them with open arms—pleased that her lodgers had taken over the whole house, saving her the trouble of looking for more—exclaiming, 'At last, madam! I had quite given you up. The weather here has been atrocious.'

There was a splendid meal soon made ready for them, comfortable beds in warm bedrooms, a footman of the landlady's own to help poor Hal carry in their boxes and other impedimenta, and maidservants to assist Polly, whose wrist still pained her. Louisa, face grey, was helped to her room where her dinner was sent up to her, daintily laid out on fine porcelain on a silver tray, while Stacy dined in lonely splendour off food which she had only dreamed of while half starving at Pontisford.

So why did she feel so desolate, so full of ennui at being, as she usually was, alone? At Pontisford she had been compelled to share her life with others, to sit at table with a pack of dependents, to listen to Matt and Jeb and the others laugh and talk companionably when she had retired to her bed behind the makeshift partition. And she surely couldn't be missing the rough fare which was all that Pontisford had supplied.

But she had never felt so lonely, she who had never felt lonely before. And could she also be missing the sound of masculine voices in this house of women?

Enough of that, she told herself briskly. Tomorrow she would visit the York branch of the Bank, to discover what had been going wrong there and try to put it right. She would have preferred to have Greaves with her, not because she wanted him to assert authority over the men whom she would have to face, but because he would have been an ally, and she might need an ally.

Poxon, the manager, when he finally met her, thought that she not only needed an ally but a keeper, she having evidently escaped from a madhouse...

Remembering her father's wise advice, Stacy had given the staff at Blanchard's, York no warning that she was immediately to descend on them. Oh, they knew that a party from the London headquarters was on the way, and that it would include Miss Blanchard herself, but they had no idea of exactly when that party would arrive—or that, improbably, it would be Miss Blanchard who would head it.

Stacy dressed herself carefully in a black gown of sober cut, with small Mary, Queen of Scots-style fine linen ruffles discreetly edged with lace at her throat and wrists, and a black leather belt with a silver buckle and a small chain hanging from it, to which was attached a tiny notebook and a pencil. Over this she wore a long black coat, caped and cut like a man's. A black fur busby completed the ensemble. The impression of cold and competent austerity was completed by her hair, which had been pulled straight back into a giant knot; a black velvet band was wound round her head and across her forehead to restrain any curls which might wish to spring loose. A single pearl depended from its middle.

The whole effect was formidable in the extreme, as was intended.

Thus accoutred, with Louisa and Hal in attendance, Stacy set off on foot to the Bank's premises, situated not far from the house which she had taken. All seemed fair outside, and inside too, as she entered, her acolytes a little behind her.

The clerks behind the gilt grilles and the mahogany counters stared a little at this procession, particularly as no gentleman seemed to be in attendance. Hal, wearing the green and gold of the livery which Louis Blanchard had designed in one of his more creative moments, was the only male in the party. He was carrying a large leather bag which held all the business papers relating to the York branch which Stacy had brought with her from London.

The clerk whom she approached stared the hardest of all. She stripped off her long black gloves and said, without giving the man behind the counter the slightest notion of who she was, 'I would like, sir, to speak to your manager— as soon as possible.'

The clerk bowed and said, 'Oh, madam, I am afraid that might be difficult. Perhaps you could inform me of what business you wish to transact? Although, forgive me, it would perhaps be better if I, or the manager, spoke to your brother or to your husband about financial matters.'

'Now that would be difficult—' Stacy smiled at him '—seeing that I have neither. Pray escort me to your manager. The business which I have with him is serious in the extreme.' And as she saw him hesitate, 'Come, sir, I have my companion with me, and my footman; it will be quite proper for him to see me with them as chaperons.'

The clerk gave way; he came from behind the counter, bowed again, and asked, a shade of insolence in his expression, 'What name shall I give to him, madam?'

'Why, sir, I prefer to name myself to him.' And as he prepared to argue with her Stacy added lightly, 'Come, I have a deal of money to dispose of, and your bank has been recommended to me as a sound one. You would not wish to lose my account, surely?'

'Indeed not,' sighed the clerk dubiously, beginning to lead the way to the bank parlour, watched with intense interest by the rest of the staff, business obviously being poor at Blanchard's that morning. By the papers in Stacy's bag, it was never other than poor.

The clerk knocked on the door, heard the answering, 'Come in,' before bowing and escorting Stacy through it, saying, 'A lady to see you, Mr Poxon, sir.' He walked by Stacy to stand at the rear of the room, his master's aide, it would seem.

'A lady?' The manager, a gross man, with the signs of heavy drinking about his face and body—he was so red-faced and barrel-stomached, put down a large glass of port and said, 'Good morning, madam. You wish to do business with me? Forgive me, but—'

'You would rather do it with my husband, father or brother,' Stacy finished curtly, refusing the chair he was offering to her. 'No, I prefer to stand.' Perforce that left him standing too, but she was unable to prevent him from seizing her hand and planting a wet kiss on the back of it. Unattended ladies—for he obviously regarded Hal and Louisa as non-existent—were fair game.

'Yes, thank you, I should care for a glass of port,' she intoned in response to his lack of an offer of it, 'seeing that you appear to be out of Madeira,' and, when he stared at her nonplussed, added sweetly, 'I will have the one which you would have offered my father, brother or husband. It is, I understand, the custom for managers to offer those who visit the bank parlour a glass of something or other and a sweet biscuit. I see that you have anticipated my arrival and favoured yourself with one. On examination you seem to have a deal of liquor and a marked lack of sweet biscuits!'

Behind her Hal gave a curious snort, rather like the ones which Jeb Priestley had been accustomed to give when his betters were entertaining him. The clerk looked as though the sky had fallen in on him.

'I had not thought…a lady…' stammered the manager, beginning to pick up a decanter, to pour a hefty share of port into a large glass. 'But if madam wishes…'

'Madam wishes,' returned Stacy. She was beginning to enjoy herself. After five hard days of battling with a man whose wit was as ready as her own, to cut this poor fool down to size was a pleasure. It might be cruel of her, but perusal of her papers back in London, Ephraim assisting, had proved to them both that if the manager was not on the take his incompetence bordered upon genius! Seeing him, Stacy didn't think that he displayed genius in any department; he was most likely a crude swindler.

'You would care for a glass too?' she asked Louisa, who shook her head determinedly.

'Not in the morning, my dear.'

'Very wise of you,' commented Stacy, draining her glass at one go, in imitation of all the men she had seen doing the very same thing when business was under discussion. 'A clear head is most necessary when one talks business. I'm sure you agree, sir.' And, as he picked up the glass he had refilled, 'Oh, no, I couldn't possibly advise you to drink further. I fear that you will need all your wits about you in the next few hours.'

She placed her glass on his leather-topped desk, walked around it and, before he could remonstrate, took his glass from his astonished hand and sat down in his high chair.

'I think that we ought to begin our business immediately. I have little time to waste,' she informed him sweetly.

The manager stared at her as if she had lost her wits. Louisa, used by now to Stacy's methods, designed to destroy confidence even before she began a merciless interrogation, sighed internally. She should have been a man, that was plain. The manager, poor fool, reached for the bell standing on his desk, to ring it to summon help. 'I will have you removed, madam. The madhouse is your proper destination, not the parlour of a bank!'

Stacy put her hand over his before he could use it. 'Not so, sir. Now, were I to be here to open an account, I should require a full and frank statement from you as to the solvency or otherwise of this branch. But, seeing that that is not my business with you, we shall come to that which is. Hal! Pray hand me my bag, if you please.'

'Certainly, madam.' Hal placed the bag on the desk before her.

The manager, face now purple, went to pick it up, to remove it. Stacy looked at him and said, her voice cool, 'Pray leave the bag where it is, Mr Poxon, or I shall ask my man to restrain you.'

'Burtonshaw!' thundered the manager at the stupefied clerk. 'Either assist me to dispose of this madwoman or fetch a constable to do so!'

'Oh, I shouldn't do that,' smiled Stacy, all deadly charm. 'Were you so unwise as to summon a constable, I should feel compelled to ask him to charge you with fraud and embezzlement, for the papers in my bag seem to suggest that you have been engaged in both, and I wouldn't like to do that until I had given you a chance to defend yourself. Besides, I wouldn't want Blanchard's to have an open scandal which might cause a run on the bank in York and damage the London house too. No, Mr Poxon, let us keep this in the room for the time being.' She paused. 'Oh, I forgot. I didn't inform you of my name, did I? Most remiss of me. I am Miss Anastasia Blanchard, come from London to discover what has been going wrong in York.' She eyed the decanter before her with distaste. 'I think that I may already have discovered part of the reason.'

She began to pull papers out of her bag, fixing the stunned manager with a basilisk eye before handing him the letter of intent which she and Ephraim had jointly signed. He took it with a nerveless hand, and collapsed into a chair as though his legs had failed him.

'And now,' Stacy contrived, holding up the first of the papers from her bag, 'we shall begin to discuss your last balance sheet, and you may endeavour to explain to me how you have managed to achieve these remarkable figures...'

'You've never seen anything like it,' a grinning Burton-shaw told the rest of the clerks in the alehouse that evening. 'She had it all off pat. Knew more about how the house ran than he did! Sat there figuring away in her head, as though she had worked in a counting-house all her life, catching him out whenever he tried to fudge an answer. *And* she did something I've never seen afore—added all three columns up at once, pounds, shillings and pence in one go—*and* got it right—while poor old Poxon was still stumbling over the pennies! Like a trick in a fair.' He mimicked a woman's voice. '"But oh, pray, Mr Poxon, how can that be? Your figures distinctly prove otherwise, unless you are keeping a second set of books for your own pleasure, of course."'

He took an almighty swig of his ale. 'Never thought I should ever see old Poxon done down by a lady who looked as though butter wouldn't melt in her mouth. Halfway through he started some tale of it not being proper for a *real* lady to be adoing all this, and why hadn't she sent Ephraim Blount to see to things? So then, so then,' he went on, relishing his tale, 'she snaps the ledger in front of her tight shut—did I tell you she had all the ledgers in *and* mastered them before you could say knife?—and says, as sweet as pie, "Very well, Mr Poxon, if you prefer not to deal with me, and seeing that Ephraim has more to do than tour Yorkshire in winter, let me go to the magistrates this afternoon and swear a warrant for your arrest.'' And *then* she says, ''And if you can't see that I'm saving of you from being transported, and saving Blanchard's name too, then you are an even bigger fool than I take you for!''

'That finished him, I can tell you. And she's a-going to speak to us all tomorrow morning, afore the bank opens. I ain't never seen such a high-stepping goer in my whole life, I ain't.' In his excitement he had reverted to the coarse speech of his youth, before he had gone to the grammar school and had become one of Blanchard's clerks aspiring to be a manager himself.

One of the younger men said, 'What right has she to behave like that, though, eh?'

'Owns the bank, don't she? And she told Poxon that while he had been making a loss in York she had been making a handsome profit in London, and so he ought to attend to her, and not the other way round...'

That silenced everyone, for the time being at least, and not forty-eight hours had gone by before all York laughed and buzzed over the doings at Blanchard's, and a small crowd gathered outside the bank each morning to see the forward hussy who had had the temerity to tell Bob Poxon what was what, and turn him off as well, before the week's end.

Even the drawing-rooms of the Minster's clergy hummed discreetly, Mrs Canon Gunter saying to her husband, 'Pray, my dear Alberic, can it conceivably be true that some un-sexed creature came down from London to dismiss poor Mr Poxon and publicly address the bank clerks in the bank's parlour?'

The Canon nodded his grey head, adding mildly, 'Al-though you might be surprised if you met her, my dear, as I was, when she discussed with me Blanchard's loan to the Cathedral of a sum of money to repair the stained-glass window broken in the recent storm, to find that she appears to be a perfect lady.'

'My dear Alberic, I have not the slightest wish to meet her.'

But the very next day, while she was dining with the Bishop, there was the Bankeress, as York society had begun to call her, being introduced to her! It appeared that she was a relative of the Beauchamps of Bramham Castle, in whose company she had arrived, and, after her work in York was ended, was to stay with them over Christmas, her mother having been Lady Beauchamp's late sister!

'It was a wonder,' Mrs Canon announced later, 'that she wasn't turning in her grave, her daughter's conduct being so unladylike.'

York society at the dinner was all agog. The more so because of the remarkable cold beauty and composure of the woman who had set the town's gossips a-roaring. If Stacy was aware of the impression she had made, she gave no sign of it. Inwardly she was less sure of herself than she had ever been.

Earlier that day she had dismissed Poxon, with the pay owing to him. Her work with the bank's ledgers and her discussions with the clerks involved had made it apparent that he had, in addition to running the bank into the ground financially, been looting it for years. Greaves, who had at last arrived in York, cured of his malaise, was in full agreement with her.

Poxon had first paled, and then gone purple. His chief clerk, Robson, who had always disliked him and had remained honest—although many had not—was, at her order, standing by, waiting to be appointed in Poxon's place, with Greaves to help him during his first few weeks.

'You hard-hearted bitch!' Poxon had ground the words out between his teeth. 'I might have known this would be the end of it when I first met you—a woman who doesn't know her place in the world. But, by God, what place can you have, other than to turn men away from their rightful employment? What man worth his salt would want to touch you, I ask myself, other than to get at your money? What mercy could I expect from such an unsexed creature as you are?'

She had heard Louisa gasp as, ruined and frustrated, the wretched Poxon had continued to pour verbal filth over her, even as Hal began to draw him away and young Greaves started forward, thinking that she might need his protection as well. But, by God, madam had courage, one had to grant her that! She never moved, her colour never changed, and when Hal had wrestled Poxon to the door, preparatory to throwing him out of the office he had once ruled, she said, her voice peremptory and as impersonal as she could make it, 'Wait!'

He fell silent. Stacy rose to her feet and, disguising her inward tremblings, said coolly and clearly, 'The mercy I have offered you, Mr Poxon, is that I have not called on the magistrates to arrest you for offences for which you might either hang or be transported to New South Wales. It might be what you deserve, but would neither benefit your poor wife, who would be thrown upon the parish, nor Blanchard's Bank. Be thankful that I have spared you that.'

He made her no answer, but allowed Hal to drag him from the room. Once the door had closed behind him, Louisa rose, went over to Stacy, whose self-control was on a knife-edge, and cried forcefully, 'You see how wrong you are to try to take your father's place. No lady should have to endure what you did just now.'

Stacy closed her eyes. 'You are more troubled than I am by it,' she said severely, which was not quite the truth. 'Allow Hal to escort you home when he has finished with Mr Poxon. Send him and Polly back for me—I have more instructions to give Mr Robson before I leave.'

Later, after she, Robson and Greaves had gone over the changes which she had ordered in the Bank's administration, she walked out of the York branch's big mahogany front doors into the narrow street. Her feet took her towards the Minster, whose towers dominated the little town which was barely changed from what it had been in medieval times.

None of the Blanchards could ever have been called truly religious, even though the founder of the line had been compelled to flee Paris because he was a Huguenot, but Stacy suddenly felt that she needed more than mortal help. She realised that during her reign at the London bank she had been cushioned from the stark unpleasantness of dismissing those who had behaved criminally. Louis Blanchard had run his business on a tight rein, overseeing everything, leaving little chance for dishonesty to flourish, so she had not encountered the more distressing aspects of business life. For the first time she understood what Ephraim Blount had been trying to tell her on the day before she had left London.

'You must be strong, madam,' he had said, blinking at her over his gilt half-moon spectacles. 'You must be aware that the York branch's poor performance is due to more than simple neglect and idleness. Dishonesty is involved, and you must deal with it as firmly as your father would have done. The Bank expects it of you.'

'Oh, never fear,' she had told him impatiently, 'I am ready for anything.' Which had not, after all, proved quite true. Worse, Poxon's accusations that she was unsexed had touched a nerve which Matt Falconer had touched before him.

It was growing dark as she walked along. Hal was carrying a flambeau on a pole before her and Polly walked by her side. 'Wait for me here, if you please,' she told them, before she entered the Minster's porch which gave access to the nave. 'I shall not be long, I trust.'

There was a brazier burning in the street before the porch, and a man was stirring the coals into flaming life.

Hal and Polly warmed themselves at its welcome heat, but the Minster struck cold as Stacy entered it—to hear the choir singing and find just sufficient light for her to glory in the sight of the great window, The Five Sisters of York, of which she had often heard tell.

Alone in the all-enveloping gloom, Stacy had never felt so lost and isolated. Every rule by which she had lived since her father's death seemed to be under challenge, not only because of what had happened to her at Pontisford Hall—and what she had done with Matt Falconer—but also because of what loyalty to the Bank had compelled her to do in York. Poxon had earned his dismissal, but she could take no pleasure in her part in it, even if, at the end, she had shown him a mercy which neither her father nor Ephraim would have done. They would have had him before the magistrates and on his way to Botany Bay without a second thought.

She needed grace. She needed to feel that what she was doing, to others as well as to herself, although harsh, was just. Most of all she needed to come to terms with her own passionate nature. Until she had met Matt Falconer she had not known passion, had, indeed, denied that she could ever experience it. A few short days had shown her how wrong she was. The memory was with her still, and to her horror, instead of being remorseful for what she had done, she was waking each morning to regret that he was not in her bed. Instead, in his guise as the lion-man, Matt Falconer visited her nightly in her dreams. Dismayingly she also knew that her body burned, not with shame but with frustrated desire.

Kneeling down, hands covering her face, Stacy prayed for help, for guidance. For the first time she—a Blanchard—almost wished that she were a Roman Catholic, so that she might confess her sins and receive absolution. Perhaps after that the memory of his lips and hands would fade away and disappear.

After a little time she rose, to see Canon Gunter standing

in the aisle, dressed not as he had been in the bank's parlour but in his robes. He spoke hesitantly to her. 'You are not ill, I trust, Miss Blanchard? You are alone. Do you need help?'

What to say? Simply, 'Is it enough for us to try to do good, sir, even if our frailty means that we not only find it hard, but sometimes impossible? And if we backslide, may we be forgiven, however gross our sin?'

'If we truly repent, my dear. Yes.'

Stacy closed her eyes. How could she truly repent her night of love with Matt Falconer, however much she ought to do so?

'Repentance is hard, sir.'

'Oh, but consider, to do right and to repent is never easy. To be easy is the way of the sinner.'

That, at least, was true. She had fallen into bed with Matt Falconer with such consummate ease, but to repent of her sin seemed impossible. She tried again to discover whether the Canon had an answer for her, but since she could not tell him why she needed absolution she doubted whether he could help her.

'And does God forgive us our sins, even if we find it hard—nay, impossible—to repent?' Stacy heard her voice shake as she spoke.

The Canon considered her for a moment, doubtless, she later thought wryly, wondering what improbable sins Miss Anastasia Blanchard might have committed that she should so desperately ask him for help and absolution.

'I think that He would prefer us to repent, but I believe that, knowing our weak natures, He might be inclined to forgive us if we had tried to do so, even if we found it difficult.'

It was plain that he was not one of the new Evangelical clergy, who would have thundered at her about hellfire and damnation lying in wait for those who sinned and did not repent. Would she have preferred him to do so? Stacy wasn't sure. As though he had divined her thoughts he added gently, 'I can only advise you to throw yourself on the infinite mercy of God if you are troubled, my dear Miss Blanchard.'

She bowed. 'I will remember that, sir, and I thank you for your help.' And she walked on, aware that he was gazing thoughtfully after her as she moved away from him to rejoin her waiting servants.

Polly said to her as they crossed the deserted road, 'Only think, madam, we thought we saw Jeb Priestley while you were in the Minster. Hal and I went a little way down the road—keeping an eye on the porch, a-course, in case you came out—and we thought we saw him going into an ale-house.'

This confidence had the improbable effect of cheering Stacy up. 'Well,' she said briskly, 'I can imagine that if you did see Jeb Priestley he would most likely be making for an ale-house, but I also think it is highly unlikely that either he or his master is here in York. I distinctly remember Mr Falconer saying that he intended to return to London as soon as his business was ended at Pontisford, and that he did not wish to remain there any longer than he needed.'

'Hal thought it might have been him,' offered Polly pertly.

Doubtless Polly's wish to meet Jeb again was father to the thought! Well, she, Stacy, didn't want to see him or his arrogant master again.

But what if, said a little voice in her head, he has made you pregnant? What then? To which the only possible internal answer was, I'll think about that if it happens, which, pray God, it won't. After all, we only spent one night together, and I am constantly hearing tales about persons who have been married for years failing to have children when they most desperately need them to provide a succession for a title or for estates, so one night's madness would surely not be enough. Would it?

The truth is, she admitted to herself, and it was something which she could never have confided in Canon Gunter, I might repent of the possible consequence of the sin of becoming Matt Falconer's mistress for one mad night, but I don't repent of the night itself, even if I wish that it had never happened—especially seeing that I don't even like the man!

And what did such an admission make of the once virtuous Miss Anastasia Blanchard?

Chapter Eight

'York?' queried Jeb Priestley, thunderstruck. 'We are going to York? I thought that you said when we reached Pontisford that we should return to London as soon as our business here was done, which it is, and take a passage back to Virginia post-haste. What are we going to York for?' And then, staring at his master, 'Oh, never tell me! You are haring after Miss Anna Berriman.'

'Not at all.' Matt made his voice as rough as he could. He was standing in his bedroom at Pontisford Hall, packing his bags, a task which was, by rights, Jeb's, only somehow he always managed to avoid doing it. 'I had quite forgotten the woman existed.' Which was a thundering lie; he thought about her every time he went to his lonely bed, and frequently in the daytime too. Which was a nonsense, considering what a cold-hearted bitch she was—except when she was in his bed. He would never have thought that a woman could show him two such different faces—as well as such a splendid body.

He swore at a recalcitrant shirt before stuffing it any old how into his bag. 'I need to see the lawyers there about some property in the town which my great-aunt owned— or so some papers I found seemed to hint—something which that ass of a lawyer in London appeared to know nothing of.'

Which was the truth. Or part of it. The real truth being that he would have taken the papers back to London with him, told Grimes to get on with sorting the whole business out, had they not provided him with the most splendid excuse for 'haring after Miss Anna Berriman'—Jeb's words—but he had to admit the truth of them. The woman haunted him. And, after so many years of loving them and leaving them, that was almost a bad joke.

'Well, I must say, I don't mind seeing Polly again, and for God's sake, m'lord, Mr Falconer, sir, or Mad Matt, whichever you prefer today, allow me to pack your bag for you before you ruin everything. You're showing a rare impatience to be off, I must say. Good in bed, was she?'

Even for Jeb this was insolence indeed. But how could you rebuke a man who had once saved your life for you, albeit you had already saved his? And who, despite his wagging tongue, was as faithful a friend as a man could have?

'Matt will do,' he told Jeb mildly, 'as I've informed you often enough before.'

'They don't like me to call you Matt here, though,' mourned Jeb, folding m'lord's fine cotton underwear. 'That poor old man Horrocks closes his eyes every time I fail to call you m'lord, and then "m'lords" you at twice the normal rate for the rest of the day to make up for my impudence, I suppose. They like bowing and scraping here, and no mistake. "Yes, m'lord, no, m'lord, pray walk all over me, m'lord, do,"' he mimicked savagely. 'You'll need a new pair of boots when you reach York. These are on their last legs. And a new coat and shirt and stockings and hat, if you hope to impress the lady. There was money there, you know. An heiress, do you think?'

'No, I don't, and I'm not going to,' retorted Matt cryptically, leaving Jeb to work out what he meant and aiming

a half-hearted blow at him at the same time, which Jeb
dodged dexterously. 'And for your information, Miss Anna
Berriman is most definitely not the purpose of my visit. I
thought that I might ride over and take a last look at my
childhood home.'

And that was another truth, and an unwelcome one.
Whether it was the passing years or the sense of having
lost something which he had not known he had treasured
until it was gone, he had been experiencing a burning desire
to see The Eyrie again. And what a terrible name that was
for the beautiful Jacobean mansion which the first Earl Falconer had built after doing some dirty diplomatic business
for James I, and which had been paid for by one of the few
grants of money made by that miserly king to a deserving
subject.

He could ride over from York to see it, if only from a
distance. He had no intention of accepting the olive-branch
which his father had offered to him. Too much water had
flowed under too many bridges for him ever to set foot in
The Eyrie again. It astonished him that he should experience such a sharp pang at the very thought of its loss.

A flash of memory showed him the room which he had
occupied after he had graduated from the nursery and before he had been packed off to be a midshipman. He had
been the third son, highly unlikely to inherit, but Frank, the
second son, had died at a badly taken fence in the hunting
field shortly after he had reached thirty—and a mercy for
the estate that he had, since his career had been one long
debauch. He had been drunk on the day of his death, unfit
to ride, but had insisted on doing so.

And Rollo, the heir, who had looked as though he might
live forever, had departed this life a year ago; how, Matt
didn't know, nor did he want to know. Grimes had started
to tell him something of it, but he had stopped him with a
sharp, 'So far as I am concerned Rollo died for me twelve

and more years ago; what happened to him since means nothing to me.'

But, astonishingly, The Eyrie did. He could see the plain of York from the turret window, he remembered, and sometimes, on a clear day, he could almost convince himself that he saw the Minster's towers rising from it.

So he told himself that it was neither Miss Anna Berriman nor his aunt's property in York and outside it which drew him there, but one last chance before he left England forever to see that window again. Even if it was only from a distance. Memory told him of the bookcase beneath its leaded panes, his treasures ranged along the top of it, and on the facing wall the old print which showed Charles II's ships firing on the Dutch fleet in one of that king's few naval victories. A Falconer had commanded a ship there, he remembered.

Only, when he reached York and discovered that his aunt had owned a house in the town, and a small manor house outside it, he decided to open the town house and stay there for the Christmas season—he might catch a glimpse of Miss Berriman. Each time that he walked the streets he looked for her—but had no luck at all. One might almost have supposed that he had imagined her, and the night that they had spent together.

He had casually asked the lawyer he had found in York, Hayes, someone jovial and rubicund, quite unlike Grimes, whether he had come across a Miss Berriman who had lately arrived in York, but that gentleman did not connect her with the Miss Anastasia Blanchard, the Bankeress, who had recently scandalised York, and had shaken his head.

'You might,' he had offered, when Matt had told him that he wished to find the lady, 'take the opportunity to visit the Assembly Rooms for the Christmas Ball. If, as you think, she is a person of consequence, she is almost certain to attend.'

Well, yes, he might attend the Christmas Ball at the Assembly Rooms, Matt told Hayes as well as himself, but not simply to meet Miss Berriman. Oh, no, that was not it at all—on the other hand he found it difficult to understand why exactly he *did* want to attend something which was the kind of event which he always avoided—the small beer of living! But how to attend, when he knew no one of consequence in York who might introduce him to the Master of Ceremonies who ruled the Assembly?

Fate was on his side, after all. By chance, walking along, admiring the Minster's east window, he met Jack Vernon, an acquaintance from his days in the Navy. Matt hailed him as though he had been his oldest and dearest friend, and Jack immediately invited him to join the party he was escorting to the Assembly Ball. Matt had remembered Jack as a man of the most undiscriminating goodwill, and his memory had not deceived him.

'I shall be escorting my wife and her sister to the dance—a classy little filly, my sister-in-law Phoebe—you not hitched yet? No? By Jove, she's just the girl for you, then, and a little fortune comes with her—not that you mind that it's little now, eh, seeing that that ne'er-do-well brother of yours has gone to meet his last rest?' And he gave Matt a poke in the ribs which left him bruised for days.

But he accepted the invitation all the same, had Jeb dress him to a turn, as he hadn't dressed himself for years, and found himself in the Assembly Rooms, part of Jack's party. He dutifully made a leg at Phoebe, who wasn't to his taste at all, thanked Jack, and was introduced all over again to Jack's cousin, Viscount Trotternish, whom Matt remembered as plain George Drummond before he had inherited.

'Matt Falconer! I do believe you haven't changed a bit since we fought together at Trafalgar!'

It was as though the scandal had never happened, or Jack and George were being tactful. Matt rather thought that they weren't. Neither of them had ever been tactful when they had been young, and they hadn't changed much with age, only grown fatter. He supposed that being a hard-working farmer himself had kept him in trim.

What Trot, as he insisted Matt call him, was interested in was heiresses.

Matt asked him impulsively, as though they were young naval lieutenants again, 'What the devil are you doing here, Trot? Not your sort of thing at all.'

'Might say the same to you, Matt. And where have you been all these years?

'Farming in Virginia.'

'Haw-haw, you always did like a joke! But I suppose you've come here for the same reason I have. Like to get your hand on the dibs even if you do have to take the great heiress as well! Now, I'd prefer little Phoebe, but she ain't got enough tin to keep the old home in lead for the roof, whereas this one—' and he raised his eyes prayerfully to heaven '—is rolling in it.'

'Now what great heiress is this, Trot? I'm not up to snuff about such matters these days.'

'Must be behindhand, then, Matt, eh, not to know the Bankeress, the Blanchard heiress? That's why there's so many unattached bachelors here tonight, and all sober. She's supposed to be coming with the Beauchamp party. Rumour says that they're all staying overnight at her place in York—and then she's off to Bramham with them tomorrow. You remember the Beauchamps, eh, Matt?'

Yes, Matt did remember the Beauchamps—just. He didn't, however, remember any rich Blanchard family in York, and twelve years out of England meant that he had little idea of what was what in the society line.

'The Blanchard heiress who is a bankeress, Trot? And what, pray, is a bankeress? You have me all agog. I don't remember any Blanchards around York.'

'Why, she owns Blanchard's Bank, Matt. You do remember Blanchard's, surely? She's old Louis' daughter. He died suddenly two years ago, left it all to her—to run!

Imagine, a female owning Blanchard's! And run it she does. She arrived at the York branch three weeks ago, and came down on old Poxon the manager like a ton of bricks. Found out that he had been robbing the bank blind, and had her footman throw him into the street. Sacked half the clerks for helping him, and read the Riot Act to the rest in the bank parlour. They say she ran the bank herself for a week before she handed it over to the new man.'

Matt might have made the inevitable connection with Miss Anna Berriman immediately, before he had so much as seen her, if Trot hadn't grabbed him by the arm, exclaiming, 'Good God, yes! There she is, with the Beauchamps. Some might say she's a stunner, but she looks a cold fish to me. Still, the Blanchard millions would make up for that, eh?'

And, like Jack Vernon, he abused Matt's ribs all over again. Not that Matt noticed—he was far too busy staring at Miss Anna Berriman, who was Miss Anastasia Blanchard, and saying to himself grimly, of course, of course. The Bankeress. I might have guessed.

Stacy had had to admit that meeting her aunt Beauchamp again had revived memories and feelings which she had thought she had forgotten. Louis Blanchard had never cared for his wife's sister, but Stacy had always found her a loving aunt until the final quarrel with her father had occurred over his training Stacy to succeed him.

She had corresponded with Aunt Beauchamp, secretly and against her father's wishes, but she had not seen her aunt or her uncle again until two days ago when they had arrived at her York home and her aunt had thrown her arms around her, crying, 'At last, my love. Let me look at you. You are as lovely as I thought that you would turn out to be! But oh, my dear, what is this I hear of you? Running the bank in York? That might have pleased your poor, dear father but I cannot say that it pleases me! And you are still unmarried. I blame your father for that.'

'Dear Aunt,' Stacy had murmured tearfully, 'do not let us quarrel, rather let us agree to disagree. I have my life and you have yours. And from now until I leave Yorkshire I shall take a holiday from work. Mr Greaves has finally arrived, quite cured of the illness which overtook him on the way here, and will look after the Bank for me until I return home.'

With that her aunt had to be satisfied, and her uncle too, that amiable, jovial man, quite unlike Louis Blanchard—or Matt Falconer, for that matter. All the same, once her aunt was alone with Louisa Landen they had sadly agreed that poor Stacy had been done no favour by her father when he had trained her to succeed him in the Bank. 'But at least she is willing to attend the Ball,' Aunt Beauchamp had said, and had looked with pride at Stacy when she'd walked downstairs to join the party ready to leave for the Assembly Rooms.

Stacy's only regret was that Louisa was not coming with them. 'You do not need me now that you have your aunt,' she had told Stacy, 'and I am growing too old for such junketings.' She had never really recovered from her illness at Pontisford, and Stacy was beginning to realise, with a pang, that the safe world in which she had lived for so long, with Louisa always by her side, was beginning to disintegrate. Change was all about her.

To her surprise she found herself looking forward to the Ball. She had dressed herself for it with great care, and walked into the Assembly Rooms conscious that she was looking her best. She was wearing a dress of pale green silk with the slightly lower waistline that fashion now demanded, trimmed with seed-pearls on the bodice and skirt, and a splendid pearl collar around her long and swan-like neck. Her fan was large, decorated with arabesques of seed-pearls and tiny emeralds. The whole ensemble served to emphasise the glowing green eyes set in an ivory face of classical purity.

Her cousin Anthony Beauchamp, who was her escort for the evening, bowed over her hand, looked into her eyes and said, 'My dear Anastasia. If only you would allow us to introduce you to Society I am sure that you would become all the rage.'

'Oh, as to that, sir,' she replied, tapping his arm gently with her fan as though she had been coquetting with men all her life, instead of doing so for the first time, 'I have no time to be all the rage; my presence is required elsewhere.'

He bowed again, his eyes hard on her. 'You must allow me to suggest that you should reform your ways to accommodate Society's demands and allow us to enjoy your charming presence.'

Well, that was as may be, and Stacy was about to answer him as kindly as she could, for she had absolutely no intention of transforming herself into a copy of one of his sisters. Their conversation appeared to centre on balls, their latest *toilette*, and handsome young men—in that order. Shrugging a little, she glanced across the room—only to see, gazing at her with a face like thunder, Matthew Falconer, Lord Radley! And where had *he* sprung from? And why was he looking at her like that? It was he who had wronged her, not she him. Worse, he was advancing towards her with that empty idiot George Trotternish by his side.

Anthony Beauchamp, staring at his magnificent presence, said involuntarily, 'Who the devil's that?' to have his mother reply,

'Why, I do believe it's Matt Falconer—Matt Radley, I suppose we ought to call him now—and goodness, how he has changed. I'm not surprised that you didn't recognise him. But what is he doing here?'

'Matt Radley?' Anthony sounded as stunned as Stacy

felt, and she could not be surprised at his astonishment. Beside Anthony's bland and civilised charm, Matt Falconer looked more than ever like some pirate out of a Minerva Press novel, come to life in all his barbaric glory.

His superb clothing only served to enhance his savage appearance: he was more leonine than ever. His coat and breeches were skin-tight, revealing the muscularity of a body which put that of every other man in the room to shame. His face was so stern and strong that ordinary canons of handsomeness seemed unnecessary—nay, even a drawback. And every woman's eye was on him.

Stacy could not tear hers from him either. Especially since his were fixed so determinedly on her that she had the unwelcome impression that she had lost every article of clothing which she was wearing. Worse still, she realised that she was looking at him and seeing his remarkable torso naked, as it had been that shameful night, in all its splendidly muscled glory, his clothing too having fallen away.

George Trotternish was, as usual, sublimely unaware, as was Jack Vernon behind him, of the sensation which their friend and guest was causing. To add to the hum of excitement which ran round the room, many of the older persons present remembered both Matt and the scandal, and were busy reminding one another of it.

Stacy saw with rising desperation that Matt neither knew nor cared about the brouhaha he was creating, only bowing impassively when Trot said eagerly, 'Dear Lady Beauchamp, do allow me to present to you my old friend and fellow sailor, Lord Radley.'

Aunt Beauchamp said faintly, 'Oh, I have known Lord Radley since he was a child—but we have not met for many years. I am surprised to see you here, sir.' For some reason she felt unable to put down Trot or cut Matt. Possibly Matt's tremendous presence and his ignoring of the fact that he was officially *persona non grata* because of his disgraceful conduct so many years ago accounted for her consenting to receive him—which meant that everyone else at the Assembly Ball would.

Matt was taking Aunt Beauchamp's hand and bowing over it. 'I have inherited property in and near York, dear Lady Beauchamp,' he told her gravely. 'I have been in the United States since we last met. I remember, though, that you were kind to me when I was a boy and sailed kites with Anthony here.'

Aunt Beauchamp said feverishly, 'Oh, he was much younger than you, and I recall that it was you who was kind to him. I must introduce you to my party,' and she began the civilities which ruled the social world over which she presided.

Matt was behaving politely and modestly, quite unlike the savage Stacy remembered from Pontisford Hall. And now it was her turn to be presented to him, and he was bowing to her and saying, as smoothly as though he were meeting her for the first time, 'An honour, Miss Blanchard. I must admit that I have heard so much about you that I feel that I know you already.' And his eyes were defying her as he came out with this splendidly ambiguous statement.

'Oh, Lord Radley, there you have the advantage of me,' she threw back at him, for if he wanted to play games with her, then so would she respond to him, 'for I am sure that had we ever met before I could hardly have forgotten doing so.' Her eyes were sparkling at him, sending him a message that she was quite unaware of.

Aunt Beauchamp was saying, as the music began, 'My dear Matt, if you have no partner for this dance then I am sure that my dear niece would be willing to oblige you,' ignoring the black look with which her son was favouring her.

Indeed, as Matt led the unwilling Stacy on to the floor for the cotillion, for she was unable to refuse her aunt's wish, Anthony turned on his dominant mother.

'I do not understand you, madam. You know perfectly well that I wished to begin the evening by dancing with my cousin. Instead you have handed her over to a man of such ill fame that I am surprised that you even deigned to receive him, never mind commit an innocent young woman into his care!'

Aunt Beauchamp watched Stacy and Matt take their position in the set and begin to move through the dance's intricate pattern. She was a woman of great character, even if that character had no real depth, and she went her own way with little consideration for what others might think—even her own son.

'My dear Anthony—' she smiled at him over her fan '—I have no wish for you to marry your cousin. Cousins shouldn't marry—bad for horses and even worse for us—and you would never be able to stand up to Stacy. Not that I want her to marry Matt Falconer—but as to receiving him, that is a different matter. I thought that he was badly treated years ago, and it is time that story was forgotten. Both Rollo and Camilla Falconer are dead, and the scandal should die with them. Now, why don't you ask pretty little Phoebe Whatever-her-name-is, Jack Vernon's sister-in-law, to dance with you? She's the sort of child you ought to marry—pretty and biddable.'

So now he had madam almost in his arms again! But she was intent on keeping him at a distance. Her hand might be in his, but that was all. Matt tried to look her in the eye, make her acknowledge him, but she resolutely kept her own gaze modestly fixed on the floor as though she were a young girl at her first ball. The result was that he was prey to the most dreadful and conflicting emotions.

From the first moment that he had seen her, tall and graceful at the other end of the room, her long neck elegantly inclined towards the young popinjay to whom she was talking, he had been unable to stop looking at her.

Really, madam was superb. As always, she carried herself with such damnable unconscious pride, but, more than that, tonight there was a glow, a radiance about her which he could not remember her possessing at Pontisford.

She even laughed lightly once, and as he moved nearer to her in the dance he could not prevent himself from mentally stripping her beautiful gown from her so that he could once again visualise her splendid breasts. He could remember only too well that he had held and caressed them with both his hands and his mouth. And as she advanced and retreated towards him, head modestly inclined, Matt was suddenly agonisingly aware that his body, constrained as it was by his tight clothes, would, if he was not careful, betray to the whole world his rampant and aroused desire for her.

Lust! That must be what he felt for her, and why he should feel it for the Bankeress, a cold, calculating machine, according to York gossip, he couldn't imagine. Down, Fido, down, he told his treacherous body, for the mere sight of her was proving his undoing. He tried to turn his mind to other things, took his eyes away from her face, only to see that now she had raised hers and was studying him as though, he thought angrily, he were an insect laid out for her to dissect.

To no avail. The memory of the night when he had wronged her, and she had so enthusiastically helped him to do so, was as sharp and clear as though it had happened only a few hours before, instead of a few weeks. He must be going mad. Even when she turned away from him, and all he could see of her was the long and lovely line of her back, the thing which held him most was the smooth elegance of her graceful and rounded behind as it moved beneath her light clothing—and the memory of his hands stroking it!

He was turning into a satyr and it was all her doing. Desire, lust, whatever it was which held him in thrall, also demanded that he needed to speak to her, so that he might hear that enchanting if disdainful voice, provoke her into saying something, anything, even if it was only something to put him down.

'You are enjoying yourself, madam?' he asked her, his voice glacial.

'Indeed, sir. And why should I not?' Stacy was retreating away from him even as she spoke, only to meet him again, hand extended, and say, 'You appear uncomfortable, sir. Do I take it that you are not enjoying yourself?'

The bitch! She was mocking him, he was sure. Did she guess the pother that he was in? Surely not. She was a maiden lady of impeccable virtue, after all—or had been until Matt Falconer had seized hold of her and thrown her upon her bed!

He felt himself breaking into a sweat while she, the cold-blooded doxy, was raising her eyebrows at him as the music brought her back to him, so that he felt constrained to say, 'A gentleman's clothing, especially a cravat, seems especially designed *not* to dance in, which explains my discomfort a little.'

Only to have her remark when next they met, 'Oh, I suppose that in the wilds of America you are more accustomed to perform clad simply in war-paint and feathers. This must make a most unwelcome change, I do agree—but you could hardly expect us to accommodate your more savage desires.'

'If I were to accommodate my more savage desires,' he told her between his teeth as he spun her around, 'you would be on the floor with me, and the company would retreat screaming.'

Well, I asked for that, was Stacy's inward response. She supposed that she ought to be shocked, but the picture which he had conjured up was such a wickedly amusing one that she was hard put to it not to laugh, especially when her next partner in the dance, her cousin Anthony, growled jealously between clenched teeth, 'If that fellow is annoying you, Cousin Stacy, do tell me, and I shall see that he ceases to do so.'

She shook her head at him and turned around, to meet Matt going the opposite way. She offered him her hand, wondering why, as he took it, a strange thrill always ran through her body when he touched her, or she him. Nothing like that had ever happened when Anthony Beauchamp took her hand in his.

Matt said, as they moved together, also through clenched teeth, she was amused to note, 'I see that you have a smile for that fribble who was entertaining you when I arrived. I suppose that you save your scowls and curses for me.'

'Of course,' she told him sweetly as the music stopped and they bowed at one another, 'for you deserve them, and he does not. After all, it was you who set upon me as though I were some lightskirt who prowls the Haymarket, while he has always behaved towards me with perfect rectitude.'

This goaded Matt into further unwise speech. 'Seeing that he is only half a man, I am sure that perfect manners are all he is left with.'

'True, and as you have no manners at all he must have inherited your share.'

'And who has inherited yours,' he asked her savagely as the music ended, 'seeing that we are an excellent match in the land where bad manners reign? My memory of your conduct at Pontisford is still fresh.'

'And I of yours, sir,' she said as they walked back to where her aunt's party was seated. 'But then, what can one expect of a savage who is accustomed to dancing clad only in paint and feathers?'

'The same as from a shrew who possesses a calculating-machine instead of a heart!' he ground back at her.

'Then we *are* well-matched,' Stacy informed him sweetly. She was astonished to find that, as before when she was with him, she had never felt so alive, every nerve in her body tingling and a strange excitement growing in the pit of her stomach. It was almost as though she wanted him to fall on her again. And, judging by his expression, if they had not been parading themselves in such a public place, fall on her he would have.

She could feel the tension in the strong body which walked so proudly beside her, and knew that it matched her own. When he looked at her the amber eyes grew ever more golden, the pupils enlarged—but she was unaware that as he betrayed the signs of sexual arousal, so did she.

He handed her into her chair, and, after the most polite fashion, as though he had not been insulting and assaulting her with every word, asked, 'You would care for a drink, madam? You look a trifle heated.' And she knew that he was tormenting her, was recognising what her body was telling her, and was taking a subtle delight in letting her know that he knew—and that he was breaching her defences.

Stacy could no longer bear to have him beside her. She was in danger of saying and doing something which she would later regret.

'Indeed, sir, a cooling drink would be most welcome,' she replied, and she watched him leave her, moving through the company as though he were a panther prowling, and truly would be more at home wearing merely paint and feathers as she had mocked him.

After that the evening became a blur for both of them, but a blur against which each saw the other plain and clear. Even when Aunt Beauchamp engaged him in conversation, trapping him into agreeing to visit Bramham Castle to bring in the New Year, leaving Stacy to be surrounded by a crowd of admirers, all astonished that the Bankeress was such an unusual beauty, they remained completely aware of one another and no one else.

'I think, Matt,' Aunt Beauchamp admonished him as they watched Stacy performing in the quadrille with Anthony, Matt with something like murder in his heart at the sight, 'that it is time that you took my niece on the floor for the next dance. For you to ask her twice would not occasion comment. More would occur if you were not to dance at all. It is the waltz, but I think that her advanced years would save her from scandal.'

'Her advanced years!' burst from Matt involuntarily. 'Pray, madam, what years does she have? And why has no one yet claimed her in marriage? One would have thought that inheriting the Bank would be a great attraction.'

'Alas,' sighed Aunt Beauchamp, 'she insists on running the Bank, and few husbands would allow their wives to continue doing so after marriage—and she is naturally fearful of fortune-hunters. To be in her late twenties and have such gifts—I blame her odious father for encouraging her to follow a course more suited to a young man than a young woman.' And she rolled her eyes to heaven as Stacy, her hand on Anthony's arm, walked towards them.

Jealousy, pure and simple jealousy, roared through Matt at the sight. He could have strangled poor Anthony, whom years ago he had found a good friend and a kind and biddable child. Now he saw only a rival. But a rival to what? Bedding madam? Ravishing the Bankeress again? What in God's name was possessing him? And how could such a cold-hearted creature as Lady Beauchamp had just described arouse such passions in him? He felt sure that the strength of them was written on his face! He had not been in such a lather since he had first become aware in his early youth of why women had been placed on earth, and what delights a man could share with them.

Perhaps, however, nothing showed. For madam seemed coolness itself. Anthony Beauchamp, ever the gentleman, bowed unwillingly at Matt as Aunt Beauchamp announced officiously, 'I believe that Matt wishes to ask dear Stacy to waltz with him. Do you waltz, Stacy?'

Yes, she *was* matchmaking, thought her son angrily,

whatever she said. And why should his mother think that his cousin ought to be handed over to such a savage disguised as a gentleman? For a moment he thought of objecting, of challenging the brute, but from long ago he remembered Matt Falconer's strength, his cold courage, and decided against it.

Which was just as well, for before Stacy could manage, Oh, dear Aunt, I am tired; I fear that waltzing is beyond me. Pray excuse me, Lord Radley, there was a sudden and excited stir around the ballroom as a party of late arrivals were bowed through the door by an obsequious Master of Ceremonies. Some great personage led them, no doubt.

Some great personage did. Quizzing-glasses were raised, ladies chattered excitedly behind uplifted fans, and by the time that the great personage had crossed the floor he and the object of his sudden interest were the only unmoved people in the room.

For once Stacy lost her own cool control a little as she saw first Aunt Beauchamp's face set in an agonised smile, and then felt Matt Falconer's whole body stiffen beside her. The newcomer, attired in the black silk court dress of the late eighteenth century and followed by a small group of splendidly turned out friends and relatives, seemed sublimely unaware of the stir he was causing.

He was making straight for them, Stacy realised, and as he did so, as he drew near, so that he was under the full blaze of the great main chandelier above them, Stacy saw him fully for the first time—and also saw something else.

Not only was he as tall as Matt Falconer, but, although a trifle stooped, he had also once possessed as splendid a body. Facially he informed her of what Matt would look like if he lived into his late sixties.

She turned querying eyes on both Matt and Aunt Beauchamp as the newcomer paused a little short of them and said involuntarily, for she could almost feel the pain radiating from the man beside her, 'Matt?'

It was the first time that she had used his name in other than despite, and he answered her distantly, not using her name as a weapon, his attention fully engaged by the man before him. 'No need to worry, Stacy. It's only my father. I present to you, Miss Anastasia Blanchard, the most noble the Earl Falconer, KG.'

Chapter Nine

'And what, Radley,' asked the Earl Falconer of his son, after he had done the pretty with Stacy, Uncle Beauchamp, Aunt Beauchamp, the Honourable Anthony Beauchamp, Viscount Trotternish, Jack Vernon and wife, little Phoebe and the assembled nobility and gentry, and the music had started again, and Trot had carried Stacy off, Matt having been cornered by his parent, 'brings you here?'

'I would prefer, sir,' was Matt's stiff reply, 'not to be addressed by that name. I am plain Matthew Falconer.'

'But I, on the other hand, would prefer to use it,' was his father's reply to that. For a moment father and son, staring at one another, were as alike as two new-minted coins, showing heads with the profiles of eagles, or lions, or whatever animal or bird of prey you preferred.

'Come, Radley, you have not answered me. I asked you why you were here. Grimes distinctly informed me that you intended to leave England as soon as your business at Pontisford was over.'

'I changed my mind,' Matt returned coolly. He could hardly bear to look at his father. All his young life he had worshipped him, but nothing he had ever done had pleased. With the benefit of maturity he now saw that they were too much alike, not only in appearance but in character. Neither man brooked being controlled by others, or bending to another's will.

'But why York? And, seeing that you have chosen to visit York, could you not bring yourself to oblige me for once, and visit The Eyrie as I asked you?'

Matt's expression was a grim one. 'Now, sir, you of all people should know why I never wish to see The Eyrie again. And have you forgotten that, on the last occasion I visited you, you ordered your footmen to beat me from the door if I tried to enter?'

The Earl's face twisted. 'If you must know, Radley, I regretted that order almost as soon as it was made...'

'I will beg leave, sir, to doubt that. I am coming to wish that I had left Pontisford only to take passage to Baltimore again. My home now is not The Eyrie but a plantation in Virginia, where a man is judged by what he does, and not what others think that he might have done, or by the bedroom he was born in.'

The old man before him, Matt saw with a savage pleasure, winced at this.

'Suppose I were to confess, Radley, that I have recently come to believe that I might have been mistaken in my beliefs about your conduct twelve years ago, that I might have been over-hasty?'

Matt, hardly able to credit what he was hearing, stared back at his father.

'Why, sir, I would be compelled to answer that such a re-examination of your prejudices is at least twelve years too late in coming. The Matt Falconer you knew then died long ago, and the new one does not need your belated forgiveness—should you feel inclined to offer it.'

His father bent his grey head in acknowledgement. 'Nevertheless, Radley...'

Matt could not bear to be addressed by that name; he said violently, 'Come, sir, I asked you not to call me Radley, and I meant it. I only knew one who bore the name, and I do not wish to be reminded of him. You say, or appear to say, that you are now prepared to question your long-established beliefs as to what happened between my brother, myself and my poor dead Camilla. That being so, I am astonished that you did not see fit to inform me earlier of your change of mind, in view of the speed with which you threw me off at my brother's lying behest.'

'Allow me to say that it is only since the circumstances of your brother's death that I began to question myself. The letter which I sent to you asking you to return to England so that we might discuss the possibilities of a *rapprochement* most probably arrived in Virginia after you had left for England. I am now in hopes that together we may review and reassess the past.'

Matt acknowledged this with a slight dip of the head, and said, 'Well, that being so, sir, I am happy to learn that you acknowledge that you *might* have been mistaken. And that, if you please, should cease correspondence between us. Twelve years ago you disowned me, and since then Matt Falconer has become an American farmer, and that is what he wishes to remain. I do not wish to discuss the dead past with you—ever. Let it remain dead.'

His cold impassivity contrasted with the pain on his father's face. That father remembered the days when this son had been famous for his youthful impetuosity, not for his cold self-control. The long years apart had brought great changes. The man before him possessed a strength of character which was beginning to convince the Earl that he might truly have wronged him. He tried again to reach beyond the cold mask which confronted him.

'Nevertheless, I must remind you, Radley, that you stand heir to a great name, and a great estate.'

Matt shook his head in wonder. 'Why, sir, as to that, I want neither. I almost changed my name from Falconer but, since that carries no burden of unwanted tradition or inheritance in my new country, it hardly seemed worth the trouble.'

The old man said grimly, seeing that the younger one refused to bend before him, 'Nevertheless, sir, like it or not, one day in the not too distant future you will be Earl Falconer.'

The music which had been playing as an accompaniment to their cold and painful conversation was coming to an end. Behind his father Matt could see Stacy in Trot's arms, being whirled into a series of spinning turns. He wondered why he could endure her being in Trot's company when the sight of her with Anthony Beauchamp filled him with jealous rage. He decided ruefully that it was because he thought that Trot was no real threat to him where the Bankeress was concerned, while Anthony Beauchamp was.

His father was saying painfully, 'You are not attending to me, sir.'

'I beg your pardon.' Matt was suddenly compelled to admit his gracelessness, if only because the desolation in the old face before him matched that which he had felt for so many years. 'But I was watching Miss Blanchard. Lord Trotternish is hardly the most suitable companion for her, I fear.'

The Earl turned to see Trot and Stacy exchanging final bows. 'Miss Blanchard? Do I understand that she is the young woman who now runs Blanchard's Bank? Are you acquainted with her, Radley?'

Was he acquainted with her? Of course he was. Had they not lain in one another's arms all night?

'Yes, sir,' he rejoined stiffly. 'I am acquainted with her.'

'Then I would wish to speak a little more with her. I knew her father—a most remarkable man. I am told that the daughter is equally so. You will do me the honour of presenting the young lady to me again. I was not fully aware of who she was when Lady Beauchamp introduced us.'

Why, the old goat, thought Matt derisively, he thinks that I may be interested in her, I do believe, and would not object to having Blanchard's Bank and Blanchard's money added to Falconer wealth! He wondered what his father would say to him if he told him the truth. That he had misjudged his son over the sad affair of his brother's wife, but if he assumed the worst in the relationship between the Honourable, the Baron Radley and Miss Anastasia Blanchard, spinster and ex-virgin, he would not be going far wrong!

'The whirligig of time brings in his revenges,' Shakespeare had once written, and Matt, reintroducing Stacy, most unwillingly, to his father, wanted to shout at him, You had better send for your footmen to attack me with their whips again, Father, for I have ravished a virgin—and the truth is I do not regret having done so. Far from that, I would have her in my bed again instantly if she would consent to come, for in it her sharp tongue and sharper mind are stilled, and she uses her intellect to promote our bodies' pleasure and not to make money!

But he said nothing at all, and watched with satiric amusement his father using all his undoubted charm on his son's late bed-mate.

'I knew your father,' the Earl was saying to Stacy, quite unconscious of the nature of his son's thoughts, thinking himself that Miss Blanchard was a fine-looking woman and that any man could do worse than marry her, seeing what a fortune she brought with her, 'and he and I were good friends. I always found his advice most useful.' He paused a moment, then added, 'I believe that I met you once, many years ago when you were quite small.'

Stacy bowed, murmured a trifle mischievously, 'I do not remember the occasion, sir, but I do have the honour of being well-acquainted with your account with us, if I may raise such a matter on the occasion of a Christmas ball!'

Clever as well as beautiful, a rare combination, and no

wonder that his son was interested in her, was the Earl's conclusion. He had seen a certain look in Matt's eye when Miss Blanchard had walked towards them, and he had read it aright. He was as aware as she was that the encounter between first Matt Falconer and the father from whom he was estranged, and now his obvious interest in the Bankeress, was causing universal comment and interest among the spectators which almost transcended common politeness. But like his son—and the woman before him—he never allowed such considerations as that to affect him.

'You know my son, Radley, I believe?' he asked her.

Now, how should she answer that? Suppose she gave him the correct answer—in the biblical sense of the word 'know', only too well! But that would never do. Some truths were best not uttered, so she remarked, a trifle undiplomatically perhaps, 'Well enough to know that he does not like to be called Radley.'

Far from antagonising the Earl, this amused him. He laughed a little. 'Yes, you do know him. I should have collected that Louis Blanchard's daughter would be blessed with judgement beyond the common run.'

Aye, thought Stacy wickedly, but what judgement did I display when I allowed your son to bed me so incontinently? She was unaware that such forbidden thoughts as these were beginning to melt the ice with which she had always surrounded herself, so that more than one man watching her wondered how anyone could ever have dubbed her cold.

They talked easily on neutral matters for a few more moments, until the Earl said, 'As a matter of interest, Miss Blanchard, although it is perhaps a question which I should not ask you, how did you come to meet Radley? On business, one supposes?'

Well, here was one truth Stacy could offer m'lord which could offend no one. 'Oh, you may certainly ask me, sir, and I shall equally certainly respond. On my way north to

York, where I had some business at the Bank and where I also intended to spend Christmas and the New Year with my aunt Beauchamp, my mother's sister, my coach broke down near Pontisford Hall during the recent great snow, and Lord Radley most graciously gave me and my entourage shelter for several nights until we were able to travel north again.'

Which was, when all was said and done, one way of telling a thundering lie so that it sounded like truth. The Earl took what she said at face value.

'You reassure me, madam. Most gratifying that my son has learned to conduct himself with such propriety. Gracious, indeed! Virginia must have had a civilising effect on him. I shall be delighted to observe it in action, for I am invited to Bramham for the New Year, and Lady Beauchamp informs me that she has also asked Radley to join us.'

The room swung about Stacy for a moment. How in the world was she going to be able to bear the constant presence of Matt Falconer in her life? She had never for one moment thought of having to dodge around him at Bramham. The effect that he had on her was so powerful, so disturbing, that she could hardly contemplate being able to endure it. The ice around her was melting with a vengeance.

More melted during the evening. She was relieved that Louisa was not there to watch and judge her. For some reason it seemed imperative that she show Matt that she made nothing of him at all, by making a great deal of such empty fools as poor Trot and the beaux from York who thought that they might have a chance of netting the Bankeress.

So light-hearted was she, so gay, that later on, after she had shared supper with Trot, Anthony Beauchamp, and a galaxy of young men who vied for her favour, Matt, who had spent most of the evening propped against the wall, looking morose and drinking over-much weak-minded punch, growled at her as she arrived back after dancing the minuet, 'A word with you, madam.'

Breathless, rosy, her lips parted, strands of her dark hair curling loose around her face, so that she gave the impression of a woodland nymph who was only waiting to be caught by her satyr, Stacy nodded in his direction. 'Of course, sir.'

'What has happened to the cold-hearted mermaid who froze us all to death at Pontisford, madam? Are you intent on snaring every man in the room, married and unmarried? Oh, yes, I saw you cavorting with my sister's husband, Bibury.'

'For shame,' retorted Stacy spiritedly. 'I only dance where I am asked.'

Matt could not help himself. The man who had vowed never to commit himself to any woman was now in the thrall of the last woman on earth who he would have thought could move him.

'It is not your dancing I take objection to, madam, but the way you conduct yourself before, during and after the dance.'

'Oh!' Stacy blazed at him. 'Who the devil are you to act as my chaperon? Recollect how you behaved yourself with me, and learn that all the men with whom I have stood up tonight have conducted themselves towards me with perfect propriety.'

He could not help himself; the words flew out before he could stop them. 'It is not their propriety which concerns me, madam, but yours.'

'Hypocrite!' she flung at him. 'Oh, base. Recollect your own lack of propriety where I am concerned before you animadvert on mine.'

'Animadvert?' he flung back, as though it were a ball which they were tossing between them, his amber eyes glowing. 'Did you learn that at the Bank's desk? It might be better if you had remained in the Bank's parlour, and then we poor devils would all be safe from your lures.'

Had they not been in so public a place that they were compelled to exchange insults in so pleasantly polite a manner that they might have been exchanging words of the deepest love, Stacy would have cracked him across the face again. Instead, she lifted her fan and turned to Aunt Beauchamp, who, slightly alarmed by she knew not what, was coming towards them. 'I am a trifle warm, madam; perhaps we could take a turn in the ante-room where I understand it is cooler.' And she gave Matt another view of her magnificent back and bottom, which had him lusting after her all over again.

Decidedly the devil was taking a hand in matters at York's Christmas Assembly Ball, and there was still the New Year to get through. He would doubtless be ready to run mad before 1819 was well on its way if he was to be exposed to the constant temptation which Stacy Blanchard presented to him when they were thrown together at Bramham Castle!

Which was Stacy's conclusion as well as his.

After that, Christmas Day was something of an anticlimax for Stacy and Matt. Particularly as both of them desperately tried to avoid thinking of the other, but both, for quite different reasons, failed in their objective.

Stacy woke up on Boxing Day at Bramham Castle feeling strange and feverish. Polly, who was herself looking a trifle green, helped her to the small bathroom off her bedroom and held her head while she vomited into a porcelain washbowl decorated with flowers, before letting go of her mistress to be violently sick into the bowl herself.

Sweating gently, her skin feeling so sensitive that merely to have had Polly's hand on her forehead was distressing, Stacy sank back into a nursing armchair standing by the big tin bath which would shortly be filled with warm water so that she might wash herself all over in it, and wondered briefly whether any of the Christmas food which she had eaten had caused such an unwanted effect.

Oh, but she knew only too well that that was not it, not it at all. What was wrong with her was that she was missing her second set of courses. Not only was her skin sensitive, but her breasts were swollen and sore, and she was not so unversed in her knowledge of the world as to be unaware that one night of passionate love with Matt Falconer had resulted in the inevitable. She was pregnant.

Once Polly had finished, and had sunk into a chair opposite to her mistress, they looked at one another ruefully.

'Oh, Miss Stacy,' Polly began, 'I hates to 'ave to say it, but I am a fallen 'oman.' Like the clerk at Blanchard's, faced with a crisis, she had reverted to her normal manner of speech before she had been trained to be Stacy's personal maid by Louisa Landen herself.

She looked half slyly, half shyly at Stacy. 'And you, Miss Stacy?'

It was a direct question, and one which Stacy was compelled to answer truthfully. 'Alas, I fear that I am breeding too.'

Servant and mistress for once shared a common predicament, and Polly, her eyes big with wonder—for were they not now bound by more than the ties of domination and servitude?—asked, 'Oh, Miss Stacy, is it Mr Matt's child you are a-carrying of?'

Stacy answered this not with a reproof for insolence but with a wry nod, followed by, 'Seeing that it cannot possibly be anyone else's, the answer must be yes. And you, I suppose, are carrying Jeb's?'

Her maid's answer was a mute nod of the head, and then a *cri de coeur* which Stacy shared with her. 'Oh, Miss Stacy, whatever are we a-goin' to do? We are both ruined— and on the same night, too!'

And that was undeniably true, and there was no answer

which she, Stacy, could make to it. Instead she asked gently, 'And if Jeb Priestley asked you to marry him to make an honest woman of you, would you agree to do so?'

Polly nodded her pretty head vigorously. 'Oh, yes, indeed. I liked him famously. He made me laugh, and he treated me like a lady, which is more than any of the other servants who came a-courting ever did.'

Treated her like a lady, indeed—by giving her an unwanted present, no doubt. And how did Matt Falconer treat me? Like a servant, perhaps. And how did I behave with him? No, I cannot answer that.

Polly felt bold enough to ask, 'And you, miss. Would you marry Mr Matt?'

'Indeed not,' was her vigorous answer to that.

'Oh, but you must marry *someone*. Think of the scandal.'

Stacy thought of the scandal and closed her eyes. Yes, she must marry someone, she supposed—but not Matt Falconer. Never Matt Falconer. Why, she hated him, did she not? And not only because he had ruined her.

You did your share of that, her conscience reminded her.

She stifled its unwelcome voice by saying to Polly, 'If Mr Priestley does not wish to marry you, then I can arrange for you to go to some farm to have the baby, and I will see that it is loved and cared for.'

'Aye—' Polly was bolder than ever '—and what about yours, Miss Stacy? Who is going to love and care for him— or her?' she amended.

Him, thought Stacy. I know it's a him.

'I shall think of something,' she announced grandly.

'Then you'd better do so soon,' returned Polly practically. 'There's not much time left before we both start showing.'

Rising rapidly to her feet and beginning to feel much better, Stacy ordered briskly, 'For the meantime we say nothing,' taking it for granted that Polly would obey her. But the peasant shrewdness which Polly possessed in abun-

dance was telling her quite another thing. For was not Mr
Jeb Priestley a bigger catch than she could ever have hoped
for? And she knew instinctively that Mr Matt Falconer
would see her right—aye, and Miss Stacy too.

It wasn't like Miss Stacy to be so airy-fairy as to think
that she could keep a love-child from the world's knowledge.

Chapter Ten

There was more than that which Miss Anastasia Blanchard could not keep from the world's knowledge, but that hammer-blow to her name and fame was yet to descend on her. For the present she contented herself with allowing Polly, once she had recovered, to help her to dress for the day. Afterwards, she went downstairs, pretending that all was well both in her private and public world.

Hardest of all to bear, she was to find, when the company arrived to celebrate the New Year, was not having Matt Falconer steadily watching her and steadily avoiding her, but the unwanted and admiring attentions of her cousin Anthony, who seemed determined to defy his mother and father's wishes by paying her the most insistent court.

The more he did, the more sardonic Matt's gaze grew. It was almost as though, across the room, she could read his mind. But what she didn't know was, could he read hers? Was he, could he be aware of the fact that she carried his child? Unaccustomed to being idle, to speaking only the nothings of polite conversation as carried on by gentlewomen, Stacy found life increasingly hard to bear. She most passionately wished that she could be back in London in the Bank's parlour, discussing policy with Ephraim, signing letters, and carrying out all the minutiae of the commercial life which had been her world since her father had first discovered her capacities when she was in her mid-teens.

Boredom rode on her shoulders. Matt found her, late one afternoon, in the gloaming hour, standing before a window which looked out over the gravel sweep which led to the front portico, watching the carriages which held his father and his father's party arrive.

'At last, madam,' he said softly in her ear, 'I have found you alone, without your cavaliers around you.' For not only Anthony Beauchamp, but Trot, who was also a fellow guest, and several other men, young and not so young, had been clustering around her like bees around honey.

Stacy did not turn to speak to him but addressed the window instead. 'I fear that I have little to say to you, Lord Radley, and you can have even less to say to me.'

He leaned forward, whispered into her ear, 'Ah, but we went beyond speech, did we not, madam?'

Her reply was a frozen one for, if she unbent at all, she could not trust herself to be able to hold him off. Even to know that he was behind her when they were not even touching was to have her shaking and quivering inside. 'I wonder you care to remind me of that, sir.'

'Unfortunately,' replied Matt a trifle bitterly, for he had never been so undone by a woman before, 'I cannot bring myself to forget what passed between us.'

'Nothing passed between us,' Stacy told the window as she watched Earl Falconer descend from his coach, Matt's sister Caroline, and her husband, Lord Bibury, following him and beginning to make their way into the house.

'I would not have thought the Bankeress's memory worse than mine,' was Matt's retort. 'Or is it reserved solely for the adding up of columns of figures or the examination of the balance sheets of failed businesses?'

Nettled, Stacy finally swung around to confront him. 'I wonder at you, sir. If I choose to forget what happened that night then the least that you can do is respect my wishes. What never happened cannot be regretted or remembered.'

This remarkable statement silenced Matt, if only for the moment. For cool pragmatism he felt that he had never met its match! Not only had the woman a mind like a knife, she also had the cunning deviousness of a politician.

He could not help himself; he finally came out with, 'By God, madam, with such deviousness at your command you should be a member of the Cabinet at the very least. More's the pity that a woman cannot sit in Parliament; you would grace the Treasury Bench itself. No ploy would be beyond you!'

Goaded, Stacy shot back, 'And is that supposed to be a compliment, sir?'

Equally goaded, Matt almost snarled, 'You may take it as you please.'

'What I please is to ask you to allow me to pass, sir. We have nothing to say to one another—let it rest at that.'

I shall never rest while I remember the night we spent together at Pontisford Hall, was Matt's secret thought. *She* may be able to forget it; I cannot. Thank God that the world has no knowledge of what happened there, else we were both ruined—and, whatever else, I do not want that for her, though, sure God, madam seems equipped to withstand anything—even that.

He took the thought downstairs with him to greet his sister and his brother-in-law; his father had already retired to his rooms. He thought Bibury, a rather dour man, if kind, looked a little sideways at him, but supposed that that was due to the reputation which had clung to him ever since Camilla's death.

Caroline kissed him warmly on the cheek and said, 'Dear Matt, how much better it is for us to meet affectionately in private, instead of having to be all formality in public. You look well. I cannot remember that you were so large and brown when we were last under the same roof together.'

Matt smiled, and kissed her back. 'Hard work, Caroline. I have been a farmer since we last met, and not a gentlemanly one, either. Hard labour is responsible for my increased size, not idleness and eating and drinking.'

Bibury, whose expression was still oddly quizzical, Matt thought—and why should that be?—drawled at him, 'You look strong enough to go several rounds with Gentleman Jackson himself, Radley.'

Well, it was useless to ask people not to call him that, Matt supposed, and when, a few moments later, Caroline took herself off to her room to change, Bibury drawled again, his hard advocate's face still quizzical, 'I should like a word in private with you, Radley, if you please,' Matt readily agreed. He did wonder, though, why his brother-in-law should be quite so formal with him. The fact that he had begun his early life as a lawyer, before his elder brother had been killed in the Peninsular War and he had inherited, was, he supposed, responsible for such a hanging-judge's manner.

They walked into the library, deserted at this hour, where Bibury sat himself down before a blazing fire and thrust his booted legs towards it, before drawing a paper from the pocket of his coat and handing it to Matt.

'I thought you ought to see that before anyone else at Bramham does,' he began without preamble. 'It will be all round London by now, and should reach York any day. Neither Caroline nor your father is aware of it yet—but they will be.'

Matt took the paper in his hand. It was a Radical newssheet devoted to scandal and innuendo about the doings of the mighty, both in Government and out of it. Bibury had run an ink mark down the side of a couple of paragraphs on the front page, headed 'Doings at Pontisford Hall—the Bankeress and the Bear'. It was brief and brutally to the point.

A country correspondent tells us that Lord R, fresh from the wilds of Virginia, while domiciled in his country home at Pontisford Hall entertained Miss A. B., commonly known as the Bankeress, to bed as well as board, when she was trapped there by the snow on her journey north. One supposes that the Snow Queen, as Miss B is also known, succumbed to the attractions of the Northern Bear and was thawed into submission. Are we to expect a baby Banker or Bankeress?

Matt stared numbly at the paper, aware of Bibury's cynical eye on him. How, he wondered, could anyone in London have learned of what had been done at Pontisford? And then he knew. He remembered the housekeeper, and her vow that he would regret turning her away. She must have gone straight to London and to the printers of the scandal sheet. She must have been told by the other servants his nickname, given to him because of his size, while he was still little more than a boy in the Navy.

He crumpled the paper in his fist and looked blindly across the library and through the windows at the wintry scene outside, avoiding Bibury's eye as he did so. 'Is this commonly known?' he asked.

Bibury shrugged. ''Fraid so. It was the talk of the Clubs.'

'And believed?'

'Oh, of course.'

'No use my denying it, then?'

'No, indeed. Silence is always the best weapon in these cases. One may hope that it will be a nine days' wonder, and then will die down.'

'But in the meantime...her reputation.'

'What reputation?' replied Bibury cuttingly and brutally. 'A female who pretends to be a man must always expect criticism. I suppose the scandal sheets have been waiting for such an opportunity to cut her up. Particularly since up to this time her reputation has been one of unbending virtue.'

He had not asked whether the rumour was true. Nor, he must have noticed, had Matt directly denied it.

He could only think of Stacy. Of his own reputation he thought nothing, for he had none. He waved the paper at Bibury. 'I may keep this?'

Bibury's face was wry. 'Oh, indeed, Matt, by all means.'

Matt was at the library door before Bibury spoke again. 'My dear fellow, you are by way of being my brother, so I feel compelled to warn you. Pray do not embark on anything rash—that can assist neither you or the lady.'

He made no answer to that, for there was none that he could make.

He found Jeb in his room, which overlooked the park at the back at the house. It was beginning to snow again. Jeb was folding his clothes. He had a shirt in his hand and an expression similar to that of Bibury's on his face. It seemed that everyone knew something which Matt Falconer didn't.

'You were saying?' he enquired politely of his unruly servant, although he felt far from polite.

'I wasn't saying anything.' Jeb was aggressive.

'No? Then you were thinking it. Out with it, man.'

'Oh, we are indeed Lord Radley today,' observed Jeb nastily.

The joke palled. Matt was too exercised by the paper in his hand to enjoy it. 'You will do me a favour by answering me.'

Matt might not be quite Lord Radley in manner yet, Jeb thought, but he was hovering near to being so.

'Very well, m'lord. It's Polly. She had some news for me this morning...' He paused.

'Had she, indeed? And is it something which should exercise me?'

'Both of us,' returned Jeb, his face one huge grin. He doubted whether m'lord would be quite so hoity-toity when he heard his news. On the other hand, he didn't feel quite so hoity-toity himself. It looked uncommonly as if Jeb Priestley might have to settle down at last.

'Polly tells me that she finds herself in the family way. We...uh...climbed into bed together the night that you and—'

Matt interrupted him. 'You are sure that it's yours?'

'Aye, and Polly's a lively lass. She'll make a good wife. I've a mind to make her Mrs Priestley—if that's all the same to you.'

'I agree with you.'

Matt found himself holding the scandal sheet as though it were contaminating him. He put it down on an armoire. Jeb picked up another shirt and began to fold it, saying, 'That's not all.'

'Not all?' Matt sank into an armchair in an attitude resembling that of Bibury—although without Bibury's obvious ease. 'What more can there be? You haven't given another wench a little packet, have you?'

Jeb snorted, rather as he had done at Pontisford when his betters amused him. 'Oh, not I, Matt. Polly's my lass, no one else. Haven't touched a wench since. No, begging your pardon, *Lord Radley*, it's you she was speaking of.'

'Me?' A dreadful suspicion struck Matt. He jumped to his feet, caught Jeb by the lapels of his coat, ground into his face, 'What the devil are you trying to tell me, man? For God's sake spit it out. I've had quite enough to try me today without you dancing me round too.'

Jeb pulled himself free, laughing, saying between splutterings, 'It's Miss Blanchard, Matt. Like master, like man, they say, and it seems that we both hit the target together— and on the same night too. Who'd have thought it?' And he continued to laugh uncontrollably, wishing that there were others with whom he could share such a splendid joke.

Matt's face was grey granite. 'You're quite sure? This isn't your idea of a joke?'

'No joke. Polly says that the Bankeress is even more overcome by her present than she is, but is carrying it off well. Of course, even the Bankeress can't carry it off forever. What suggestions do you have, *Lord Radley*, to help her out of her unfortunate situation?'

He would have to marry her to make matters right. He couldn't leave her to the tender mercies of a society which had already agreed to despise her, and would despise her the more when this news broke. He had thought that the existence of the scandal sheet was bad enough—but this... How could he have put her into such a compromising situation? What madness had overtaken them both that night at Pontisford?

He pulled himself together. Jeb was saying, 'I've already asked Polly to be my wife, and she's agreed. Says she doesn't mind going back to America with us—that is if *Lord Radley* still wants to return there.'

Lord Radley didn't know what he wanted. He bit back at Jeb, 'Lord Radley isn't likely to be as fortunate as you are. Somehow I doubt whether Miss Anastasia Blanchard will fall into my arms as quickly as Polly has fallen into yours. And as for returning to Virginia—what you have just told me is likely to alter everything.'

'Well, as to that,' remarked Jeb agreeably, 'I would be prepared to say that if she has any common sense at all Miss Blanchard had better make up her mind to be Lady Radley well before another month is out.'

Which was all very well, but Miss Anastasia Blanchard's version of common sense might not be the same as Mr Jeb Priestley's. Matthew Falconer, Baron Radley, didn't know whether he had any common sense left at all!

Stacy was taking tea with Caroline Bibury, whom she was finding an agreeable soul, ready to discuss matters other than dress and scandal, being happy to comment on Lord Byron's *Manfred* which she, like Stacy, had just finished reading. She had met him, Caroline told her, during his short and unhappy marriage to Annabella Milbanke, and he had struck her as a man of intemperate passions, exactly like those heroes of whom he wrote. 'The very model of *The Pirate*,' she finished laughingly. 'Just the kind of handsome and passionate reprobate whom we all ought to avoid, for who knows how we might behave if confronted by such a charming monster?'

Who knows better than I, indeed? thought Stacy ruefully, watching Matthew, Lord Radley, enter the drawing-room, remembering the passionate reprobate with whom she had shared a bed, and the consequence which had flowed from *that*. She also thought that Matt looked *distrait*, not at all like his usually damnably controlled self, and wondered what was troubling him. She knew only too well what was troubling her.

He came over to sit with them, and to drink tea as though it were wormwood which he was consuming, so that even Caroline noticed his strange manner and asked him whether he was ailing.

Matt shook his head. 'No, indeed. I find England strangely dark after the clear bright air of Virginia.'

Caroline questioned him about his life in the United States and he began to answer her with passionate enthusiasm. 'And you work, yourself, in the fields?' she exclaimed.

He nodded, and when he spoke his eye was on Stacy, not his sister. 'I would not have it otherwise. There is a cleanliness of spirit and a satisfaction about manual labour when it is performed for the love of it and not as a duty, enforced on one by others. I do what I choose, and what I please, and no one there thinks my labours odd. Imagine the brouhaha there would be if I toiled with my hands in the fields around The Eyrie!'

Stacy suddenly saw him, stripped to the waist, his tawny head blazing beneath a golden sun, his big body etched against a clear blue sky. The sensation this unexpected vision produced was so exquisite that she could almost have cried aloud. Ever since she had known that she was carrying his child the sensations of faint nausea which she occasionally felt were linked with a heightened sense of awareness of everything about her.

And the thing that she was most aware of was Matt Falconer. It was almost as though she were a part of him, so that for a moment she shared his memories of the life he had left behind him. She listened, also aware that Matt Falconer was talking to her, rather than to his sister, reminding her that he had a life of which she knew nothing, and to which he wished to return.

Or so he said.

Later, when Bibury and the rest came in, and Matt's father looking tired from his journey, Matt took the opportunity to ask her to examine some of the family portraits on the walls of the corridor which led to the drawing-room, a pretext so nakedly obvious that Stacy smiled at it.

'Come, sir,' she asked him as soon as they were alone before the portrait of an Elizabethan Beauchamp, gallant in huge ruff, pearl-sewn doublet, and trunks and hose of pale pink, 'what is it that you wish to say to me?'

Matt smiled ruefully—rueful seemed to be the only word which fitted his thoughts these days.

'I'm sorry if I appeared clumsy,' he began.

Stacy's exasperation showed. She was used to being spoken to directly, not to having men make pretty speeches to her on the way to being direct.

'I doubt whether anyone else noticed,' she returned, 'but I could not help being aware that you were becoming increasingly impatient at being constrained to speak to me before others—that you wished to speak to me privately. Something is troubling you, I collect.'

She did not say that where he was concerned she had acquired a sixth sense.

'Well, then, madam—' and Matt was suddenly savage, and as direct with her as she could possibly have wished '—allow me to tell you that I would have preferred that you had informed me that you were carrying my child, rather than have discovered it from the lips of Jeb Priestley. I'm not sure what etiquette governs these matters, but I cannot but believe that, as the child's father, I should have informed him, should I have so wished, rather than he me.'

'Oh!' Stacy was enraged, and could not help but show it. 'I particularly instructed Polly that she should keep that piece of news to herself, not go tattling it around Bramham.'

'Just so, madam. Did it not occur to you that you had a duty to inform me even before you informed Polly?'

'Etiquette, you said. What book of etiquette exists to assist an unmarried pregnant woman on the right line to take with the man who so incontinently made her so?'

'Oh, madam—' and Matt's smile was deadly '—the same book which instructed you so well in how to fall incontinently into bed with the father!'

Now what could she say to that? Nothing but, 'Your being the father is an unfortunate accident. My child will be rich enough to be able to dispense with a father.'

'Would that matters were so easy, madam. I fear that any hope you might have entertained that you could somehow have your child and its origins remain anonymous have already been dashed. You had better read this.' And he handed to her the Radical broadsheet which Bibury had given to him.

If he had thought to overset her, he was mistaken. She took the paper from him and read it without so much as changing colour. She might as well have been casually examining something as innocuous as the latest *Book of Beauty*.

'So?' she remarked, handing it back to him.

'And is that all you have to say, madam?' His face was

suddenly suffused, Stacy was fascinated to notice. He looked as he had done that night when he had fallen on her—and she on him.

'What is there to say?' she answered, her heart thumping, but determined to stay as cool as he was hot. 'It is the truth, is it not? Or are you prepared to dispute it?'

She was prepared to drive him mad, that was it. Regardless of the fact that they might be interrupted at any moment, Matt seized her by the shoulders, ground out between his teeth, 'Are you determined to destroy yourself as well as me? That you care nothing of what is written there is one thing—but what of others who read it? That paper will reach Bramham in the next few days—and what reputation shall we have then? How shall we—you—face our fellow guests? If it were not for the fact that you are carrying the consequence of our madness, then we could deny what is written there, say it was concocted out of spite—as I believe it was. But nothing to that, madam, nothing to that. Our guilt will shortly be obvious to the whole world—unless you are prepared to say that the child is not mine—which would brand you a slut, as well as careless. Is that what you want?' And he began to shake her.

They were back at Pontisford, before they fell upon the bed. He had only to touch her and she was lost. Oh, she had dreamed of him in her arms night after night, as he had dreamed of her. Only the fact that a few yards away the assembled guests sat, innocent of the passions being released in the corridor outside, kept them from falling on to the floor to consummate those passions.

Both of them had been solitary beings so long, denying themselves, enduring passionless lives, telling themselves that fulfilment was not for them—each for their own different reasons—that they found it difficult to surrender, to admit what was burning so fiercely inside them.

Eye to eye, breast to breast, heart to heart again, wishing

only to be united, but strongly denying the wish, they breathed and trembled together.

Finally, Matt released her, to lean against the wall shuddering with the force of passion rejected. He lifted his head, muttered hoarsely, 'There is nothing for it, madam. You must marry me and soon—before you grow big and all is lost.'

It was the most ungallant, unloverlike proposal a man could have made. But it was not that which enraged Stacy; it was his cold assumption that she had no choice.

Shuddering herself, burning, caught in passion's toils, Stacy murmured, her voice so low that Matt could hardly hear what she was saying, 'I suppose I should have expected that. You may keep your proposal, sir. And what you say of that paper's news is yours to say. I shall say nothing.'

'Mad,' groaned Matt, 'you are mad. You cannot refuse me. Ruin lies before you, not me. I am already ruined— and you are a fallen woman. You will be a pariah.'

'I am already a pariah, so that is nothing new.' She came out with this splendidly, as though she were carrying a flag with the words emblazoned on it into battle. 'I am tolerated only for my fortune and the Bank. Men want to marry me only for my fortune and the Bank.'

'I want neither your fortune nor the damned Bank,' Matt growled at her. 'I want him—my child—to have a name, and his mother not to be called a whore. Is that so wrong?'

'Him?' And Stacy's voice was a reproach, even though her secret wish was that the child should be a boy—and look like him. 'Him? It might be a girl.'

'Boy, girl, whatever it is,' gritted Matt through clenched teeth. 'I won't have it farmed out.'

'I have not the slightest intention of farming my baby out. It will be brought up as a Blanchard—and, boy or girl, it will inherit the Bank.'

'It will be a pariah, too. You are a clever woman, Stacy.

How can you be so stupid as to deny your child a name and an inheritance? Unless you marry me your child—our child—will have no name. Can you really want such a thing?'

Stacy. He had called her Stacy, not madam. And did she really want such a thing? If only he had shown her some affection, had put an arm around her, had said, I understand how you feel. Marry me and all shall be well. But he hadn't. He was worrying about the child, and her good name, not about Stacy Blanchard herself.

But what he had said about the child having no real name had struck her hard. Was she being fair to this unborn creature which she carried beneath her heart?

Her expression changed, softened. Matt saw it, and pounced. 'You will consider my offer,' he said eagerly, and put a hand on her arm, showing her for the first time some small sign of affection. Afterwards he was to ask himself why he had been so hard with her, but somehow the passion which ruled him whenever they met so appalled him by its strength that he wished to deny it, and denying it he denied her.

A mute nod was Stacy's only answer. He followed up this small advantage. 'We need marry only for show,' he assured her, for he was certain that she could not love him, since she never unbent to him, only showed him her indomitable will. 'I shall apply for a special licence. We can remain married until after the child's birth, give it a name, and then we may part on agreed terms—you to the Bank and me to Virginia. There, I cannot say fairer than that.'

Before she could reply they heard the door open and footsteps come towards them. Matt seized her by the arm, half ran her along to examine another portrait, so that the advancing party, seeing them thus engaged, could have no idea of the passions which had ravaged them the moment before, and which were plainly written on both their faces.

Only, when he handed her towards the stairs, Matt whispered hoarsely in her ear, 'And you will give me an answer, madam, and soon, I hope.'

To which Stacy answered, 'Yes,' which was saying anything—and nothing.

Nor would Stacy say anything more, merely mounted the stairs to talk to Louisa, who was still a semi-invalid, as though nothing in the world had happened to overset her. Matt must wait for an answer—but what answer she would give him was as unknown to her as to him.

Chapter Eleven

'And Mr Anthony Beauchamp, who dances such attendance on you, Stacy, my dear— what would your answer be to him if he were to propose himself to you? He would be so much more suitable a husband for you than Lord Radley—as I suppose you realise. Such a charming and pleasant gentleman!'

Louisa and Stacy were seated together, each of them stitching away at a pair of tapestry cushions, before the blazing drawing-room fire at Bramham Castle. Caroline Bibury had been playing Haydn to them, a pleasing, tinkling piece, light and airy, not at all matching the dark and troubled thoughts which lay behind Stacy's apparently composed countenance.

Louisa had asked her question in a quiet voice, so that no one should overhear her, although she and Stacy were seated well away from the rest of the company, who had begun to play spillikins as though their life depended on it. The noise that they were making quite drowned out anything which Louisa might care to say—or Stacy, when she replied to her.

She jabbed her needle viciously into the likeness of a hen pheasant and murmured, almost below her breath, 'I have no mind to marry anyone, Louisa, as I have so frequently told you. I like my cousin Anthony, but not as a future husband.'

'I can see that there is no pleasing you,' sighed Louisa sadly.

No, indeed, thought Stacy. Sooner or later I must give Matt Falconer an answer, for sooner or later my condition will betray itself, and I still cannot make up my mind as to the best course of action to follow.

It had begun to snow again and a group of gentlemen who had been riding earlier came in, exclaiming at the cold, the hard ground, and the inclement nature of the weather, as though every January did not find them saying the same thing.

Matt, walking beside his father, was wearing his usual expression these days, Stacy noted clinically. He glowered. He was waiting for the unwelcome news in the scandal sheet to reach Bramham. So far it had not done so, but so far his Lady Disdain had refused to make up her mind to accept the inevitable and marry him.

Yesterday, catching her in the library, he had said, 'If you accept me, madam, before the scandal about us breaks here, then it cannot be scandal. You understand me, I'm sure. Cannot you give me an answer now? To do so would be to the advantage of both of us. Every time that the post arrives I live in a sweat of fear that all will be revealed.'

So did Stacy. So why was it that she could not say yes to him? He was so unloverlike, that was it! But why was that it? Had she not scorned all talk of love and romance these many years? So how was it that now she was like a green girl waiting for her beau to shower her with compliments, promising her moonlight and roses? Instead he showered her with practical, rational, logical advice, plainly, almost rudely offered, with no intent to deceive her by pretending that he loved her—the kind of behaviour which she had always told herself that she expected, and would welcome, from a man. But, alas, now that she *was* receiving it, she found that she didn't welcome it at all!

A coach was being driven along the sweep, passing the drawing-room windows on its way to Bramham's superb front door, with its noble flight of steps. Bramham, although still called a castle, had been rebuilt in the classical style in the 1770s. Matt watched a uniformed flunkey alight and begin to unload the boxes and sacks of mail which it was carrying in lieu of passengers. No, there was one passenger, a black-clad lawyer—Grimes. He of the rueful countenance and impudent disapproval of Matt Falconer and all his works. What the devil was he doing here?

No need to ask, Matt thought dismally, and no need to worry this time what the sacks of letters, newspapers and parcels might contain. He gave a short exclamation, rose from his seat and walked over to where Stacy sat, the picture of virginal and untouched innocence. A picture which only he knew was false. He was aware that Anthony Beauchamp was watching him sourly, and knew that, whatever Anthony hoped, Stacy would never accept him—least of all now that she was pregnant by another man.

Ignoring Louisa, after a brief polite nod to her, he murmured, almost below his breath, so that only Stacy could hear him, 'The time grows short, madam. It may be already too late for us to emerge from this with any credit. Give me your answer. Now.'

Had the man no manners? Stacy saw Louisa's head lift itself sharply from its concentration on her work, and said reprovingly, 'I have no idea of what you speak, Lord Radley. As to the answer I promised to give you—that will arrive in due course.'

He leaned forward to hiss into her ear so that no one else might overhear, 'At least before the child arrives, I hope!'

'We are watched,' Stacy told him severely on hearing this sally. 'You grow indiscreet.'

'*Our* indiscretion is about to be announced to the world. I am sure of that, madam. You have left us no way out.'

He watched Grimes being ushered into the room by a footman, watched the tea-board accompany his entry, to be set out for him on a low table, saw his father speak to him, saw Grimes bend his head deferentially to say—what?

Lifting the silver teapot to pour both himself and his powerful patron a cup of tea, Grimes was muttering quietly, 'It is of all things essential, sir, that I speak to you in private, and soon. You ought also to ask Lord Radley to be in attendance to be called in to consult with us when we have finished.'

'And what, pray, has Radley done this time?' queried the Earl, a look of extreme anger on his old face.

'That I cannot speak of here. Later.' And Grimes drank his tea and ate a ratafia biscuit with all the appearance of extreme enjoyment.

Matt Falconer felt no enjoyment. Instead he put out a large hand to grasp Stacy's small one, to prevent her from continuing with her stitchery. As usual her extreme composure was driving him rapidly, not slowly, mad. Added to his thwarted desire to bed madam again, her refusal to give him an inch was the most exquisite form of torture she could have devised for him.

'Attend to me, madam,' he whispered fiercely, aware of Louisa Landen's horrified eyes on him. 'We have but a few minutes left, and your refusal to face facts is becoming dangerous.'

'Unhand me, sir,' hissed Stacy.

'No, indeed,' he told her, his voice rising a little, 'not until you answer me plainly.'

'Here is your plain answer, sir,' she told him equally fiercely. Before he could stop her she used her left hand to pull her needle from her right hand and stabbed him with it in the back of the hand with which he was gripping her.

This was so unexpected that Matt, taken unawares, let

out a roar of anger, mixed with surprise, and, yes, admiration for her spirit. She was looking him full in the face, and was smiling at him. Yes, dammit, the bitch was smiling at him! No, dammit, she was laughing at him! At the predicament he was in, and at his inability to retaliate against her for what she had so incontinently done.

Every head in the room had swung towards them at the sound of Matt's bellow. Louisa, unbelieving, frozen with horror, watched Stacy throw down the offending needle and take Matt's damaged paw into her hand, to dab at it with her tiny lace handkerchief.

'Oh, sir!' she exclaimed, all innocence. 'Pray forgive me. I had not seen that your hand was in the way. Allow me to stanch your wound.'

The wound was light, and the pain was small. It was surprise which had wrenched the cry from Matt's lips. He saw his father's cold eye on him, and then Anthony Beauchamp was beside them, saying sharply, 'Cousin Stacy, is this fellow troubling you again?' and the look he gave Matt was a malignant one.

'No, not at all,' Stacy carolled, having discovered inside herself a fount of mischief which she had not known that she possessed. 'I wouldn't say that you were troubling me, would you, Lord Radley?'

Matt, holding her handkerchief over his damaged hand, looked up at Anthony, who was eyeing him as though he were some mad animal which ought to be shot on sight.

'No, not at all, Miss Blanchard, rather the contrary, I would say.' Which masterly and devious reply nearly overset Stacy, and had Anthony puzzling over its meaning. There was no doubt about one thing, was her inward judgement—Matt Falconer liked to sail close to the wind. She forgot that she was inclined to do the same.

Fortunately for decorum, for Anthony had just worked out the true meaning of Matt's reply and was squaring up to him again, the little lawyer came over to them, bowed, and said in his dry way, 'Miss Blanchard, Mr Beauchamp, sir, you will forgive me for intruding, I trust, but the matter is urgent. Your father, Lord Radley, would like you to accompany us for a discussion in m'lord's private suite.'

He bowed so obsequiously that the company forgave him on the spot, particularly since he was rescuing them from a situation which was rapidly becoming embarrassing. Matt allowed himself to be led away, promising himself grimly that dear Lady Disdain would pay for her pin-prick if it was the last thing she did.

But she was already having payment exacted, first by Anthony Beauchamp and then by Louisa Landen.

'My dear cousin—' Anthony was all indignation '—I cannot understand what you see in that rude fellow. I collect that he works like a peasant in his fields in Virginia, and now he has come over to behave like a peasant in polite drawing-rooms. If he is really troublesome, pray let me know, and, as I offered once before, I will deal with him.'

'That is very noble of you.' Stacy was all sweetness and light, having put Matt in his place and now being determined on putting Anthony in his. 'But I am well able to deal with Lord Radley myself. Pray do not exercise yourself over the matter. Should I ever need assistance, I would ask for it. You may be sure of that.'

He was a little mollified, spoke to her for a moment about a variety of things in an effort to soothe her, though she needed no soothing, and then left her to Louisa.

Louisa, shocked to the marrow by the wild behaviour of both Stacy and Matt, moaned gently at her, 'Oh, my dear, however could you conduct yourself so outrageously? I own that Lord Radley spoke a trifle brusquely to you, but that was no reason to assault him with your needle. I am beginning to think that all the wildness which you should have worked through in your earlier years is being expressed in your maturity instead. Is it not enough that your conduct already attracts attention because of your running the Bank, without you behaving like a hoyden and thus attracting even more censure?'

'Oh, pooh to that, and to everything else.' Stacy was on her high ropes, and had no idea why that should be so. She had seen Matt's face immediately after she had stabbed him, and she knew that had they been alone he would have inflicted the most condign punishment on her. And oh, how her body ached and wished for it. Yes, she *was* going mad, and it was all much more exciting than being continually staid and proper as she had been for so many years.

At the same time she could not help wondering what Grimes and the Earl were saying to Matt—and then it struck her, so that her face paled, and she swayed a little. What a fool I am! They have seen the scandal sheet—and everything which Matt has repeatedly told me would happen will happen.

Louisa caught her arm, said feverishly, 'Stacy! You are not ill?'

'Oh, no,' she told her old companion. 'I can't afford to be ill now, Louisa. Most injudicious of me. But I should like a cup of tea, and would wish you to ring for one for me. That should set me up to be ready for anything.'

She was not wrong. Grimes, who for all his dried-up manner and appearance relished the more scandalous aspects of his work, had given the Earl the scandal sheet to read, and when m'lord threw it down, disgusted, said, 'I have spoken around London and it seems that they did spend a night alone together at Pontisford. I thought it might be my duty to inform you before anyone else did, remembering that Lord Radley has been involved in a similar brouhaha once before.'

'But I have been recently led to understand that we might have been mistaken over that.'

'Indeed.' Grimes was smooth. 'As there may be a mistake over this. I would advise you to discuss the matter with Lord Radley immediately. He may not be aware of this—' and he flicked a finger at the sheet '—and the talk which is going around London. There will be others who will find this in their post today.'

'No doubt.' The Earl rose and paced to the window to look out of it. The snow had stopped, but before it had done so had created a white world. The bridge over the lake, the little pavilion to which it led, the trees beside it were ornaments of silver filigree against a blank landscape. 'I had hoped that Radley and myself were coming to some kind of understanding—but this…' And he shook his head, began again, 'To destroy the honour of a young woman who has always possessed a reputation for extreme virtue… This is too much, and this time must be remedied.'

'There may, of course,' murmured Grimes smoothly, 'be a reasonable explanation. Might I advise that you speak to Lord Radley before reaching a final judgement?'

'Exactly so. You said that he was outside. Pray ask him to come in at once.'

Matt was in the ante-room. Restless, unable to sit quietly, he had been pacing the floor, examining cabinets containing rare china and curios from a dozen countries in the near and far east. He knew perfectly well what news Grimes had brought his father, and for the life of him he could think of nothing to say in extenuation of the conduct which the scandal sheet imputed to him.

If Stacy had already accepted him, then that would have been that. But she had not, and doubtless his father would put the worst interpretation on what he was supposed to have done.

Supposed? He had done it, and therein lay the rub. So, when Grimes beckoned him in, he squared his shoulders as he had done when a boy at Eton, waiting for old Keate, the headmaster, to beat him. And now, in his middle thirties, he was still in no better case!

Grimes withdrew with a bow and his father thrust the

paper containing the record of his delinquency at him. 'I should like an explanation of this, Radley. I understood from you that you were not at your old disgraceful games again, but I see that I was wrong to believe you.'

This was easier to answer than Matt had thought possible. 'Hanged, drawn and quartered before I say a word in my defence, eh, Father? Still the same old story? Except that the old story was a lie, all of it, as I tried to tell you to no avail.'

'To the devil with the old story,' growled his father. 'It is this new one which exercises me now. Were you aware of this, sir?'

Matt said as coolly as he could, 'Aware that this sheet existed, yes. But I must tell you that I am not prepared to discuss with you, or with any man or woman, my relations with Miss Anastasia Blanchard.'

His father's face grew slowly red. 'You are not denying this vile libel, then, I see—'

Matt interrupted, 'Neither affirming it nor denying it. It is no affair of yours—or any man's.'

'This—this,' exclaimed the Earl violently, waving the paper about, 'makes it my affair! If a lie it impugns your honour, and the lady's. Hers most of all. If true then I have no words for you, sir. No words at all. Indeed, true or false, words fail me.'

Impudence was all that was left to Matt, and, dismally, he knew that it was the only weapon in his arsenal which he could use. Stacy's refusal to accept his proposal had deprived him of all others.

'Why, sir, that comforts me—to know that there are to be no more words from you on the matter. In that case, I will leave you, unless there is anything further of moment which you *are* prepared to discuss with me?'

For one moment he thought that he had gone too far. Behind his outward bravado he could hear the inward bells of regret tolling. Since he had met his father again in York it had almost come to seem that they might become father and son once more, Camilla and Rollo's ghosts no longer coming between them. But now it was Stacy who had replaced them as a living and breathing barrier.

The Earl's hands curled into fists. He was a young man again. Had he a whip in his hand he would have struck his son with it. Lacking a weapon, he used the only one he had left to him: his tongue.

'You are no son of mine, sir, if your answer to this gross libel is silence, and a refusal to defend a lady's honour. How will she be able to withstand the inevitable shock of scandal when this...becomes known to the company?'

Matt couldn't defend himself. He couldn't answer his father's just anger as he might have wished by saying, The lady and I intend to marry. What is printed on that paper is neither here nor there. We both ask you for your blessing. Then and only then would gossip be silenced, and his father not be shamed by his son.

He bowed. 'I will leave you, sir.' He refrained from saying, Reflect that, as you were wrong about my behaviour towards my brother's wife, you might also be wrong about this, because the paper was telling the truth.

His father said heavily, 'Yes, you may leave, Radley. I have nothing more to say to you. Except that I am sorry for the lady. Her life is difficult enough, I understand, without this.'

He could have said, Her choice, Father. She has left herself open to scandal by refusing my honourable offer of marriage. But no decent man could interpose a woman between himself and obloquy. In any case, the whole business had been his fault, and no one else's. The affair had been precipitated by his act of folly in pretending to be the butler, and had been further compounded by his falling upon her that night when they had been alone in her room. That thereafter she had co-operated with him most willingly and lustily did not lessen his own guilt—he was the older, the more experienced and the stronger. He should have stopped... He was suddenly aware that merely to think of being in her arms was to excite him...

He turned to let himself out, trying not to hear his father telling him that he was no son of his, that, after all, he had come back from America more unregenerate than when he had left, and that the best thing he could do would be to return there.

But none of that would help Stacy.

She knew. Oh, yes, she knew. The post had arrived and been distributed. There were letters for her, all dealing with business. Reports from Greaves at York, longer ones from Ephraim Blount in London, and a letter from Hamburg where the Bank had been doing business with some merchants of the old Hanseatic League, and her opinion was wanted on certain matters of importance.

But the letters of those around her were quite different. They were from friends and relatives, and their letters were chatty, gossipy, retailing the *on dits* which flew around London, or the great houses to which the nobility and great gentry—or, as it was sometimes known, the cousinry—retired during the winter months. And with the letters came newspapers, and among them, she knew, would be the sheet retailing the scandal about herself and Matt Falconer.

Even if the story had been a lie it would have stuck to them. But it wasn't a lie, and what Matt had forecast was coming true. More, the moment she walked into the drawing-room she knew that many there had already learned the delightful news: that Matthew Falconer, the renegade Lord Radley, already the leading player in one delightful scandal, was now the leading player in another. And, even more than that, the other player was the eccentric Bankeress, long known as an icy virgin, but who had been melted not by the summer rain but by the winter's frost!

Matt they had called the Bear. Quite wrong. He was her

lion-man, and she was coming to understand that by refusing him she had been selfish, for it was he who stood to lose the most, just when the old scandal which had ruined him had finally died.

She sat on her own. None came near her. She had dressed in virginal white, as much to defy everyone as to proclaim to the world what was no longer the truth. She wore her collar of pearls again about her long and graceful neck, with one giant ruby, set about with seed-pearls, depending from it above her bosom. The dress itself was of the most elegant simplicity, with floating panels of gauze depending from the high waist above the smooth satin of her skirts. Her fan was white, her gloves and shoes equally so, and the small circlet in her hair was again of pearls.

Louisa came over to her, her face agitated. 'My love,' she began, her eyes brilliant with shock, 'I feel that you ought to know...'

Stacy leaned forward, put a gentle finger on Louisa's lips as though she were the old and wise one and Louisa her charge. 'Shush, my dear, I already do know, have known for some days. And so, I fear, does everyone else. We will not speak of it.'

'But...' began Louisa when the finger was removed.

'No buts, dear Louisa. You must be brave as I will be.'

How could she be so cool? was her companion's only thought. Caroline Bibury came in, moved straight to Stacy, took her hand and said, her eyes swimming, 'My dear, I am so sorry. I would have such creatures who write filth about us shot if I were in the Government. Bibury says that I must not exercise myself. He told me that you have known for some days... What can I say or do but offer you my most profound sympathy, and my admiration for your moral courage? We, by virtue of our rank and station, stand to be attacked, but this...this is the outside of enough. And poor Matt...'

Stacy's eyes filled with tears as the most extraordinary

mixture of sentiments warred in her breast. For she knew that she was not innocent, and Caroline was assuming that she was, and she felt a cheat and a rogue for deceiving her. She was not sure how much Louisa knew or guessed, but kind Caroline was a different proposition altogether. She pressed the sympathetic hand which held hers. Looking about her, though, she noticed something odd. Only the senior men of the party were present. Earl Falconer, whose old face was so sad that she knew that he too had read the scandal sheet, was seated by the roaring fire. Beside him was Uncle Beauchamp, pulling his watch out to examine it as the normal hour for dinner had passed by and half the company were not yet present. The lawyer, Grimes, was sitting mumchance in a corner, watching, his eyes sardonic. And night was beginning to fall as the afternoon wore on.

She stood up, worried by she knew not what.

'What is happening, Caroline? Where is your husband and Anthony Beauchamp, Trot and the rest? Where are they? What is to do?'

Caroline, Lady Bibury, who had never run a great bank, watched for signs of change in the money market, picked up hints and ideas from the movements of stocks and shares and the contents of speeches by members of the Government, had noticed nothing untoward. She looked puzzled, stared about her, said slowly, 'I only know that Bibury told me to go ahead. You are right. All of the younger men are absent. What can it mean?'

Stacy said, in the voice which she had often employed to dominate Ephraim Blount, Greaves, assorted bank clerks and the thieving manager at York, 'I don't know. But I intend to find out.' She picked up her fan. Louisa made to follow her, to have Stacy say, still in that cold, businesslike voice, 'No, stay where you are, I beg of you. I don't want anyone to follow me.' She waved down Caroline, who was beginning to rise, her face anxious.

Every female eye was on her as she crossed the room,

straight-backed, head high, making for the door which led to the great entrance hall. Opening it, she saw at the bottom of the main stairway all the young men of the party. They had been lying in wait for Matt, who had just reached the last turn of the stairs before they opened on to the ground floor.

Anthony Beauchamp, his back to her, stood a little in front of the main group. He advanced on Matt, saying in a loud voice, 'Damn you, Matt Falconer. I want satisfaction from you for the slur you have brought on my poor cousin. I should have asked my father to have had you beaten from the door by the footmen before you ever set foot in Bramham. As it is, take this,' and before Bibury, who was plucking his sleeve and advising caution, could stop him, he struck Matt as hard as he could in the face, knocking him to the ground, and when Matt tried to rise was on him again.

Bibury and Trot pulled Anthony away. He was still raving, his face purple. 'Satisfaction,' he roared at Matt. 'I want satisfaction from you, Falconer. You may choose what weapons you like. I shall take pleasure in killing you whatever the means I have to use.'

Matt had made no effort to defend himself. He was conscious of his guilt, of the misery which he had brought upon himself and Stacy by his own rash and ill-considered action. He rose slowly, said, his voice low but steady, 'I don't wish to fight you, Beauchamp, but I shall, and it will not be my own honour I shall be defending, but Miss Blanchard's.'

Which had Anthony raving again, shouting, 'You are not to name her. I will not have her named.'

Bibury said sharply to him, 'Be quiet, man. You heard what he said. Now let him choose his weapons, and we will decide the time and place for the action. Until then, all must be decorum. You must name your second, Radley—as must

Beauchamp—and if you have no one here who will stand your second, then I shall do so, for form's sake.'

Stacy watched them, mute for once, and shaking inwardly, aware that her own delay had caused this. She decided to stop the folly being enacted before her. She might play a man's part when she ran the Bank, but she thoroughly disapproved of the whole code of honour which governed the lives of the men who belonged to the gentry and aristocracy. In the moment of silence which followed Bibury's statement she chose to speak.

'There will be no need for any action to take place. You, Cousin Anthony, are quite mistaken if you choose to provoke Lord Radley to a duel. He has already asked me to marry him, and I have agreed to accept his proposal. No one's honour is at stake here, least of all mine or Lord Radley's.'

All the men had turned and were staring at her, a different version of shock on each face, shock that not only should she have been present, but that she had chosen to speak so publicly before a party composed only of men. And of men engaged in an affair of honour—an occasion where women had no place.

Bibury released Anthony Beauchamp, who said hoarsely to Stacy, 'Cousin, you should not be here. It is neither fit nor proper. I am about to teach this fellow a lesson he will not live to remember.'

Stacy could see only one face, and that was Matt's. She had begun to shiver internally, but quelled the shivers, said in her best Bankeress voice, 'Oh, what nonsense, Anthony. Why should I not speak when I collect that the matter between you and Lord Radley is that of my honour, and that you are quite mistaken over the part he has played? Lord Radley and I have been grossly libelled, but it is no matter. We were waiting until we left Bramham before we announced our betrothal to the world but, seeing the misunderstandings that our natural desire for privacy has created,

I release him from his vow of silence on the matter. We shall be married by special licence when we reach London, shall we not, my dear sir? No need for duellings and bravado; you may all wear wedding wreaths instead.'

She saw Matt walking towards her, the bruise on his face where Anthony had struck him slowly turning purple. He wore a small bandage on the hand which she had stabbed. He went down on one knee before her, said, 'Miss Blanchard, I honour you for your courage in speaking for me after such a public fashion. I respected your wish for silence, and respect the reason why you have now reversed it.'

A small hum of sound ran round the watching men. Anthony opened his mouth again, to protest, to reproach, no doubt. Bibury took him by the arm and said loudly, 'No need for bravado, indeed, Miss Blanchard, nor any need for a duel. Let us all go into dinner. I, for one, am hungry.'

Anthony, his face white, hissed something in Bibury's ear as they all walked towards the drawing-room door, Matt and Stacy leading, her hand on his strong arm. Bibury shook his head and said mildly, 'You heard the lady, Beauchamp. There can be no grounds for reproaches, none at all. The first toast at dinner shall be to the prospective bride and groom.'

He threw open the door, and escorted Matt and Stacy through it. Matt had taken Stacy's arm, and led her to where Caroline, her face white, sat with Louisa Landen and Earl Falconer, all looking equally troubled.

'Caroline, my love,' Bibury told her gently, 'I think that your brother and Miss Blanchard have something important to tell you and your father.'

Chapter Twelve

The announcement that Matt Falconer, Lord Radley, was to marry the Bankeress, and soon, was exactly designed to set the Bramham house party alight. It would not be true to say that everyone was pleased by the news: Anthony Beauchamp, for one, was not, and it was to be supposed that Trot and the other young hopefuls were afflicted by the dismals once they realised that England's richest heiress outside the ranks of the nobility was denied to them.

Among those who were pleased was Matt's father, who was quite bemused by the news, coming as it did on the heels of the distressing interview with his son. Why in the world could Matt, once he had been challenged so ruthlessly, not have told him that he had proposed to, and been accepted by, the very lady whose virtue he had accused him of tampering with? He would never understand his wilful son, never.

It was perhaps as well that the exact truth was never revealed to him. Questioned by his father later that night, once they were alone and Stacy had retired, Matt offered no explanations, no extenuation for his strange behaviour. The fact that Anthony Beauchamp had secured the backing of the younger members of the party, before publicly challenging Matt over the insult offered to the woman to whom he was already secretly betrothed, could not be concealed from the rest of those at Bramham who were not in the know, and added to the Earl's confusion.

Anthony Beauchamp and Bibury were both reprimanded by Uncle Beauchamp, Anthony for his rash hot-headedness, Bibury for not having the sense to hold him in check. 'But by God, sir,' Anthony had exclaimed, exasperated, 'their betrothal having been secret, how could anyone be expected to know of it? As her nearest young relative it was my duty to defend her name. And, come to that,' he added, his blue eyes bright with suspicion, 'when *did* they become betrothed? They have hardly met since Pontisford, and what occurred there must be a matter for conjecture.'

'Then let it remain so,' his father instructed him. '"All's well that end's well", as the Bard once said, and for Radley to settle himself so well must be a source of congratulation to his father and all his relatives. As for the lady you and she are not suited to each other. She is older than you are, and doubtless a self-willed man like Radley will be better able to hold her in check than you would have been.'

'But I love her,' grumbled Anthony, half beneath his breath. 'And I doubt whether Matt Falconer does.'

'And that is no matter, either. There are plenty of pretty, biddable young girls who would be delighted for you to make them your wife.'

Again below his breath Anthony muttered, 'I don't want a pretty biddable young girl, I want Cousin Stacy.'

Cousin Stacy didn't know what she wanted. Somehow she had endured the polite uproar which had followed the announcement of her betrothal to Matt. His father had come over to her and said, 'Madam, I could hardly have expected my son to have made so worthy a choice. I understand t̶ you both wish to be married as soon as possible. It ̶ tunate that Grimes is here. He may set all the ̶ malities in train straight away. But it is not t̶ ercises my mind, it is my pleasure at welcoming you into my family. As I told you before, I knew and respected your father. I hope to love, as well as respect, his daughter.'

Whatever might be said in private, all that was said in public was as proper as could be. Poor Trot, poor in every way, could only moan inwardly at the wretched luck that had handed the Blanchard wealth to a man who would be as rich as Croesus without it when he finally inherited the Falconer estates. But he, too, said all the right things on that interminable afternoon and evening which followed the revelation at the bottom of Bramham's stairs.

The only person to whom Stacy did not speak at any length was Matt himself. They were being watched so closely that they both, being a man and woman of some maturity of experience, in order to give nothing away, said as little as possible which was not light and innocuous. The private meat of their conversation, so to speak, would have to wait for the public hors d'oeuvres of it to be over.

Louisa, walking with Stacy to their suite of rooms, said timidly to her before they parted for the night, 'My dear, exactly how long is it since you accepted Lord Radley? I must say that I was as surprised by your news as the rest of the company.'

'I accepted him at exactly the moment at which it was proper for me to do so,' returned Stacy elliptically, and Louisa had to be content with that.

The servants were, as usual, wiser than their masters, knowing more of the truth than they did. Stacy and Matt's insistence on such a speedy wedding ceremony came as no surprise to them.

Matt, weary in body and soul, tired at having to behave in public with such circumspection, entered his bedroom to find Jeb there, laying his nightwear on the covers of the big four-poster bed which, he had been told, had once been slept in by the great Duke of Wellington himself.

Jeb, who would have had no more respect for the Duke

than for Matt, said, 'So, you are to be turned off at last? Do I congratulate the Bankeress for capturing you? Or should my felicitations be more properly addressed to your good self? My own regret is that you didn't put a bullet into that pretty young fellow who calls himself her cousin.'

'My good self,' grated Matt, beginning to pull off the skin-tight clothing which was the current fashion, 'has only one wish at the moment, and that is for a good night's sleep. As for my future bride's cousin, however many bullets *he* had put in *me*, she would never have married him. Had she done so she would have eaten him in a week!'

'But you will eat her—or will the meal be mutual?' Jeb enquired suavely. 'At least your child will be legitimate now.' And he began to laugh. 'Is that why she accepted you?'

Matt, now naked, began to sponge himself down from the bowl of warm water which Jeb had poured out for him. He said, his voice muffled a little by the towel which he was using to dry himself, 'I don't think that she thought once about whether her child would be legitimate. It's my belief that she announced our engagement to stop an unseemly duel—for which I am grateful. I suspect I am more than a match for Anthony Beauchamp with either pistols, swords or fists, but honour alone would have prevented me from proving that I was.'

Jeb began to laugh uncontrollably. He threw Matt his nightshirt, spluttering, 'What a woman to win. By God, I'm reasonably happy to marry my Polly. She's a good girl, or was until I cozened her into bed, but she ain't a patch on the Bankeress for guts. I shall purely admire watching her tame you!'

A tawny head emerged from the ruffled neck of Matt's nightwear. He said gruffly, 'I shouldn't take any bets on that. I suspect a draw will be the result.'

Jeb wasn't the only man that night to discuss the outcome of such a bet. The comments of the women were more discreet, but followed roughly the same line. And, naturally, the question of whether the marriage was a forced one also exercised many minds.

The only response to gossip, Stacy felt, was to behave as normally as possible, to eat her breakfast, to talk briefly in the drawing-room to Caroline, and finally to retire to her own rooms—to sit by the fire, wondering what exactly she had done in handing herself over to Matt.

There was a knock on the door, not a timid knock, and of course it was Matt, looking larger and sterner than ever. He bowed to the rapidly departing Louisa—who was acknowledging that a betrothed couple might, ever under the strict etiquette then prevailing, safely be left alone together.

'I have come,' Matt told Stacy stiffly, 'not only to thank you for honouring me with your hand, but also to thank you for saving me from having to allow your cousin Anthony to put hole in me which might have proved fatal. I couldn't have put a bullet in him when he was in the right and I was in the wrong. I shall always remember, and treasure, your courage in speaking out.'

Stacy had never respected him more. She was suddenly aware that behind Matt's unconventional exterior was a man of impeccable honour—which made the details of the scandal which had destroyed his social position in youth even stranger. Stranger still was the manner in which he had behaved to her at Pontisford.

She murmured, 'It was the least I could do for you, sir, seeing that it was my dilatoriness in accepting your proposal which had brought you to such an unfortunate pass. I hope, also, that our betrothal has restored your credit with your father.'

None of this was what she wanted to say, it was all so stiff and stilted. And he was as stiff, too, running a hand under his carefully tied cravat and saying in a distant voice, 'Of course, the condition on which I offered our marriage still stands. One of convenience only, until our child is born—and after that we may honourably agree to go our separate ways. I have no particular wish to marry, as I am sure you have not—'

Oh, dear! Stacy's heart fell into her elegant kid slippers. She should have known. He didn't really want to marry that strange and eccentric creature the Bankeress. He must have had a syncope at Pontisford, and ravished her in the middle of it. He didn't, couldn't, care for her at all.

'I didn't want to marry in the first place,' she snapped at him, 'but, things being as they are, and seeing that for some reason which I cannot fathom we both ran mad at Pontisford, marriage is what we are doomed to. I must tell you that I have no intention of giving up my management of the Bank until my coming child compels me to do so. What you care to do with your life is of no consequence to me.'

And oh, what a damned lie that was! She cared most desperately, but if he was going to speak to her as bloodlessly as Ephraim Blount did, then she could not let him know that, whatever else he had done at Pontisford, he had caused Anastasia Blanchard to fall in love with him. She could no longer blind herself to that unwelcome piece of knowledge. And he, plainly, felt nothing for her—he cared only that their child might be legitimate.

'Nevertheless,' pursued Matt doggedly, wishing that his dear Lady Disdain would offer him something better than the cold face which she probably used when she was having thieving managers thrown into the street. He was a fool to think that she might care something for him—other than the moment of lust which had overcome them at Pontisford. 'Nevertheless, I have a duty to tell you what my plans will be once we *are* married.'

'Oh, that,' said Stacy as carelessly as she could, 'yes, that would be a piece of common courtesy, I agree.'

He wanted to jump on her, lift her out of the chair where

she sat surveying him as coldly as if he were an insect—a stare he remembered from their earliest encounters—and shake her and kiss her until she lay panting against his heart.

And what a savage she would think him if he did any such thing. No, he must be as cold as she, and resign himself to having had her as his love, even if only for one night, only to lose her to the kind of marriage which he had always despised. A man and a woman tied together simply for the sake of two pieces of land and a son and heir to them. It was only too grimly appropriate that the busiest set of people involved in their marriage would be their lawyers, working out the details of the settlement of her estates and his. Grimes would be in his element.

'My plans,' he began, dragging his mind away from the cheerless prospect of an arranged and convenient marriage, the reason for which—an heir— had already been accomplished, 'are as follows. I regret that I shall have to leave England as soon as is decently possible to return to Virginia to settle the management of my estates in the United States. It is being borne upon me that my future, now that my brother has died, lies here. I shall be Earl Falconer one day, and the duties of a great estate will devolve upon me. I cannot neglect them, even though I might like to. I shall leave Jeb behind to be the overseer of my farm. I don't think that he wishes to stay here. His spiritual home is across the Atlantic.'

He did not say, As is mine, although he was thinking it. He had not wanted Rollo to die, however much he had disliked his brother, because alive he would ultimately have become Earl Falconer and Matt would have remained a simple American planter. That dream was as dead as Rollo.

'I am sorry,' Stacy said truthfully. 'I know how much you love your adopted country.'

Matt waved a dismissive hand. 'No matter,' he told her. 'My one regret is having to leave you so soon after marriage, but I wish to be with you when our child is born, and to do that I must leave speedily, so that my early return is assured.'

He was speaking to her in the emotionless language of the world of banking and commerce—a language which Stacy had once thought was the only one which she would ever use. Pontisford had briefly introduced her to another, but that language seemed fated to be denied her in the future.

What would he say if she cast herself at his feet, crying, Damn everything, your and my duties, the Bank and the Falconer estates, and take me to Virginia with you, to stay there, for all I want is to be your true wife, and everything else can go hang?

Almost she did so, only unfortunately he continued, still emotionless, 'I know how much this marriage irks you, that you have no wish to surrender your independence. You may depend upon it that I shall make it as easy as possible for you to live as though it had never happened.'

His face was averted a little when he spoke, for he could not bear to look at her, knowing that they would be parted so soon and for so long. He remembered Camilla, thought bitterly, are all my loves to be doomed? But at least this love of mine is a strong woman, so I must be strong too.

Unknown to him, his strength was written on his face. Stacy, seeing it, stood up, began to move towards him, to say something of what was in her heart—and then, if he insisted on denying her, she would accept that denial, and learn to live with it.

She compelled him to look at her by the simple process of standing before him, her green eyes earnestly on his tawny ones. To be so near to him started her inward tremblings again, as though the child within her were already able to move, to tell her of his presence—something which she knew would not happen for another few months.

Unknown to her Matt began to tremble too. Her scent, a

compound of lemon and spices from the little bags of herbs which Polly had made up to store between the folds of her clothes, and from which the laundress at her London home had created the soft soap which she daily used, was temptation itself to him.

'Stacy,' he said hoarsely, putting out a hand to touch her chin, to lift it. His tawny eyes were suddenly glowing, the icy manner in which he had been speaking to her was suddenly gone. 'Oh, God, Stacy...'

He got no further. The magic moment which they were beginning to share, with Stacy turning longing eyes up towards him as he started to speak, was shattered. The door was flung open, to reveal Polly.

'Oh, Miss Stacy!' she exclaimed, taking in the scene before her as Matt stood back and the light which his impulsive action had lit in Stacy's eyes began to die. 'I'm so sorry. I thought that you were downstairs. I came...no matter...' And she shot out of the room as quickly as she had entered it.

Too late. Both Stacy and Matt had lost the impetus which was suddenly bringing them together. They were apart again, the spell broken.

Stacy put her hands behind her back and clenched them tightly. A lifetime of obeying her father, of suppressing her emotions, was preventing her from telling Matt what he would most have liked to hear. As for Matt, he was so afraid of coercing her, a legacy of what had happened at Pontisford, that his usual forthright nature was strangely subdued.

He took up where he had left off, was busy outlining his—and her—future plans. 'We must, I fear, leave for London as soon as possible. My father will also be making plans to open Falconer House, off the Strand. I have spoken to Lord Beauchamp and I understand that he wishes to be present at the ceremony, and be responsible for you as your nearest living relative. I collect that you have no Blanchard relatives.'

Stacy was fascinated by this passionless and businesslike recital, which seemed to be leaving so little to chance. 'Only a very aged great-aunt,' she told him, 'who has had nothing to do with either my father or me since I was a baby. She is now in her late eighties, lives at Bath, and has not left that city for these thirty years!'

'As Lord Beauchamp informed me. My father wishes us to be married at Falconer House, but I believe that your uncle and aunt Beauchamp would prefer the ceremony to be at their place in Bedford Square. I think that the decision should be yours.'

Stacy would have married Matt over the anvil at Gretna Green if she had believed that he loved her, but, seeing that he was all business, then so would she be.

'If Aunt and Uncle Beauchamp wish to extend such a kindness to me, then let it be Bedford Square.'

Matt nodded, still passionless, she noted sadly, the spark which had been so nearly lit between them quite extinguished. 'Most proper of you, madam, but no more than I would have expected of you.'

'You did not always think me proper,' Stacy offered a trifle dejectedly.

'You have my word,' he returned earnestly, 'that I most truly regret my wretched behaviour to you at Pontisford and elsewhere!'

Which wasn't what she wanted to hear from him at all. She remembered the burning fire which had raged between them from the moment that she had mistaken him for the butler, and which had consumed them both on that fatal night. Whatever could have happened to it? Oh, it still raged in her heart, but it could find no outlet, no way in which it could light a similar fire in him.

The rest of their conversation was conducted in the same sad and emotionless tone. They would live at Stacy's home

in London until Matt took ship for the States. Polly and Jeb
were to be married quietly on the same day as Matt and
Stacy, and would accompany him to Virginia. Stacy would
work at the Bank until she grew too big for decorum and
would then settle herself wherever she thought proper—in
the country, he hoped, where she and the child could
breathe the pure air, so unlike London's smoke and fumes.

At last they were finished. There was another knock on
the door. This time it was a footman carrying a silver salver
with coffee for them, and all that he interrupted was an icy
exchange of courtesies.

Matt became a little more human, said, as Stacy poured
coffee for them, 'I see, madam, that you are looking more
in health than you were when you first arrived at Bramham.
The child does not yet discommode you?'

The child, the child. He would never have offered her
marriage if it had not been for the existence of the child,
living proof of their scandalous behaviour which would,
without marriage, effectively have ruined them both.

She replied, her throat closing as she did so, 'No, I am
well now. I had some sickness when I first came to Bramham, but that has passed. If, once we are married, I do
experience distress, I shall be able to send for a doctor. At
the moment common sense must be my guide, since no one
must yet know that I am already pregnant!'

'Ah, yes.' Matt was almost satirical. 'Common sense!
That has always been your guide, I believe.'

'Except once!' she could not help shooting back at him.
'Except once!'

And that, Stacy was dismally aware, was enough to stop
any further conversation between them, other than on the
most neutral matters such as the probable date of their departure from Bramham, the wedding, and her own plans to
notify her lawyers to meet Grimes and his cohorts as soon
as possible. The impossible marriage was to be put in train.

Chapter Thirteen

'So,' Matt remarked halfway through dinner on their wedding-day, 'it is accomplished. For good or ill you are Lady Radley now. I offer you a toast, madam. To you and our future.'

Stacy raised her glass to him and, as cool as he, offered him a toast in exchange. 'And to you, sir, and any child which may spring from our union.' Which was as plain as she dared be, surrounded as they were by servants who might suspect why they had married so precipitately but could not actually know.

He smiled a trifle ruefully at that, and later, when they had moved to the drawing-room, a stately place which owed everything to Louis Blanchard's taste and nothing to Stacy's, she said to him, looking around at its ornate splendours, 'Had you ever thought of visiting this room, I doubt that you could have anticipated the reason why you might find yourself in it!'

At last she had provoked his stern face into something resembling genuine amusement. 'Perhaps, madam, the speed with which I have arrived here after our first meeting is as remarkable as the reason for my being here at all.'

Stacy's response was a mute one, a nod of agreement. Indeed, long afterwards, looking back at her wedding-day and the events which led up to it, she always marvelled at how short a time it had taken to turn her life upside-down. There she was at the beginning of November, living the life which she had led since her late teens and then, in a few short weeks, all was changed, and changed forever.

She had thrown her reputation to the four winds, been initiated into the delights of the bed, become pregnant and accepted marriage from a man whom in the terms of their world she had barely become acquainted with and wasn't sure she even liked—lust being a different thing. After that she had been united to him in the most hurried wedding-ceremony, although their union was merely a legal one, the body having nothing to do with it, and in consequence had seen the old Stacy Blanchard disappear to become Lady Radley—and who was she?

Always, when thinking of it, her thoughts became as breathless as that time itself, as though, the grammar of her life having been destroyed, the grammar of her expressing what had happened to her had disappeared as well!

Their wedding-day had been fine at first. Later, after the ceremony, a winter thunderstorm had followed, out of a clear sky, as though the gods were expressing their anger at the hollowness of what she and Matt had done. They were to spend their empty honeymoon at Stacy's London home, which Matt had visited for the first time twenty-four hours before the wedding. The cool nature of their first meal together as man and wife was to set the tone for their married life before Matt left for Virginia, taking a tearful Polly and a happy Jeb with him.

On that last late January day, when he came to see her before leaving London to take ship, Stacy was seated at her desk in what had been her father's study. She had cancelled her visit to the Bank, but was working on some proposition which Ephraim Blount had put before her. She was trying not to think of what Matt's departure meant to her.

He had been scrupulously kind and distant in manner to

her from the moment that the Bishop had made them man and wife. No one could have been more considerate. Only afterwards, when he had gone, did she realise that since the ceremony he had not so much as touched her, indeed had scrupulously avoided all contact with her.

And so things had remained. In front of others they were charmingly polite, the very picture of a newly married pair. But once alone the politeness remained, and some of the charm, but the rapport which Stacy had hoped that they might somehow find was missing.

So now he was standing before her, dressed for travelling. She thought that he looked gaunt, that since their marriage he had lost weight, so that the cheekbones in his face were starker than ever, adding to its strength.

'Madam,' he began, and then fell silent. There was nothing of the semi-bantering, semi-mocking manner which he had adopted with her before they were married. All was deadly seriousness. Stacy thought that she preferred the lighter manner of their illicit relationship to the gravity of their legal one—but she could not say so.

Over the few weeks of their marriage she was coming to understand that, however much her father's tuition had made her ready to run the Bank, it had done nothing to enable her to express the feelings of her heart.

'Yes?' Stacy prompted, trying to help him, but in the doing she remained so calm that Matt, who had thought that before he left her he might fall on his knees before her and tell her how much he had come to love her, how little he wished to leave her, was quite daunted by such cold composure—the composure that Louis Blanchard had bred in his child, unaware that it might act like a killing frost quelling an unspoken but truly felt love.

Also, at the last, he didn't want to leave her—and miss how much she would change and blossom as the child grew in her. Some intuition, foreign to the hard man he usually was, told him that the coming child would change her, was already changing her, and this he would miss—although he fully intended to return well before their child was born. Would she always remain his dear Lady Disdain, so cold and controlled that his heart wept within him, that heart which he had once thought that he had left in the grave with his dear, lost love Camilla?

'I have to tell you, madam,' he said, as cold and controlled as she was, for he would not force himself on her, as that would be to behave as Rollo had behaved to Camilla—with such shocking results—'that all is ready for my journey to Virginia. Jeb, I need hardly inform you, can scarce wait to be gone. Polly, now, is a different matter. She wails that she does not like to leave her dear Miss Stacy to the ministrations of a half-trained girl, but she knows that her duty to Jeb, and to their child, demands that she make a new life for herself in Virginia.'

And I, thought Stacy, screaming inside herself, could not I make a new life for myself in Virginia? For there is only the Bank to keep me here, but you have never once expressed the wish that we might settle there as Jeb and Polly are doing. But I suppose that true love lies between them, and it is plain that you regret what we did together at Pontisford, since now you can scarce bear to touch me.

She forgot that she was giving him no reason to believe that she felt for him anything other than mere tolerance for someone who thought that he owed her reparation for having forced himself on her and caused her to commit an act which she had subsequently bitterly regretted. The loneliness which had been the constant companion of both of them throughout their lives had only been endured by their proud rejection of any form of surrender in the way of asking anyone for love and pity. Even Louisa had never broken through the shell of pride which had hardened around Stacy's heart.

Matt, likewise, had taught himself to depend only himself—to love was, in the end, he discovered, to experience punishment and pain, and his heart shrank, as Stacy's did, from commitment to another. Worse, ever since he had married her he had feared to touch her, for he knew that to do so would result in rousing him to the degree where he might force himself upon her as he had done at Pontisford. And that he had vowed never to do again.

Stacy, still a prisoner of her upbringing, said, in that deadly polite fashion which had Matt hungering to smash it, but not knowing how to do so without injuring them both, 'I hope that you have fair winds on your journey, both to the Americas and back again. I shall write to you in the hope that some of my letters may reach you.' For she knew how untrustworthy communication was across 'the steep Atlantic stream', as the poet Milton had it.

'Indeed—' Matt bowed '—and I know that you will look after yourself, and our child, for the one thing which I most admire in you, madam, is your practicality—a trait few women share with you.'

Well, doubtless he meant that for a compliment, but Stacy would have traded it for any sign of true affection, however small. But, asking for nothing, she received nothing. She rose, accompanied him to the door, to the entrance hall where Jeb and Polly were waiting, and Louisa stood in the shadows.

Polly was tearful again, flung her arms around Stacy and sobbed her farewells. Jeb bowed before giving her his hand, as though she were a man, and then, suddenly, impulsively, as though they were equals, not mistress and almost-servant, he took her in a giant bear hug—of the kind she would have liked from Matt. He whispered in her ear before he released her, 'I will look after him for you, madam, and see that he returns in one piece, and by then I hope that you will have the wit to find one another, for you were meant to be the two halves of a broken coin brought together, or a split apple, if only you and he had the wit to see it!'

Matt, astonished, watched as, impulsively and warmly, Stacy kissed his friend on the cheek, thinking jealously, Why could she not favour me like that? But, like Stacy, asking for nothing, he received nothing, and she watched him follow Polly and Jeb out of the ornate front door and into the waiting chaise which was to take them on their journey north to Liverpool, where they would take ship for Baltimore.

The chaise was driven down the short avenue which led to the iron gates which separated them from the road to central London. Stacy's eyes followed it. Outwardly she stood calm and composed beside an anxious Louisa, who was worried for her charge. Inwardly she was shrieking, He is my love, and I have been cruel to him, and I have sent him away. If he could but have granted me one word of love, or had asked me properly, I would have gone with him to the ends of the world, shoeless and in rags, rather than live here in my meaningless wealth and comfort.

All the years of her father's instruction were being stripped away from her, and the final words which haunted her as, straight-backed, she walked into the house with Louisa were, Too late! Too late!

And Matt Falconer? Looking out of the chaise window as he was whirled away out of her life, he also was consumed with the most bitter regret, that he had left her without telling her of his love, and the same words echoed in his head, even to the moment when he boarded ship and watched England's shores slide away into the distance.

Too late!

Inexorably the world swung around the sun, and the seasons changed, and with those changes Stacy changed too, the child growing big within her. The day finally came when she left the Bank's office, not to return, she said, until the child was born. Nothing came from America, which was no surprise, until one day in late May a packet arrived containing letters from Matt, Jeb and Polly. They had docked safely at Baltimore, and were on their way to Virginia.

'I trust, Lady Radley,' Matt had written in a hand as big and bold as himself, 'that you and the child thrive, that my business here will soon be conducted, and that it will not be long before I see you again. I remain your most devoted husband and servant, Matthew Falconer.'

'Devoted husband and servant'. Well, they were hardly words of love, Stacy thought, but they were better than nothing. The rest of the letter was like himself, straightforward, telling of the sea journey—that Polly had been ill, so that her coming child had been feared for, but that she and the child had survived the crossing, and were now well and fit. Jeb and Polly's letters were like themselves too. Polly's was full of ill-spelt excitement, and her sadness that 'Miss Stacy'—and who was she now?—had not travelled with them. Jeb's entertained her by its impudent bluntness.

> Mad Matt is madder than ever, and I know that it is because he regrets that we are not all of us, including Mad Matt's wife, returning to settle permanently in Virginia. When I taxed him over his desire to return to the land of the unfree, his reply was as stiff as you might suppose it: that he had his duty to perform to all his vast estates in England now that he was the heir, and now that he himself was on the way to having an heir. I made so bold as to suggest that he might as well have put a deputy in charge of what he owned in England as easily as he was putting me in charge in Virginia, and stayed in Virginia himself! I then had to endure a sermon on logic-chopping for my pains.

Almost as an afterthought, with a different pen and in different ink, he had written:

I pray you, madam, for the love and gratitude I bear him—he having saved my life—that when he returns to you you prove kind to him, or shall I advise him, that failing that, he must return to Virginia and I will make a burnt offering of myself by returning to run Falconer lands in England! You see what a sacrifice I am prepared to make for you both.

Tears gathered in Stacy's eyes as she put the letter down. She rose and walked to the window to see coming up the drive, towards the house, a coach with the Falconer arms on its side—a white shield with a black falcon, its wings outspread on it, a ring in its silver beak. She knew that Caroline Bibury was due in town, and had written that she would visit as soon after her arrival as was possible, but surely she would have come in her own carriage, not her father's?

She turned away from the window, but not before she had seen the footmen jump down from the box, one to throw the door open and the other to hand down the Right Honourable the Earl Falconer, Matt's father. Now, what was he doing, visiting his errant son's wife?

Stacy was soon to find out. The butler came to enquire whether she was receiving and, on being told yes, presently escorted my lord in, alone, no Caroline with him. She thought that he had aged since she had seen him at Christmas, was a little more stooped.

He bowed over her hand, and then Louisa's—Louisa being fully recovered from her Christmas malaise. Once again Stacy saw the resemblance to Matt, and saw that in his youth he had been as vibrant a man as his absent son was.

'It is good of you to receive me,' he told her, before taking a seat. 'I arrived in town but two nights ago, and I do not intend to stay long. I am merely here to do some necessary business. I visited Blanchard's this morning to pay you my respects, only to be told that you will be away until after your child is born. I trust I see you well?'

Stacy smiled at him. 'Very well, sir. And you?'

'Tolerably, madam, tolerably. As well as one of my advanced years is ever well in London. I shall not be truly well until I am back in the Yorkshire countryside again. It is of that which I wished to speak to you. I cannot think that being in London during the summer is good either for you or for my coming heir, and since it has been the practice these many years for the Falconer heir to be born at The Eyrie—most fitting a name in the circumstances—I am here to ask you to remove to Yorkshire until the birth is over.

'My dear Caroline and her husband will be returning with me, and it would please an old man to look after his son's wife in his son's absence. It is commendable that not only does his duty demand that he give up his home in Virginia, to devote himself to his life as the Falconer heir, but that also his duty demands that he return to see that his affairs are wound up there in proper form.'

He had been speaking with great conviction and great formality, and then, suddenly dropping all formality, he said, almost as blunt as Jeb would have been, 'Oh, madam, my son and I have been at outs these many years, and it is now my one wish that we shall be at ins again, and what better thing can I do than care for his wife? I shall send for the best doctor from London for you, well before my grandchild is born, so have no fears on that score.'

What could she say? The old Stacy, if she had accepted his offer at all, would have made a cool and distant answer of acceptance, not letting her emotions show, but the months of carrying his grandchild and Matt's child had changed her, had softened her. Impulsively, her eyes filling with tears, she put out a warm young hand to take his cool old one which lay loosely on his black silk-clad knee.

'Oh, sir,' she told him, 'you do me a great honour. Of

course I will come. I have never been part of a family, you know, have only ever had my dear Louisa to care for me. I am sure that Matt...Lord Radley...would be happy to learn that I shall be staying in his childhood home. He said before he left that he hoped that I would leave London to have our child in the healthy country air.'

This pleased the old man, she could tell, almost as much as her agreement to go to Yorkshire did. She would form part of his train when he travelled home again, he told her, 'And I have already sent word to The Eyrie that all must be made ready for you by the time we arrive.'

All the way north Stacy could not but think of the last journey she had made through the cold and the snow, and that the result of it was that she arrived at The Eyrie under the summer sun, a woman who was happy to live in idleness, so that her child might be born safely—even though both the Earl and Caroline protested a little when she insisted on walking out each day, as she had always been accustomed to.

Her rooms looked out over a lake with a folly in the shape of a miniature temple before it. It was there that she walked each day, sometimes with Louisa in attendance and sometimes Martha Williams, Polly's successor. There she sat in a large armchair, or reclined on a sofa fetched from the folly, watching the ducks paddle by, dozing a little, doing tapestry-work, reading, and altogether being as idle as a fine lady was expected to be, instead of being the Bankeress, that unfeminine model of diligence. It was as though she was making up for all the years of hard work which she had spent first with her father and then alone, after his death.

The only thing lacking was Matt himself, and, as if to remedy that lack, after many months' absence from them he suddenly began to walk in her dreams again. He was the lion-man, golden against the blue of the sky, tawny all over, skin and hair both. Sometimes he was walking and sometimes he was running on a parched and sun-baked plain, a dog, a large one, something like a wolfhound, following him. Sometimes he crouched by a cave at night, feeding a fire, the dog now lying beside him. Always the dog was present and always the dream ended in the same way. He would suddenly see her. His eyes would light up, she would run towards him, and he towards her, to take her in his arms, to…

And then she would wake up, to find herself alone, the ready tears about to fall, asking herself whether when… if…he returned she would still be able to be as frank and free with him in reality as she was in her dreams.

'Did Matt ever have a dog?' she asked the Earl one evening when they sat together talking after they had finished playing a rubber of whist.

The Earl answered her, looking a little puzzled by her question, 'Oh, I don't think so, no.'

Caroline, who was helping her husband to put away the impediments of the game, looked up to say, 'Oh, but he did, Father, don't you remember? He had a wolfhound, Prince; he was very fond of it, and Prince was very fond of him. When Prince was…killed Matt was broken-hearted, said that he would never have another dog. I would have thought that you would remember how he grieved over him.'

'Killed?' Stacy's voice was almost that of the Bankeress again, cold and hard, detecting a false note in something which she had been told. She saw the Earl change colour, saw that Caroline's own colour was high. 'How killed?'

Her voice was so peremptory, so commanding that Lord Bibury looked curiously at her, and Caroline answered her unthinkingly. 'It was an accident,' she said slowly. 'Rollo shot Prince by mistake… Matt took it very badly.'

So Rollo, the brother whom Matt never mentioned, whose wife he had supposedly run off with, had shot Matt's dog—and the Earl had chosen to forget that he had done so.

'How old was he?'

'Who, the dog?' Caroline appeared to be genuinely bewildered.

Stacy's sigh was impatience itself. She was the Bankeress again, questioning a prevaricating clerk, and the whole company, which included Caroline's other sister, Georgiana, and her husband, Dean George Tranter, were staring at her, good manners forgotten.

'No, Matt, I meant. How old was he? And Rollo—how old was he?' Stacy had thought it odd that no one ever spoke of Rollo, who had after all been their eldest brother and the heir, and had died comparatively recently.

'He was thirteen. Rollo was twenty-one. Matt was the youngest of us.'

Georgiana, a handsome woman, a little thrusting, determined one day to thrust her husband into a bishopric, exclaimed decisively, 'Oh, come, Caro, you were always too tender-hearted! You knew perfectly well, even if Papa didn't, that Rollo shot Prince because Matt loved him so. Matt and Frank could never have anything without Rollo wanting it. Rollo asked Matt to give him Prince and Matt refused. A week later Rollo shot Prince—accidentally, of course.' Her sneer as she said the last sentence was palpable.

An appalled silence followed. Stacy had got the answer she wanted and had, intuitively, half known was coming. Or was it the dream, where Matt roved a strange countryside, always with a dog beside him, which had told her? She had never seen him with a dog in real life.

She shivered involuntarily. The Earl saw her do so and said, 'Georgiana, I am surprised that you should make such an accusation about a brother who is dead, and cannot defend himself. If Rollo said it was an accident, done when we were all out shooting, as I now remember, then an accident it was.'

Georgiana sat down, picked up her canvaswork, abandoned for the game of whist, shrugged, and drawled, 'He never lacked a defender so long as you were there to defend him, Papa. Even now he's dead you can't acknowledge what a beast Rollo was. It's time you faced the truth. I heard him laughing about what he'd done with that groom of his. If he couldn't have Prince then he'd make sure Matt wouldn't, was the gist of it.'

The Earl's face was grey. He turned to Caroline, who was twisting her hands nervously together. 'Do you believe this to be true, Caroline?'

She nodded reluctantly. 'Yes, Papa. I was with Georgie when we heard him telling Yates—that was his groom's name, I remember—what he had done.'

Another silence fell as the Earl digested a bitter truth which he had long refused to recognise as a truth. Stacy was suddenly horrified at what she had uncovered, even if the sad story which she had just heard might make his father think a little differently about Matt. She avoided everyone's eye, cast off the mask of the Bankeress, picked up her own canvaswork and began to stitch as though her life depended on it. Silence fell again as each member of the party took refuge in some occupation, however trivial.

The Earl rose heavily, looking old. 'I should not be ungrateful to you, Caroline and Georgiana, for at long last telling me something which I should have known before. I think I will retire early, if you would all excuse me. I would like to reflect over what I have just learned when I am alone.'

Everyone, including Stacy, stood—to watch him walk slowly away, his years suddenly pressing heavily on him.

George Tranter began to reproach his wife, 'No need for that, my dear—' only for her to interrupt him spiritedly.

'Nonsense, my love. It's time he faced that, and even

worse truths, about Rollo. Matt was always Rollo's victim, and it was not the worst thing which Rollo did to him, by any means—'

This time the Dean managed to silence her by thundering, 'My love, *no*. You have said enough. Matt's wife is here. You will distress her.'

Stacy shook her head, replied as steadily as she could, 'No, it was my own insistent questioning which provoked this…incident, and I apologise for it.'

Lord Bibury, who had had a soft spot for her ever since the night when she had publicly proclaimed her betrothal to Matt, came over to sit beside her and take her hand— she had laid her embroidery down. 'No, my dear. You must not reproach yourself. You naturally wished to learn about your husband's past. It was your bad luck that you hit upon something which had long been hidden.'

No, it had not been bad luck at all. She had, after some curious fashion, known what she was doing, even as she had badgered Caroline. She often knew when people were lying, or concealing the truth from her, as Caroline had been doing when she had spoken of Matt's dog. It was a talent which she had inherited from Louis Blanchard, and of which, when she had spoken to him of it, he had said, 'All the Blanchards have possessed it, my dear, and whether it is a blessing or a curse, who is to say?'

Later, in bed, she asked herself what the real truth was in the story of Matt's running off with his brother's wife, for there was a false note in that tale, she was sure, and one day, for Matt's sake she would try to find out what it was. Meantime, she must watch and wait for him.

Several days later Stacy was doing exactly that in front of the little temple. Martha had wandered off—doubtless to meet an off-duty footman, she was sure—and she was quite alone, a book of Lord Byron's earlier poems on her knee— all her reading was frivolous these days; she had no time for Blackstone now.

The afternoon was warm, she was reclining on the sofa which had been carried out for her, and she could see the ducks on the lake, and one small rail, who had left the water and was skittering about in front of her. The sun and the silence lulled her into the easy sleep of a woman who was now more than seven months gone. She realised with a sense of shock, just before consciousness left her, that Matt had come back into her dreams on the very day when she had felt his child stir within her.

So it was natural that he should come to her again, as she lay sleeping in the grounds of the home that he had loved, and that she should, in her dream, stretch her hand out to his dog, and call him Prince, and that Matt should smile at her as she did so. This time he didn't embrace her, but took her hand, the dog walking along behind them. And how had she known that Matt had once owned a dog and had loved him? She had never seen him with one, which was strange for a man who loved animals and the countryside.

This afternoon his embrace came at the end of their walk, and as he took her in his arms she awoke, as she always did—to see him standing there, tall and bronzed, an expression almost of awe on his face at the sight of her, big with his child...

Chapter Fourteen

Busy though he had been during the short time he had spent in Virginia, Matt had found that he could not banish Stacy from either his daytime or his night-time thoughts. Camilla's death, and the manner of her dying, had made such a strong impression on him that he had told himself that he would never marry; any dealings he had with women would be both passing and superficial. He had never deceived his partners: he always made it plain from the beginning that any liaison he entered into would be temporary.

And now, in any pause in his work, when his mind began to wander, he found Stacy there with him. Always she was as she had been on that fatal night: wild-eyed, face aflame, her whole body vibrant and ready for him. Oh, he hungered for her as he had never hungered for anyone. With Camilla he had been her knight—protective, always ready to defend her, his love a gentle thing, as she had been gentle. He had been little more than a boy, after all, and chivalry as much as love had motivated him from the first moment he had ever seen her, shy and out of her depth at a grand ball, waiting for someone to rescue her—which he had done.

But Stacy! From the first she had been as fierce with him as he had been with her. She had traded him word for word, had stared him down, and when finally they had fallen into bed together it had been a contest of equals. As for shyness and needing to be rescued... He chuckled to himself a little wryly whenever he thought of the night when *she* had rescued *him* from the unwanted duel with Anthony Beauchamp. She had faced everyone down, had turned the whole business around, had been as bold in public as she was reputed to have been in private in York when dealing with her dishonest manager. She was quite the last kind of woman whom he could ever have imagined himself as finding attractive—but being absent from her told him that he loved her to distraction, that what he had felt for Camilla, although sweet and true, paled beside it.

He had concluded his business as quickly as he could, seen Jeb and Polly settled into the home which had been his, and had taken the first boat back to England on which there was a spare passage. All the way from Southampton to London he had had but one thought in his head and that was the hope that she was waiting for him. He had never thought of the child at all. It was as though once he had left Stacy behind in England she had turned back into the Amazon she had been at Pontisford, defying and mocking him every time they met.

By God, she was a woman in a thousand, and so he would tell her, and when he had done so they would celebrate his return in the most time-honoured way. He was burning as his coach turned into the drive of her home...

Only to discover that she was no longer there, had travelled to Yorkshire, to The Eyrie, of all places, to have her child. So there was nothing for it but to go and see Grimes, to discover that the improvements which he had asked to be made at Pontisford so that it would be habitable again had all been set in train, and then to race north to be reunited with her.

Impatience rode with him until The Eyrie came into view, and he was being welcomed into the entrance hall.

Servants had gathered to strip his chaise of his luggage, to escort him to his room, except that that was not the thing which was most on his mind.

'Lady Radley,' he said eagerly, waving aside enquiries about his journey from Talbot, his father's secretary. 'Will someone please inform Lady Radley that I have returned?'

It was his father who, drawn by the noise of his arrival and coming to discover what was toward, told him that his wife was in the grounds by the lake, as was her wont on fine days.

Matt found himself so impatient that he was barely able to be civil to anyone, either his father or his sisters. Habit and long training rendered him apparently so. He allowed himself to be exclaimed over, congratulated by his brothers-in-law on his healthy colour—which his sisters deplored—and answered his father's questions on how he had fared in Virginia.

Finally he allowed himself to say, 'Pray send no messenger to Lady Radley. I will inform her myself of my return,' and was out of the door, still in the clothes in which he had travelled from London.

The Earl raised expressive eyebrows, but said nothing. If there were times when he had had doubts about the depth of his son's feelings for the remarkable woman whom he had married, then Radley's obvious desire to be with her again as soon as possible went a long way towards dispelling them. He had assumed that the marriage was that strange thing in their world, a love-match, by the unorthodox way in which it had come about, and Radley's conduct seemed to bear this out. What his son's wife felt for her husband was another matter.

Half running across the park to find Stacy again, Matt remembered himself and settled down into something resembling a determined stroll. With his good long sight he could see that she was alone, lying on a sofa, unmoving, a book upon her knee. Neither Louisa nor any other escort appeared to be with her.

His last few strides brought him before her. She was asleep, but it was not that which knocked the breath from his body, but the sudden sight of her, big with his child. He shook his head disbelievingly. How could he have thought that after all these months he would find her as he had first seen her, tall and virginally slender? Instead, lying before him was no airy nymph but his wife, a fulfilled woman…who opened her eyes to look at him at the very moment when the reality of her condition smote him hard.

Matt had thought often and often of how he would fall on his knees before her, to tell her of his love, of the passion which he felt for her, and would shortly hope to demonstrate… What a fool he had been, for here was a woman who carried his child, who was smiling at him, trying to sit up and finding it difficult because of her condition. How graceless of him it would be to babble of love and passion to a woman who was carrying the result of it—she would think him a heartless boor to try to force himself upon her in her present state. She deserved his care, his compassion, more than anything else.

'Matt!' she exclaimed as he bent over her solicitously to kiss her rosy cheek, his face tender.

'Oh, madam—' and his voice was thick with emotion '—do not discommode yourself, I beg of you. Lie still. There is no need for formal greetings between us, no need at all.'

Stacy smiled, but her answer to him was as forthright as anything which the Bankeress would have said before she had met and surrendered to the man in front of her. 'Oh, Matt. I am not ill. I am having a child, and that is a condition which most women endure, and I have no desire, no desire at all, to be carried about before it is necessary. And now let me tell you how well you look, and, in return, you must tell me all your news.'

He was drinking in the soft lines of her face as she settled herself back on the pillows. She had blossomed and matured since he had last seen her. Her beauty was no longer so sharp, so haughtily dominant; there was a touching quality about it; at least, it touched him. Was this what happened to a woman when she ceased to add up columns of figures, or was it the effect of the child within her?

But Stacy's outward appearance, he noted with amusement, had not changed the cutting edge of her mind. She was as keenly intelligent as she had ever been. She listened to him as he told her of his adventures, saying as he finished, 'You remind me of what Shakespeare said when he wrote of Othello telling Desdemona of *his* adventures at the beginning of their tragedy: "She lov'd me for the dangers I had pass'd, And I lov'd her that she did pity them." I hope our play has a better ending than theirs!' And her green eyes teased him.

'Loved, madam, loved?' he repeated softly, bending forward. 'You said "loved". Is that a current description of your feelings for me, or a forecast?'

Stacy trembled beneath the intensity of his tawny gaze. He was more leonine than ever. He had pulled his cravat loose and she could see the bright golden hairs at the base of the powerful brown column of his throat. For once she regretted the child—which leaped inside her to reproach her for her desire to be slim and graceful again so that she would be able to demonstrate her love for him without having to wait.

'Time will serve to reveal all. Of that I am sure,' she began, her eyes mischievous, but before she could continue the child kicked her again, so that she cried out.

Matt's eyes widened; all thoughts of love fled at once. 'You are in pain?' he exclaimed. 'You must tell me if it is too much for you to sit here talking to me.'

To his surprise, Stacy smiled gently, even as her mouth twisted a little at the end, as the child reminded her of its existence. 'Oh, no, the pain is light, but it comes unexpectedly, without warning, so that I cry out with it. Your son and heir wishes to remind me that I must not give all my attention to his father. See—' and, to his surprise and astonishment, as well as his pleasure, she took his large hand and placed it on the curve of her stomach so that he could feel the wave of movement which a tiny kicking foot was creating.

They sat thus for a moment, eye to eye, Matt's wide. He thought that her forthrightness was so admirable that he wished that there were some tangible way in which he could reward her, other than by a passionless kiss. The lack of passion was for his sake: he was still afraid to touch her for fear of what that touch might do to him, especially after so many months of abstinence.

To walk his mind into neutral ground he told her gravely, 'By the by, madam, I forgot to tell you that Mr Jeb Priestley asked me to give you his respects.'

Stacy blinked naughtily at him. 'Now *that* I do not believe. Jeb has never respected anyone.'

'Oh, but he respects you. He told me that had I not existed, and he had met you, he would have done his best to convince you that despite the difference in station between the pair of you a marriage with him would have been made in heaven.'

For a moment Stacy was silent, contemplating a world in which Matt did not exist and Jeb Priestley pursued her. What a strange might-have-been that conjured up!

'But he has Polly,' she offered gravely.

'So he has, and she is good for him. She ignores his flights of fancy, and her only care is to look after him.'

'Now that might be a text for me to follow with you, when once our little monster is born,' she told him, her eyes closing.

No matter what she had said, Matt thought, looking at the delicate mauve shadows below her eyes and the white line around her mouth, carrying his child was tiring her, and he could suddenly understand why she had found refuge in The Eyrie.

To his astonishment he saw that she had fallen gently and sweetly to sleep again, even as they spoke, and when Martha returned he ordered her to look after her mistress while he walked back to the house to find the chair in which his mother had been pushed around the grounds when she was carrying him. He would push Lady Radley home, he said. 'And you must be sure to await my return,' he told Martha a little severely, 'for I know that your mistress will try to walk back: her will is stronger than her body at the moment.'

His head was awhirl, as Stacy's was when she awoke to find him and the wheeled chair waiting for her. There was such tenderness in his strong face that she wanted to cry gently at the sight. Tears had come easily to her during this last stage of her pregnancy, and the reality of Matt's presence was so much stronger than the image of him which walked her dreams that she was almost overwhelmed by it.

Matt was surprised by the transformation which the Bankeress had undergone. He had thought that she might resent her coming motherhood; he had not imagined that she would embrace it with such passion. But then he remembered how hard she had worked under difficulties at Pontisford... Yes, his heart told him, she puts *her* whole heart and mind into everything she does. And, knowing that, I also know that if she is to be a mother, then she will, no doubt, be the best of mothers.

Another thought struck him, an unpleasant one. And shall I see her after the birth, or will she insist on the strict letter of our agreement, that once the child is born and settled we part? In the joy of seeing her again he had quite forgotten the conditions to which they had agreed before he had gone to Virginia!

Unaware of all these seething emotions boiling about her,

Martha trotted happily beside them, holding a parasol over Stacy's head to shield her from the sun. Together she and Matt helped her from the chair and into the house. Stacy had found walking troublesome these last few weeks for the child was large, and she had begun to worry that the birth might be difficult because of it.

Matt, however, seemed determined to save her from all discomfort, for once she was out of the chair he carried her into the house to the drawing-room, where, although dinner would shortly be served, Caroline Bibury had ordered tea for them as soon as their small procession had come into sight, and had had the big glass doors to the garden thrown open so that they might sit in the shade of the awning above it.

The warmth of early July enveloped them. Caroline had tactfully left them alone. Stacy gave a small sigh of pure contentment. Matt leaned forward, said softly, 'Did you miss me, Stacy? I missed you. How strange it is that I calculate that we have spent less than a month in one another's company, that in our early time together all we did was quarrel, and yet every day I turned to say something to you—and you were not there.'

Stacy's heart beat in time with her child's. Now it suddenly beat in time with his words. Surprisingly she found her throat thick with tears. She remembered words he had said then, and also Poxon's, flung at her in rage and contempt on his last day at the York bank. Was it possible that Matt could truly feel for her what she had come to feel for him?

She could not help herself; she muttered in a low tone so that Matt had to strain to hear her, 'You do not now consider me a high-nosed bitch, then? A woman lacking all the womanly arts which give my sex grace?'

As his own words, spoken early on that fateful night at Pontisford, came back to haunt him, Matt's face twisted in pain. 'God forgive me,' he told her, his own voice low and

broken. 'It was my rage and temper speaking then. I could
not forgive you for tempting me so, for calling to me, albeit
unwittingly, in a way which no woman had ever done
since…my first and only love died. No, whatever else you
are, Lady Radley—' and he tried to speak lightly to lessen
his pain and hers '—you are not lacking in womanly arts.'

His reward was a watery smile, and the words, 'Yes, I
missed you,' but behind those simple words Stacy was registering 'my first and only love'. What, then, does he feel
for me? And if it is only friendship, a meeting of minds,
and, yes, of bodies, but not love, then I will accept it, and
not bore him with my love.

Which was exactly what Matt was thinking as they
moved away from the dangerous ground which lay between
them—and which each was refusing to explore.

So, in the happy days which followed, when they
laughed and talked together, and Matt pushed her around
the grounds or drove them in Rollo's curricle, a magnificent
thing, picked out in scarlet and gold, as far as the boundary
wall, neither spoke openly of the love which might lie between them. They talked of everything—and nothing. Both
of them usually silent souls, found in the other a partner
whose tastes and attitudes matched their own.

Forthright himself, Matt began to love Stacy's forthrightness. A hater of shams and hypocrisy, Stacy found Matt's
similar attitude towards them admirable. They liked the
same books and the same music, which Caroline played for
them in the evening.

So much were they at evens that they began to wonder
how they could ever have been so much at odds. Except
that Stacy, laughing, raised the matter as they sat alone one
evening in the dusk, before the candles were lit, by saying,
'I suppose the reason why we were so fierce with one another when we first met is because we are so much alike,
both determined to have our own way, and in those days

our ways differed,' and then, looking at him almost shyly, 'I wonder why they don't differ now?'

Matt drew a sharp breath, took her hand to kiss it, and answered her, with an admirable lack of sentimentality, 'That, madam, is because the coming child constrains you. When he has arrived, and you are bounding about, full of *joie de vivre*, you will be as harsh with me as you ever were, and I shall be compelled to point out once again where you are going astray!'

Was that true? Stacy wondered. Or, now that they were coming to know one another, were they both beginning to find in the other virtues that they were not previously aware they possessed? Could it be that they might come to love one another? Perhaps the coming child, which she had once resented a little because Matt had seemed to consider it more important then herself, was responsible for bringing them together? Or was it the long months of separation which had revealed to each of them that they had, as Jeb would have put it, lost their other half?

She was not to know that Matt was thinking the same thing! For strong-willed and determined people they were strangely diffident towards one another, even now, so far as their emotions were concerned, Matt because he was still afraid of commitment, and Stacy because she had not completely cast off the shackles which Louis Blanchard had bound around her. Neither could quite say to the other those magic words: I love you. To do so would be to surrender, and neither of them had ever willingly surrendered anything to anyone. But those about them saw more than they did, as onlookers often saw more of the game than the players did.

The Earl had summoned his son to his study soon after his return, to speak to him of the duties which he, as the heir, must take on, and of the way of life which Matt must then follow. As he had wryly said to Matt, 'The land owns us as much as we own the land.'

Afterwards, as Matt had prepared to leave, his father had said slowly, 'Stay a little longer, Radley; there is something which I must say to you.'

Matt, who had risen, sat down again, to hear his father continue, his face grave, 'I have learned a lot, during the year which has passed, of the true nature of my late son and heir, your elder brother, and what I have learned has not been pleasant. I know, for example, and I think that you ought to be aware of it, that he died a shameful death in a brothel, in a fight over a whore when he was drunk, and that he had squandered the fortune which came to him at your mother's death. I am ashamed to admit that I arranged that the cause of his death be hushed up.

'Because of what I have subsequently discovered about his mode of life, I fear that I may have misjudged you over the matter of Camilla, his wife; that what you said in defence of your behaviour at the time was most likely the truth.

'I have no proof of this, nor do I wish to seek any, for to set agents on your and Rollo's trail after so many years would be demeaning to you. I believe, from all that I have seen of you since living with you again, that you have a strong sense of honour, and your choice of a wife demonstrates that you possess common sense too. Shall we agree to put the past behind us—if you can forget my wilfulness in misjudging you—so that we may start again as father and son, living in harmony, if not always in agreement?'

This speech was so remarkable and so unexpected that Matt was almost stunned by it, and said so.

His father smiled sadly. 'Let us shake hands on it, sir, and then you may believe that I am sincere, and the past may no longer haunt us.'

Well, that was something which he had not expected. Time and chance had done their work, and now he might walk about The Eyrie with a sense of pride again. Matt no longer cared what the world thought of him, but his father's opinion was quite another matter.

From that day on one of the ghosts which had haunted Matthew Falconer, now Lord Radley, for so many years passed from his life. He would try to remember Rollo as he had been when Matt was a boy and Rollo was in his teens, before drink and dissipation had begun to destroy him. But the other ghost, that of Camilla, still walked with him. His father's forgiveness could neither exorcise her nor make him forget the manner in which she had died.

'I do believe, sir, that you are at last becoming civilised! The lion has ceased to roar, and the bear to rove the hills.' And Stacy moved her backgammon counter along the board to take her a little nearer to victory.

Matt muttered something rude beneath his breath about calculating women who could play chess and backgammon better than most men he knew, before he rattled the dice-box again.

'I should have known better than to play with you,' he told her ruefully a few minutes later, when victory became inevitably hers.

'But you lose so much more nicely now than you were wont to do when we first met.' And Stacy lay back against her pillows. She was now into her eighth month, and the doctor who was to supervise the birth was due to arrive at The Eyrie before the weekend. He was to take over from the one who rode twice-weekly from York to stare at her, and comment that 'Lady Radley is in great fettle, and by all appearances preparing to give birth to a fine boy'. He was to be the London man's assistant when he arrived.

'I can't recall that we played backgammon together when we first met,' retorted Matt, who was busy gathering up the counters and the dice. He thought that she looked particularly well that afternoon, with a fine colour on her—the pallor which had been hers before she had conceived seemed to have disappeared.

'No, indeed,' riposted Stacy, 'but we played other games, as you well know, and losing them appeared particularly galling to you.'

'But I can't recall losing any kind of game,' he replied, grinning at her as he carefully replaced the backgammon board in the ornate inlaid box which held it, the dice-box and the ivory counters. 'On the contrary, I distinctly remember winning.'

'Oh, yes, the last one.' Stacy's tone was careless, and the eyes she lifted to look at him as he towered over her were full of shameless mirth. 'I grant you that. For, behold, as a consequence of it you have reduced me to a condition in which I am fit for nothing but to be carried about and petted.'

'To make up for all the years in which you weren't,' he told her briskly, and bent down to kiss her warm and rosy cheek. Yes, madam looked particularly fine today, fine enough to drive a man mad, particularly a man who hadn't touched a woman since he had last taken the woman before him to bed.

The rapport between them was so strong now that Stacy leaned forward to take his hand and kiss it, being unable to lift herself up to kiss his cheek. 'I do believe,' she had said that morning, 'that I am about to give birth to a veritable giant. It must be a boy; I could not wish a girl to be so large.'

'You wish to renege on our bargain?' he asked her now quietly, so that Caroline and Georgiana, sitting on the other side of the room and chatting about a ball which they were due to attend at York, could not hear them.

'Bargain?' Stacy repeated dubiously, as though she had never heard the word before—and when had she learned to be so teasingly naughty, so that she was provoking him with every word she uttered? 'I can't remember a bargain, sir. On what piece of paper was it written? Remind me, so that I may refresh my memory as to the details of it.'

Matt had dragged up a chair, to sit on it facing her. He leaned forward and took her happy face in both his hands. 'You witch, to tease me so! You know perfectly well to what bargain I refer. The one to which we agreed before our wedding—that our marriage would be in name only, and that we would part after a suitable interval, once our child was born.'

He was still holding her face and gazing into her eyes, regardless of what his sisters might think, when she answered him. 'Oh, that bargain! I believe it was one which you proposed. I cannot remember any countersigning on my part.'

Matt drew in his breath sharply, and took his hands from her face. He leaned back, said hoarsely, 'Have you no idea, madam, of the effect which your words have on me? And that I am helpless before you in your present condition. Stop playing the Bankeress with me and remember that you are my wife, and that you promised to love, honour and obey me! Did none of those words mean anything to you, madam?'

Stacy decided not to taunt him further. There was a look almost of agony on his strong face. The lion seemed to be wounded. She murmured softly, 'As much as you wish them to mean, Matt. As much as you wish...'

The air between them vibrated, was full of a strange magnetism. It was as though they were completely on their own, out of space, out of time. The room they were in, the people near them, had gone. Everything but the other disappeared.

'Are you saying, madam, what I think you are saying?' Matt finally ventured, only to have Stacy return,

'Now who is playing with words, sir?'

'You taught me,' he answered her, all brevity.

'Then you are an apt pupil, sir, who does credit to his teacher.'

'And if the pupil told his teacher, and the client told the Bankeress, that he wished to renege on the agreement, and wondered what strange maggot had invaded his brain that he could have ever conceived of such a thing, what then?'

'Why, then the teacher, as well as the Bankeress, would answer that the same maggot must have invaded her brain to cause her to agree to such a proposition, and furthermore that an agreement entered into by two persons whose sanity was in doubt at the time could hardly hold—so let us agree to forget it.'

It was, Stacy afterwards thought, typical of them both that they could declare the love they had come to feel for one another in such a roundabout and oblique fashion—the magic words were still unsaid.

But Matt's response to her invitation was not oblique. He gave a sudden shout of laughter so that Caroline, being timorous, started and dropped her needle, and Georgiana, being fiery, glared at him. "Pon rep, Matt,' she exclaimed, 'think of your poor wife! You will overset her with your noisy ways.'

'Overset her?' choked Matt, taking Stacy's hand and covering it with kisses. 'By no means, never. My dear wife is never overset—least of all by her husband. No, she makes a practice of oversetting him! And now, to celebrate her latest feat, I will, like the magician in the fairy-tale, tell her that I will grant her any wish she cares to make, seeing that she has granted me my dearest one. Come, madam, wish!'

He was transformed. Usually stern, and a little forbidding in his bearing, like his father—as that father was coming to recognise—he was suddenly all playfulness. Georgiana was to say afterwards to her sister and her father that marrying Miss Blanchard was the strangest thing that Matt could have done, but was quite the best. 'She is turning him back into the man he was before he lost Camilla, and for that we should all be grateful.'

'I have no wishes left,' Stacy told him, 'since my one wish has been granted.'

'Come, there must be something. A diamond necklace, perhaps?'

Stacy shook her head. There was one thing which she *had* come to wish for in the last few days as they had driven about the park, and perhaps, if she asked him nicely, he would agree to grant it, even if it was only a small thing.

'No, Matt, I have enough jewellery to make the Tsarina of all the Russias envious. What I would really like is to leave the grounds, for you to drive me, not around the park, but into the open country. Pleasant though it is here, I have begun to feel a little imprisoned.'

Matt said, laughing, 'Is that all? A most frugal request for the Bankeress to make. But are you sure that you are fit to undertake such a drive? You would not be overset?'

'No, indeed. I would like a breath of the wide world. and so, I think, would you.'

'When I think what you might have demanded of me! A fortune perhaps—and all you wish is an extended drive. So be it. Tomorrow, then, if it be fine, and, if not, the first fine day. We must celebrate, must we not?'

Georgiana overheard this last. 'Celebrate, Matt? What's to celebrate?'

He could hardly tell her that they had just agreed to be truly man and wife, seeing that they were already married! Instead, he answered her airily, 'Why sister, we have just decided that if the child is to be a boy, then he will be Henry, after our grandfather, I believe, Adolphus after my father, and Louis, after Lady Radley's. Is not that a splendid thing?'

'Well, I think so,' agreed Stacy, to whom Matt's fertile invention had come as a surprise, almost as big a surprise as to learn that he had been thinking of what to call his future son, if son it was. 'Especially since he has left to me the choice of names if it is to be a girl—but I have not yet made up my mind what they are to be. He is before me there.'

'Bravely said,' replied Matt, thinking that once again Stacy had trumped his ace so to speak; after having had a boy's name sprung on her she had counter-attacked by claiming the right to decide on a daughter's name. Oh, he could see that life with madam was going to be lively, full of surprises. He wished with all his heart that their child would soon honour them with his or her presence so that they could start living that life as soon as possible.

And if she wished to go on being the Bankeress, then so be it. Somehow he would arrange to let her have her wish—if that was what she truly wanted.

That night they were more loving than they had ever been, and Matt came to Stacy's room after she had retired, and sat by her on the bed, holding her in his arms, enjoying the sweet torment which that provoked in him, and thinking of all the sweeter ecstasies which were to come…

Chapter Fifteen

'You are quite sure that you are well enough to undertake such a long ride in the country?' Matt asked anxiously. 'After all, so far we have stayed inside the park on easy roads and pleasant ways. You will not find the motion too distressing?'

He had already lifted Stacy into her seat in his curricle; grooms were holding the horses' heads to prevent any chance that they might rear before he was fully in control of them and cause her discomfort—he did not think that she would be frightened, for nothing seemed to frighten her.

She shook her head as he sat beside her, taking up his whip. 'No, indeed. I ailed a little in the first few months, but of late I have felt most amazingly well. Today I feel that, if it were not for the burden which I carry, I could move mountains. Truly, I have never felt so well in my life.'

She gave him an enchanting sideways glance, which had him trembling again, before adding, 'Why, I do believe that you are going back on your word.' Stacy was still revelling in her new-found powers of mischief and of teasing gaiety, which she had been unaware she possessed until she had met Matt. It was as though he was getting the benefit of all the flirting which she had never done, but now felt able and willing to do.

'Never,' he told her, with a grin, as the grooms released the horses and they started off. 'But if you *do* feel any discomfort you must tell me so immediately and we shall return home at once.'

Home. Matt had spent many years denying that The Eyrie had ever been, or could ever be, his home. As for Stacy, it was odd to think that she could call somewhere home which she had only known for a few months, but she had already come to love The Eyrie, which would one day be truly hers and Matt's.

It felt strange to reach the big gates and turn out of them on to the York road, and then to make not for York itself but for the open plain. The Eyrie was situated between York and Selby, in open country criss-crossed by small lanes and ditches which were even more primitive than the road on which they were travelling, the one which the mail-coaches took.

They had taken no groom or tiger with them—not that Matt possessed a tiger—something which he was later to regret—but he did not intend to be out for long, and he had become accustomed to living informally during his years in Virginia. It had taken him some time to grow used again to the press of servants who were needed to make The Eyrie run smoothly. Once he had taken them for granted, but after Virginia he would never do so again.

'He's a good man to serve, the new lord,' the staff at The Eyrie had agreed, 'not like the bastard, his older brother.' There were those who remembered Matt as a boy, and thought that he had grown into someone who commanded affection as well as respect.

'Oh, do let us go along there!' Stacy suddenly exclaimed as they came to a side-road which led gently down to a small valley through which a stream, a tributary of the Derwent, ran beneath over-arching trees. 'I would love to be able to paint it.' Then she added wistfully, 'There are times when I wish I had not given up painting, but Father said that, like music, it was a waste of time best occupied by more serious matters.'

It was unguarded disclosures like these which told Matt something of the rigorous life which Louis Blanchard had inflicted on his daughter. If it had made her a strong woman, it had also deprived her of many of the small pleasures of living. He had already made a private resolution that once their child was born he would encourage her to enjoy herself by indulging in all those innocent amusements which one by one her father had vetoed in favour of the stern regime which had come to dominate her life.

Matt shook his head, murmured, 'I am sorry to disappoint you, my darling, but we have already come quite a long way from The Eyrie. I think that we ought to turn for home. The plain of York is a lonely place.'

'But peaceful,' said Stacy, and then, 'It also seems a long way from the Bank. Please, Matt, let us go just a little further before we turn back.'

She accompanied this plea with such a charmingly wilful expression that he felt compelled to give way. 'Very well, my naughty minx, just a little further. I see that having our child is making you lose all your high-minded caution.' And he touched the horses lightly with his whip and they turned into the narrow lane. Any narrower and he would have refused to go down it at all.

Here, among the scents and smells of the open country, Stacy found it hard to believe that the Bank existed, that it had been the centre of her life for so long. Her father had become a distant figure, no longer the demi-god who had dominated her, and he was fast receding into the past. It was not that she no longer loved him, or his memory, but she was at last freeing herself from the prison of lovelessness into which he had unintentionally thrust her. Ephraim was sending her regular reports, and she dutifully commented on them and wrote back suggestions, but it was like posting letters to Mars, or the outer planets, she sometimes thought.

She turned to share this odd notion with Matt after he had negotiated a bend in the lane and was turning for home again—he had already told her that the road, such as it was, was growing too poor for them to go much further—when disaster struck.

They were bowling happily along when they disturbed a large nye of pheasants, which, the cock-bird leading, exploded out of the bushes which lined the lane, straight into the path of the horses.

Neighing and snorting, both horses reared and stumbled. That alone might not have caused an accident, but the nearside horse, despite all Matt's efforts, lost his footing, tried to recover it, lost it again, and, as he did so, took his companion down into the ditch with him, the curricle and its occupants following. The nearside horse broke his neck immediately, his fellow his leg. Matt, half stunned, landed among the ruins of his carriage, with Stacy beside him. She lay there unmoving. One moment she had been enjoying the afternoon sun, the next she had been flung sideways, and now was hardly aware of where she was.

After a little time, through the almost pleasant haze she was lying in, she heard someone say hoarsely, 'Stacy, oh, my darling Stacy. I have killed you in my folly. Dear God, not twice. I could not bear this to happen again.'

In her dazed condition she thought that she was lying in the wreck of her coach in the November snow, and she could not imagine why Hal should be saying such strange things to her. A horse was making a dreadful noise, as though it was in great pain.

She tried to sit up, but found that she could not, and then someone was freeing her, lifting her and carrying her some little distance to lay her down on the ground—in the snow? What a strange thing to do. Someone—could it possibly be

Hal?—had his arms around her, and was holding her tenderly. She looked up to find out who it was, but at first all that she could see was the sunlight shining through the trees—and then she saw Matt's agonised face—and remembered everything...

It was not November, it was July. And she was no longer Anastasia Blanchard, but Anastasia, Lady Radley, expecting her first child, and it was her husband who was holding her, and begging her to speak to him, if she could. Yes, they had gone for a drive, they had driven down to a stream, and then away from it, but after that...nothing...

Her head began to clear. She said, weakly at first, then more strongly, 'Matt, what happened?' And now she could see him properly. His face was white. There was a great bruise on his cheek, his coat was torn, but otherwise he didn't seem to be hurt.

'Pheasants flew at us,' he told her, 'frightened the horses. I couldn't control them—I doubt whether anyone could have done...which is no excuse...' He held her tightly to him. 'Oh, God, Stacy, what have I done to you?'

Her voice muffled, because he was holding her so tightly against him, she answered him, 'Nothing; I don't think I've taken an injury...' She paused, then continued doubtfully as he released her a little, 'I must have caught my head on something, for it feels very odd, but it is growing better now. And I have a pain in my back. I think I must have twisted it when we fell. But what about you?'

'Oh, me,' he answered her dismissively. 'I think I might have damaged my ankle—we're both lucky to be alive. Fortunately neither of the horses fell on us, or kicked us. Unfortunately one is dead, the other badly injured, and the curricle is done for.'

That must have been the horse which had been making a noise and was now silent. She was to learn later that while she was still semi-conscious Matt shot it with one of the

horse pistols which he always carried when not riding in
the park.

'God forgive me for not bringing a groom with us, but
I have grown out of the habit of having servants trailing
around after me. Forget that,' he said anxiously. 'I can see
a cottage not far away. If I can get you there you can shelter
in it, and we can send someone to The Eyrie for help. Do
you think that you could manage to walk?'

Her head was still misbehaving, but Stacy said, as
bravely as she could, 'If you will help me up I shall try.'

It was almost a question of the blind leading the blind,
for Matt was limping badly—his ankle was more sprained
and swollen than he had admitted—and the pain in Stacy's
back was so severe that she found difficulty in walking.

She could tell that he was in pain, so she tried not to
lean on him too much, but as they made their way up the
track, to where a cottage stood on a small rise in the
ground, she felt such a sharp pain in her back that she gave
a little cry, and sat down abruptly on the ground.

Matt was squatting beside her immediately, his face more
drawn than ever through pain and worry. 'Stacy! What is
it?'

She looked up at him, trying to control herself. 'Oh,
Matt, I'm sorry to make a fuss, but the pain was so strong
and came so suddenly, without warning...' She gave another small gasp. 'It's not continuous, it's coming and going, which makes it hard for me to bear it.'

Stacy had not thought that Matt could grow any paler
than he already was, but he did, and she felt the arm which
he had put about her shoulders tighten, but he said only,
'Try to walk, my darling, but if the pain grows too bad,
then I will carry you.'

But she didn't want that, and somehow, half leaning
against one another, they drew near to the cottage.

Matt, who was not suffering as Stacy was from the after-
effects of a blow to the head, saw before she did that some-

thing was wrong. The cottage looked neglected; it had once possessed a garden, but it had been allowed to run wild. A dirty child in ragged clothes played in it, casting feral looks at them as they approached, before running through an open door. No, not a door, but an opening where one had been.

His heart sank. He helped Stacy into the garden and laid her down on a small patch of rank grass beside some bedraggled fruit bushes which had run wild. The child reappeared—it was difficult to tell whether it was a boy or a girl. He asked, trying to keep his voice gentle and steady, 'My dear, is either your mother or your father at home?'

Matt thought wryly that he might have been speaking Greek for all the impression he made on the wild creature before him. He started for the doorway in order to enter the cottage, to see if anyone was there, but the child ran before him, darting in, to come out again dragging with him a woman, as ragged and dirty as he was. The woman stared at him. She was as feral as the child. For the first time he saw that a tinker's cart stood near to the cottage, but there was no sign of the tinker.

The woman said slowly, in an accent so wild and strange that he could barely understand her, 'What's up, maister?'

Nothing in Matt's life had prepared him for such indifference as she was showing him. Even as he spoke to her her eyes ranged away from him to stare into the distance while he tried to explain what had happened, that he was Lord Radley, and that he would like someone to go to The Eyrie to fetch help, for he did not wish to leave his wife on her own. To his dismay she didn't answer him, but shouted unintelligibly at the boy, who stared at him again and then began to run away from the cottage, towards the lane from which they had so painfully walked.

He saw that Stacy was sitting up, and was holding her back. The woman walked over to her, said something which Stacy could not understand, and then she put her hands into Stacy's armpits, pulled her erect, and began to walk her into the cottage. She said to Matt as she passed him, 'Coom in, then. Thy missis is having thy child.'

'Having thy child!' The world spun around Matt. He cried hoarsely, 'No!' Time turned in on itself. He was in an inn, and a woman was saying fiercely to him, 'Couldn't you see that the girl you have brought here is about to give birth? Shame on you for dragging her around the country-side in such a state...'

He was back on the plain of York again, walking into a small, dark room. There was a table, a bench, a rude fire-place without a fire in it, and something which passed for a bed in a corner. His brain told him that the tenant farmer who had lived here was long gone, and that a tinker's fam-ily had taken over the derelict cottage. Where the tinker was God only knew. All he knew was that he had brought Stacy to this terrible place, and history was about to repeat itself...

The woman sat Stacy down on the bench and fetched a clean blanket from a wicker basket which lay on the dirt floor before the empty hearth. Matt joined Stacy on the bench. She turned a white face towards him, exclaimed feverishly, 'Oh, Matt, she says that I am about to birth the baby! Do you think that she can possibly be right?' Even as she spoke her face contracted again, as the pain in her back struck harder than ever this time, and she said numbly, once it had subsided, 'Oh, I do believe she is, but surely the pain is in the wrong place?'

All that Matt knew about the birth of babies was that Camilla had died trying to deliver one—something of which even now he could barely think. He pushed the thought away. The woman came over and put the blanket on the bed, saying to Stacy as she passed her, 'Coom on, then, gal. On to the bed wi' ye. Stay there while I fetch old Grandam Outhwaite to help yer. He—'and she jerked her thumb at Matt '—will 'ave to look after ye until she cooms.'

Stacy looked wildly round the room. The bed did not appear to be particularly dirty but, apart from the blanket which the woman had just laid down, wasn't particularly clean either. Whenever she had imagined having her baby she had never foreseen anything like this! She had seen herself on the large bed in her room back at The Eyrie, servants coming and going, perhaps faithful Louisa sitting in a corner, Matt striding along the corridor outside as Georgiana had told her her husband had done when her first child had been born. One of England's most famous doctors would have been in attendance; the best doctor in York was to have been his faithful aide.

But the only person attending her was Matt, and all that she was being promised was some peasant midwife, who was probably having to be fetched from the nearest village—wherever that might be. This was certainly not how she had visualised giving birth to the heir to all the Falconers!

For once even her brave spirit faltered. Matt saw her face change and came to sit beside her on the makeshift bed, to lift her up a little, to hold her against his chest, to say anxiously, 'Oh Stacy, my darling, what a time to tell you. I should have told you before, but for some odd reason I never found the courage to do so... I love you so dearly that I can hardly bear to see you suffer. I think that I have loved you ever since I opened the door at Pontisford and saw you standing there, so brave and defiant, and look at you now, at what I have done to you... How can you love me after this?' His voice broke on the last words and she could feel his poor heart beating furiously as he held her against him.

They were the words which Stacy had always wanted to hear him say, and what a time to choose to tell her! Even through her pain and rising fear she felt that she had to reward him by saying, her voice hoarse and broken as she fought the all-consuming pain, 'Oh, Matt, you must surely know that I have loved you since Pontisford, and what we did there was done together—together we made our child, and I was as willing and eager as you were...'

And then the pain took her, and this time it was he who held and comforted her, not she him, and he felt with her the pain which was tearing her apart. After it had passed they rested in one another's arms, until Matt said tenderly, trying to control his own rising fear that he was in danger of losing his wife and child just as they had found each other, 'Is there anything I can do for you? Have you any idea how soon it is likely to be before the baby arrives?'

Before she could answer him another pain—they were coming thick and fast now—tore through Stacy with such force that she could not prevent herself from writhing and crying out, putting her fist into her mouth to stop herself from screaming. This time the pain was in the front, and when it had passed she told Matt what she thought the woman had said: 'It won't be long, me duck.'

'Won't be long!' Matt muttered something blasphemous under his breath, and then, 'And how long before she returns with this old wise-woman, and how useful will she be?'

Stacy didn't answer him; she was too busy trying to cope with other things—one a great gush of water which she knew, from questions which she had compelled the York doctor to answer, was the breaking of the waters which preceded birth.

'Oh, really, Lady Radley, I do not think my place to discuss such matters with you, nor would it be proper for you to know of them,' he had twittered at her.

To which she had replied in a voice of steel, 'Well, it is I who am having this child, sir, so kindly do as I ask. I have no wish to die as the result of ignorance like the late lamented Princess Charlotte.'

He had also told her that the pains she would feel would come more and more rapidly as the time for the birth neared, and there was no doubt that this was beginning to happen. Once the latest pain had subsided a little she told Matt so, adding, 'You are going to have to help me if you wish your son and heir to be born alive, for there is no one else here to do so.'

She could not have anticipated his reaction to this news. She had felt him shaking when he had taken her into his arms, and now she felt him begin to shudder violently. She twisted her head a little to find that he was not grey, but yellow, and looked as though *he* was about to faint.

'For God's sake, Stacy,' he muttered, 'do not say so. It is not half an hour since the accident, and I always understood from what I heard of my sisters' talk, and from the women on the plantation, that birthing a baby usually takes a day at least.'

One thing was certain, he learned immediately, and that was that Stacy's fiery spirit had not been quenched by what was happening to her.

'Well,' she told him bluntly, 'you had better pray that the baby does come soon, for one thing is certain—a day of pains such as these would be the death of me—' and then she was writhing again in such agony that he gently laid her down on her back again, thinking that that might ease her.

He remembered being present after Camilla's agony, and after the birth of one of the black servants on his Virginia farm, and that on both occasions there had been blood everywhere—although the black servant's child had lived and Camilla's had not. Stacy would need some clean linen, and water. She had begun to sweat heavily, and he used his fine cambric handkerchief to wipe her face tenderly—but she would need more than his handkerchief if the child was coming.

'Listen,' he murmured urgently, during the interval between her pains, 'if the baby is coming soon, which God forbid, then I must try to find some water—there will almost certainly be a well at the back of the cottage, or a running brook nearby. Do you think that you could hold on for a moment or two while I reconnoitre?'

It was the last thing Stacy wanted, to be left alone, but there was no help for it. She offered him a twisted smile and a murmured, 'Yes,' while she concentrated on preparing to withstand the next pain.

When it came she closed her eyes, gripped the corner of the blanket and thrust it between her teeth to stop herself from screaming at its force, so that on Matt's return some little time later, carrying a bucket of water and a battered pewter cup, she was able to offer him a brave face.

'There *was* a well,' he told her, 'and the water looks and tastes sweet. Would you like to drink some?' For he thought that she was now beginning to show the effects of severe pain added to the shock of the accident.

Stacy took the offered water, drank it greedily, and then watched with some astonishment as Matt took off his jacket, untied his cravat and pulled off his fine linen shirt, which he began to rip apart, creating from its back one large piece, and tearing off long strips from its sleeves and front. He put his jacket back on again, and offered her one of the strips. 'To bite on,' he told her, 'when the pain become too great to bear. That's what the surgeons did on board ship after a naval battle when they were looking after the men. The others will do for later, when the child comes.'

Taking the linen strip, and doing as she was bid, Stacy didn't inform him that she had already used the blanket for that purpose. He looked so ill and worried that one might almost have thought that he was about to have the baby himself! Surprisingly, even through her pain, the thought made her want to giggle.

For a time nothing changed, the pain came and went, but after about an hour, by which time the pains were coming continuously and she could no longer suppress her screams at their strength, Stacy's body began to tell her that the baby's birth was imminent. She was now half sitting up again, Matt was holding her, and when she turned to say to him, 'Oh, Matt, I think that the baby is about to come,' it was at this point that he broke.

He laid her down on the bed, put his head in his hands, and groaned, 'I can't, Stacy, I can't bear this, not again, not twice. Oh, God, I don't think that I shall be able to help you!' He had, unknown to her, gone back more than ten years. He was in another room, the bedroom of an inn, and he was looking down at poor, dead Camilla, at her child who had been born dead, and the ghastly evidence of a painful, mismanaged birth all about them. It had unmanned him then, and he had tried to suppress the memory of it, but, faced with Stacy in a similar situation, he was unmanned again. Was he to lose another, and stronger love in the same painful way as the first?

Stacy, overcome by surprise as much as by shock when Matt buried his face in the blanket on her bed, stared at him, even through her agony. She was sweating, her hair had come down and hung in wet tendrils around her face, and the man whose strength and courage she had always admired, the man who had saved Jeb's life, rescuing him against fearful odds when his farm had been attacked by roving brigands, was telling her that he was unable to help her to bear their child. Whatever could be the matter with him?

'Matt,' she almost shouted over the pain which was destroying her, 'you must help me. Look at me, Matt, look at me! Of course you can help me. How many mares have you helped to bring their foals into the world?'

He lifted his head to show her a face nearly as agonised as hers. 'But you are not a mare, Stacy, you are my wife, and—'

'And bosh,' she roared at him rudely, the Bankeress *in Excelsis Gloria*, as an irreverent wit had once named her.

'What am I now but a two-legged mare, about to let her foal slip into your hands? Would you do more for your horse than you would do for me?'

Slowly, unwillingly, as the memory of Camilla's death-bed faded from his mind, driven away by the strength of his wife's words, he gave a slow and reluctant grin at her unquenchable spirit.

'By God, madam,' he told her softly, 'you rightly rebuke me. Yes, we will birth our foal together.'

'Then see to it at once, Radley, do you hear me? For I shall shortly have little more reason left than your mare, and it is you who will have the greater burden—Ah, God, Matt—' and she gave a shrill scream '—I believe he is nearly here.'

This time he was ready for her, his courage restored, and for the next few hectic minutes, as Stacy panted and pushed their child into the world, Matt was helping her and encouraging her, as though she were the mare she had claimed to be. And when at last the baby emerged into the cruel world, crying its protests at being born at all, it was Matt who caught him in his large hands, who wrapped him gently in the remains of his father's linen shirt—for yes, he was the boy whom Stacy had always claimed that she was carrying. And it was Matt who showed him to his mother and let her hold him for a moment, saying, 'Hal, my boy, you must meet your mama at last. Stacy, my darling, here is your foal.'

To which she replied weakly, but with a smile, 'Oh, no, Matt, he is my lion-cub. See, when his hair dries it will be as tawny as yours!'

Matt thought that he had never seen anything so beautiful in his life as his wife as she lay there, cuddling their child, never mind that she bore about her all the stigmata of a difficult, if rapid birth. And so he told her, the pair of them sharing broken endearments over the head of their child.

And finally it was Matt who carried the protesting Hal

over to place him in the wicker basket from which the blanket on the bed had earlier come.

As he bent down there were shadows and noise at the door, and the woman who had earlier gone for the wise-woman entered. Behind her came an older woman, bent and wrinkled, who took in the scene before her—the large man holding the howling baby, the exhausted woman on the makeshift bed.

Grandam Outhwaite said in a cracked voice, 'Why, I believes as 'ow yer didn't need me arter all,' before she went over to Stacy to finish the business of birthing, finally washing both her and the baby down with an infusion of herbs which she had brought with her in a little blue bottle.

The heir to all the Falconers had been successfully born, on a blanket in a deserted cottage in which a family of tinkers had been squatting, with only his father and mother to help him!

'I am sure that something must be dreadfully wrong!' Caroline Bibury was wringing her hands. It was late after-noon and Matt and Stacy had been gone for some hours. They had been expected back long before. 'Matt would surely not have taken Stacy on a jaunt as extended as this in her condition.' And she looked helplessly around at the assembled company.

Earlier that afternoon the Beauchamps had driven over from Bramham, and Anthony, still smarting from losing Stacy to 'that fellow', muttered ungraciously, half beneath his breath, that, 'Nothing that Radley did would surprise me.'

His father cast warning glances at him, so he subsided, but if he didn't speak again he thought a great deal. The Earl ordered the grooms and stable-hands to ride out in the direction which Radley had gone, but so far no one had returned with any news. Aunt Beauchamp persuaded Uncle Beauchamp to stay longer than they ought to do before returning home, in the hope that they might see Stacy safe before they left, but even so they finally had to make ready to take their leave.

The Earl and his family, by now seriously worried, walked to the stable-yard to see the coach for the Beauchamp parents driven out; Anthony had ridden over on his horse. The Earl did them the honour of coming out himself. He was leaning on his stick, his mind in turmoil as a result of Radley's non-return, when a ragged child who had been lurking about the yard suddenly sprang at him, howling something incomprehensible.

Thwaites, the head groom, who was busy supervising operations, leaped forward to remove the child bodily. 'Danged little tyke bin a botheration to us all arternoon,' he grunted. 'Shouting and roaring his nonsense at us. You mind your manners, lad. 'Tis the Earl you're saucing.'

At the mention of the Earl the child howled again, trying to escape Thwaites' strong arms. This time the Earl thought he heard something familiar.

'You heard that,' he said to Anthony Beauchamp who was making ready to mount. 'He distinctly said Radley. Now how would he know that? Let him down, Thwaites. Let him come and speak to me, since that is what he wants.'

Thwaites, muttering, put the child down. He immediately ran to the Earl, fell on his knees before him, and began to speak. The name Radley was now distinctly heard by all of them in the yard.

'He's trying to tell us something about Radley,' the Earl announced incredulously. 'Slowly, lad, slowly.'

The child nodded his shaggy head, mouthed at the Earl so that he could make out that Radley had had an accident and, ''E's at whoam, 'e is. At whoam.'

'And where's home?' the Earl asked him gently.

The child pointed towards where Selby lay, took the Earl roughly by the sleeve and began to pull him in that direction. There was no doubt that he was trying to tell him that he knew where Lord Radley was, and that he was to go with him to find him.

'Is Lord Radley injured? Hurt?' he added, when he saw that the child had not at first understood him.

The child shook his head, said something incomprehensible, and repeated it when he saw that the Earl had not understood him. This time, 'Nay, the ooman,' came out quite plainly.

Anthony Beauchamp said feverishly, 'My God, it is Stacy who is hurt. We must go to her at once. Cannot the child show us the way? If necessary I will go alone.'

The Earl shook his head. 'No,' he said, 'I will ride there, and you may accompany me if you wish.'

And so it was that they came at last to the lane below the cottage, the child riding with Thwaites and pointing out the way, the Earl and Anthony Beauchamp following. They passed the ruined curricle and the dead horses lying in the ditch. Anthony swore blackly below his breath and the Earl's heart sank within him. But when the boy slid off his horse and began to run up the track to the cottage, he dismounted and set off after him, fearful of what he might find.

He and Anthony had not reached the cottage before Matt came out to meet them, after hearing the sound of men and horses. He had been helping Grandam Outhwaite to undress Stacy and put her into a coarse but clean nightgown, after giving her a draught from yet another blue bottle—'Poppy,' she had told him briefly. ''Er 'll sleep soon.'

He had such an expression of joy on his face as his father had never seen. The grim, rather dour man had gone: he had the manner of the happy boy he had once been. 'Father!' he exclaimed, and there was joy in his voice as well. 'I knew that you would come to find me if the lad could only find the way.'

'Your wife?' panted the Earl, sinking on to a bench beside the door.

'Stacy—what have you done to her? We saw the ruins of the curricle on our way here,' burst from Anthony, who was privately vowing to kill Matt Falconer if any harm had come to Stacy.

Matt was still wearing that queer look of triumph. 'She's as well as can be expected,' he said. 'Come.' And he waved them into the cottage.

To their astonishment they saw Stacy lying propped against a pillow, covered by another coarse blanket. She was half asleep, already under the poppy's influence, and gave them only a distant smile, while Matt bent down to a basket by the hearth, to lift from it his son, who, roused from peaceful sleep by his father, gave a howling welcome to his grandfather.

'Your grandson greets you, sir. Allow me to introduce Hal Falconer, not yet an hour born. He came so rapidly into the world that his mother and father were hard put to see him into it properly.'

Anthony looked aghast. 'Here!' he almost moaned. 'The poor child had her baby here—with only you present!'

'Aye,' said Grandam Outhwaite, bobbing an indifferent curtsy to the gentry, more as a mere token of respect than anything else, 'an' what better place to have it, wi'out a pack o' useless noddies dancin' around her, but wi' her own true love helping her, and me to see her right when 'twas all over? Sleep now, me duck,' she told Stacy firmly. 'Tek no notice of 'em. The maister and I will look after ye until ye are fit to travel 'ome agin.'

Stacy's last sight before she fell into a black pit of healing sleep was of the Earl's half-amused face and Anthony's outraged one as the old woman ordered them about. The last sound she heard was that of her protesting son, whom Matt was still holding as though he never intended to lay him down again. He was to ask himself afterwards whether the fierce pride he had felt for the boy-child in his arms was because he had assisted at his birth, not been fetched in when all was over and shown a spotless baby lying in a spotless cradle covered in lace, as though he had been dropped from heaven clean and washed and clothed in the finest garments!

Instead little Hal Falconer wore nothing but the remains of his father's shirt, and was to do so until Thwaites rode back to The Eyrie with the news of his birth. He carried with him a request that many of the baby-clothes wrapped around bags of lavender and lying in the drawers of the waiting nursery should be brought to the poor cottage where the latest Falconer had been born, along with his mother's nightrail and enough bedlinen, towels, soap, perfume and other etceteras to make the cottage a more suitable place for the Falconer heir until he and his mother were fit to be carried back to The Eyrie.

The small, dark room seemed smaller and darker still, filled as it was with more people than it had known for many a day. The Earl looked round it and said, 'I believe that a yeoman used to live here, but he died some years ago, unmarried, leaving no children behind. The land being marginal and hard to farm, I never let it out again. I take it that this poor woman and her child are squatting here, for want of anywhere else to go?'

'Then, whoever you are, you takes it wrong,' a harsh voice told him as the owner of it stepped into the room. 'And who the devil are all of ye to be in my whoam? And who the devil's she?' And he was pointing at Stacy, happily asleep, all her problems solved, dreaming that she was roving across a great plain, Hal in her arms, Matt by her side, and a large dog following them…

Chapter Sixteen

'Well, one could hardly blame the poor man for being surprised. To step into such a galaxy of great men, all sitting in his one small room, and me asleep on the only bed in it, must have been a great shock for him!' Stacy was responding to Matt's tale of what had happened while she had been happily unconscious after Hal's birth. 'I hope you were all suitably kind to him for the shelter his wife gave us. Otherwise Hal might have been born in the open!'

'Oh, Father is arranging that,' responded Matt, who had been on his highest ropes ever since Hal had been born and Stacy had survived his birth, 'and if he hadn't done so I would. After all, you were given bed and board there for several days until the York doctor allowed that you might safely be moved.'

Stacy laughed again as she remembered the great man's shock on hearing how Hal had come into the world, and a letter had been sent to the even greater man in London telling him that his services were no longer needed.

She had been back at The Eyrie for some days, in her own bed again, and was waiting to feed Hal, reluctant to disturb him while he was sleeping peacefully. Louisa was distressed by Stacy's insistence that she feed Hal herself, and was constantly worrying her over it, 'Are you sure that you would not be better with a wet-nurse, my dear?' being her usual refrain.

'Perhaps I should,' Stacy had told her robustly, 'but seeing that master Hal arrived so incontinently into the world that there is none available, nor will be, I am told, for another few weeks, he is going to have to be content with his mama.'

Whether it was Matt's ministrations during the birth, or Grandam Outhwaite's herbs, potions and care after it that did the trick, as Matt was fond of saying, Stacy recovered amazingly quickly from what Anthony Beauchamp, Caroline and others persisted in calling her 'ordeal'. Far more rapidly, Georgiana said acidly, than *she* had ever done with her more conventional *accouchements*.

It had seemed like an ordeal at the time, Stacy thought, but afterwards, well, that was quite a different thing. Like Matt she thought that she loved young Hal the more because they, and only they, were responsible for his presence. Not simply in creating him, but in seeing that he was safely born.

'So brave, Stacy,' everyone said, but Stacy always maintained that Matt had been the brave one. Anthony and others had tried to blame him for taking her to such an out-of-the-way place when she was so near to her time, but she wouldn't have that either.

'Why, I was the wilful one,' she always said, 'not Matt, seeing that it was I who insisted on going down that final lane where the accident happened, when Matt had wished to turn for home earlier. So, there's no more to be said.'

But there *was* one more thing to say, and when Matt came into her room to see how she and Hal were faring she patted the bed and asked Matt to come and sit by her. 'For,' she told him, 'there is a question I must ask you, sir.'

'Oh,' said Matt, gazing at her fondly, 'and what question is that?' He thought that since Hal's birth she looked more beautiful than ever. Motherhood had softened her, put a faint blush in once pale cheeks, had rounded her even more delightfully in every direction. Only her sharp intelligence remained unchanged, which was all to the good, he thought, for he was coming to treasure it, and could not imagine why so many men wished to have fools for their wives.

'I am curious,' she said, speaking slowly, 'as to why a man whom I know to be brave out of the common run—no, do not contradict me, sir, Jeb Priestley told me of your exploits in America—should behave so strangely when his wife was having their child. I thought at one point that you were about to faint. Most unlike you. I would have imagined, beforehand, that you would have taken all in your stride.'

To her surprise he changed colour, and then rose to walk to the window and look out of it at the golden afternoon, before he turned to speak to her.

'If I said that most men of any sensitivity would be distressed at the sight of their wife giving birth then I should not be speaking the entire truth. There was more to it than that...' He paused.

After a time Stacy said, 'Yes, I thought so. You said something odd at the time. "Not twice," you said. "I can't bear this, not again, not twice."' And then swiftly and tenderly she added, 'Oh, my dear, if it distresses you to speak of it, then pardon me for having raised a matter which might hurt you.'

He came back to the bed to sit by her again and take her hand before saying quietly, 'No, it doesn't hurt me now. Not like it did. Indeed, I think it might be better if I told you why I was so distressed.' He paused again. Stacy pressed his hand, and he pressed hers back. Since their child's birth they had been more tender and loving with each other than she could have believed possible. One day, soon, when the pains of the birth were behind her, they would celebrate their love as it deserved to be celebrated, wildly and fiercely, no doubt, as it had been that night at Pontisford, but for the present simply to be together, and Hal not far away, was enough.

'I was a happy child,' he began slowly. 'I was the youngest and a little spoiled. I never knew my mother; she died when I was only four years old—she had never been strong, they said. And while I was very young Rollo seemed not to resent me. I realise now that when they grew up he resented both his brothers, as though we were somehow his rivals. So when I grew older he changed towards me. I was given a dog, a wolfhound. Prince, I called him. Rollo wanted Prince, simply because he was mine, I now think. He asked me to give him Prince. I said no, Prince was mine. I loved him and Prince loved me. He said nothing when I refused, only softly, "You'll be sorry."

'I didn't really understand what he meant by that. I did about a week later. We were out on the moors shooting, the dogs were with us, and Rollo shot Prince dead. He always claimed it was an accident. Only he and I knew it wasn't, that it was quite deliberate. After that I was careful never to show that I cared much for anything when he was about, for I knew that if I did he would do something like that again, or would take it away from me.

'And then I met Camilla. It was at a ball at York Assembly Rooms. She was not at all like you. She was a little thing, with silky blonde hair, eyes like cornflowers and a tender, delicate face. She was shy, and was seated quite alone, with an old aunt by her side, while the young men fought over her three elder sisters. I fell head over heels in love with her. I wanted to protect her, to make her smile. I asked her to dance, and, seeing that I couldn't dance with her more than twice or cause gossip, I sat by her and talked to her. She seemed to like talking to me.

'She was the youngest daughter of a family of gentry who had lost their money through unwise speculation in the late wars. They lived in a tumbledown manor house

near York. All the older sisters married early and, if not
well, quite decently. Her parents were naturally overjoyed
when I began to show that I was serious in my intentions
towards her. After all, I was Earl Falconer's son, even if
only a younger one, and he would see that we had a decent
living one way or another.

'My way was to go into the Navy, and before I left for
my first service in it it was agreed that when I came home
on leave the arrangements would be made for us to marry.
Both our parents thought that we were a little too young to
rush into marriage straight away. I suspect that for some
reason my father delayed it—her parents were much more
eager.

'At first she wrote to me quite regularly, although as was
the way at sea I often got a whole budget of letters at one
go, after receiving nothing for months. Suddenly the letters
stopped altogether, until one day I received one from her...'
He stopped, turned his face towards Stacy, and she could
see that he was not with her; he was reliving the pain of
that day again.

'It said, quite simply, that she no longer wished to marry
me, that what we had shared was a boy-and-girl love—that
Rollo had proposed to her and she was going to marry him!
It was the story of Prince, and a score of other hurts, all
over again. She wasn't the sort of girl whom Rollo had
ever shown any interest in before. He liked them big and
showy. It was just that she was mine, and he was taking
her away from me. I learned afterwards that her parents
brought enormous pressure on her to throw me over. After
all, if they had thought Earl Falconer's younger son was a
great catch, imagine what they made of it when his heir
offered for her, a virtually dowerless girl. Perhaps she was
a little dazzled by him, too; he was considered to be very
handsome. Although now I think not. I don't think that she
ever cared for him, but she dared not defy her parents.

'I'm not sure what my father thought. Probably that all

she and I had shared was puppy-love, as they say, and Rollo at that time was the apple of his eye; he could do no wrong. Later was a different matter, but by then it was too late.

'They were married when I was at sea. I didn't come back to The Eyrie for a long time after that, not until I was wounded at Trafalgar and they sent me home. I was put on half-pay, so I lost even my navy career, the thought of which had been something of a consolation to me after losing Camilla. Father wanted me to go into the *Corps Diplomatique*. He had a lot of influence then, but what subsequently happened put an end to that.

'When I went home all that I could think of was that I would see Camilla again. What I never thought of was how much she might have changed. She had always been delicately pretty, pink and white, with a charming manner and what I had thought was an enchanting laugh. Nothing of that was left. She was sallow and haunted-looking. When I met her again she turned her face away and could hardly look at me.

'Rollo's manner to her in public was always correct and loving. He claimed to be puzzled as to why she was so constantly ill. She was breeding, he told me carelessly, and that was probably why she looked such a fright.

'"I hope to God she looks a little more *comme il faut* when she has had the heir," he drawled at me. "I can't stand all this weeping and wailing; she's forever having the vapours, and never seems fit enough to perform her wifely duties." I think that he talked like that about her to taunt me.

'I wasn't feeling very well when I first got back to Yorkshire, but as I recovered my strength Camilla's condition worried me more and more. Seeing her again had revived all my old love and compassion for her. Oh, I know now that it was quite a different sort of love from that which I feel for you—there was no passion in it, and what would have happened if we had married sometimes worries me.

But then, I was ablaze with anger at what I clearly saw was Rollo's mistreatment of her. And my father couldn't seem to see it.

'Matters came to a head one day when I came across her in the gardens; we had been avoiding one another. She was sitting in the small gazebo, looking away from the house, not the folly you used to sit in before Hal was born. She had been crying. I remember that it was a warm day and she was wearing quite a heavy shawl. She was so different from the little fairy that I had fallen in love with that I could hardly believe that she was the same person.

'I remember that I asked her if there was anything I could do for her, since she was so plainly unhappy. She shook her head and said no, nobody could help her. She couldn't help herself. She had made a mistake in marrying Rollo, and that was that. I couldn't help myself; I put an arm around her. God knows, I meant nothing by it; she was big with my brother's child and I was only trying to comfort her.

'She gave a great cry and pulled herself away from me, and half-shrieked, "No, don't touch me, don't." I don't know why I did it, but as gently as I could I pulled the shawl away, and then I saw. All the great bruises down her arms, and even on her neck. I knew then why she wore long sleeves in the height of summer, and dresses with high collars.

'I remember sitting there trembling, saying to her one word—"Rollo"—because her condition explained so much. She put her thumb in her mouth and whispered through it, "He mustn't know you know. He'd kill me." I asked her why she hadn't told my father, and she said that she was afraid of him. Not that he had done or said anything unpleasant; he was always kind to her, but he thought the world of Rollo... I could see that it was hopeless; Rollo had broken her spirit.

'I didn't know what to do. I was still little more than a

boy, only twenty-one, and despite my hard life in the Navy, and all I had seen and done there, I was still inexperienced in the ways of the great world. For several days I debated what to do to save my lost love, and then events took their own course. My father went away to London—he had a minor post in the Cabinet—which gave Rollo the freedom to practise even more cruelties. That last afternoon he drank too much at dinner, snarled at me, snarled at Camilla—I remember how she shrank away from him—until finally he took her by the hand and dragged her off to their rooms. He shouted at me as he left that he was tired of seeing my hanging-judge's face, and couldn't wait for me to leave.

'I went to my own rooms. About an hour later I heard noises, running feet, Camilla's voice raised. She was outside, in the stable-yard—my room overlooked it—talking to one of the grooms, a boy who was always ready to do things for her.

'He was doing something for her, something he should not have been doing. He was readying one of the small chaises for use. I saw that Camilla had a bag in her hand; she was calling feverishly to him to hurry. Finally she climbed into the chaise, the groom was on the box and they were off, clattering out of the yard. There was no sign of Rollo.

'I picked up my coat and ran downstairs. I ran into the yard and roared at Beckett—he was Thwaites' predecessor—Where is Stephen taking Lady Radley?

'He looked at me as though I were witless. "He's not taking her anywhere, Mr Matt."

'I said something like, Don't treat me like a fool, Beckett, and then Sim Farrell came running up. "He's taking her down to London to her folks, Mr Matt, and about time too. We all know what m'lord's been a-doing to her!"

'Beckett was as nonplussed as I was, and roared at Sim, "You fool, Sim, that's your job gone!"

'I stood there, my head whirling. She was very near her

time, and setting off for London with only an ignorant boy with her was the last thing that she ought to have been doing—and where was Rollo?

'Beckett was so shocked he was almost witless himself. As well he might have been—he was turned off for not having the gumption to stop Stephen—even though he had no idea what Stephen was doing.

'I had only one thought in my head; to go after her and help her. Saddle my horse, I flung at Sim. I'll ride after them, try to get her back.

'That ride passed in a dream, a nightmare. I finally caught up with them after changing horses at Selby. I nearly rode past the inn where they had stopped to change horses again, but fortunately, or unfortunately, I recognised the chaise as I rode past the inn-yard.

'Camilla was sitting in the parlour. She looked worse than ever. I ran over to her, said something wild about whatever did she think that she was doing.'

He was suddenly not with Stacy any more. He had gone back in time. He was in the parlour, holding Camilla's hands.

'You must come back with me, Camilla. You're not fit to travel to London when you're so near your time.'

She looked up at him, the once cornflower-blue eyes dark with suffering. 'I won't go back, Matt. I will kill myself rather. You have no notion of how dreadfully he treated me. This afternoon he started to beat me so cruelly I began to fear for my baby's life. I fought him. He was so drunk he found it difficult to overmaster me. I hit him over the head with one of the bronze statuettes from Pompeii. He fell down and didn't get up again. I know that I didn't kill him, for he was still breathing. He was only stunned. I can't stay with him, Matt. Don't make me go back. I want to go home to my father and mother. I know that they're in London.'

She said all this in a tired, matter-of-fact voice which

had Matt trembling. 'You must go back to The Eyrie,' he told her desperately, for he knew that her father and mother would not stand by her. They had sold her to Rollo, and that was that. 'I shall go to my father and tell him the truth.'

She began to shiver and shake, her hands writhing together, her face ghastly. 'I won't go back. I would rather die in a ditch than go back. I have an aunt in Chelsea; perhaps she will take me in.' Then she added almost inconsequentially, 'You know, Rollo often told me that he only married me to take me away from you. He said that you wouldn't want me when you saw what I had turned into.'

Matt took her into his arms as gently as he could and told her the truth. 'I shall always love you, Camilla, and I shall always try to help you.' But he had never felt so helpless. In the face of her determination and her suffering he could no longer argue that they should return to The Eyrie.

Stephen came in. Matt said wearily, 'I suppose you know that you'll be turned away for this?'

'So?' Stephen shot back at him. 'A fine sort of man I should be to stand by and see what I have seen without doing something. I'm surprised at you, Mr Matt. Want her to go back for him to beat her again, do you?'

'No,' he said, and made up his mind. 'I'll take her to her aunt at Chelsea, if that's what she wants.'

He told Stacy, whose face was now as white as his as she listened to his long and painful tale, 'But, of course, we never got to Chelsea. Twenty miles further on her pains started. I had left my horse at the last stop and was travelling with her. The postilion was driving, Stephen beside him on the box. I stopped the coach at the next inn and carried her in, as I carried you into the cottage where Hal was born.

'But Camilla's baby was born dead. It had been dead for some little time. And Rollo had probably killed it, if what

Camilla said to me in her delirium after his birth was true. I cannot tell you how much she suffered while her child was being born, and how long it took.

'I was not with her. But I sat on the inn stairs and could hear all her agony. The landlady thought that we were eloping; she was certain something discreditable was happening and she raved and shouted at me for making a woman in such a condition travel at all.

'They let me in to see her when it was all over, and even now I can hardly bear to think of it. I had seen what a warship looked like after a battle, but what I saw in that bedroom beggared description. And my poor Camilla lay there dying, killed by my brother as surely as though he had run a sword through her heart... So now you know why I was not brave when Hal started to arrive, and why I thought that I was going to lose you. That I would have two loves and would lose both of them in the same cruel fashion.'

'But you were brave in the end,' riposted Stacy, squeezing his hand lovingly. 'Without you Hal might not have survived. And, now that you have shared your story with me, I understand why you felt and behaved as you did. The only thing that I don't understand is why everyone blamed you, why you had to leave home and were given such a bad name. After all, you only went after Camilla to save her.'

Matt's smile was a twisted one. 'Oh, when Rollo came to, and found out what had happened and started after us, he arranged everything so that the blame fell on me. Stephen and Sim were turned away and told that if they betrayed what had actually happened he would make sure that they would never work again, which was enough to silence them. Beckett, too, was bought off. By the time my father was informed and arrived on the scene, several days later, it was fully established that Camilla and I were running away, that we were guilty lovers. Rollo couldn't pretend that Camilla's child was mine, but everything else which could blacken me was thrown at me.

'The landlady at the inn didn't help; she blamed me for making Camilla travel when her time was so near. Nobody helped me, or would listen to anything I said in my defence. My father believed every word Rollo said. Camilla's parents accused me of killing her. If I hadn't persuaded her to run away with me, they said, then the child would have been born alive at The Eyrie and Camilla wouldn't have died.

'No one thought to ask themselves where in the world I could have been taking Camilla to, without a penny in my pocket, and no home of my own. I didn't help myself much. I was incoherent with grief and anger. When I tried to tell anyone—even my father—the truth of the matter concerning Rollo and Camilla I was called even worse names for attempting to blacken the character of the grieving widower. One of the reasons I was so harsh to you at first, at Pontisford, was because you reminded me of all the fine ladies who had torn my poor Camilla to pieces after her death.

'She was given a hole-and-corner funeral, which I was not allowed to attend, and when I said that I wanted to leave the Navy—the Navy didn't want me anyway—and go to the small estate which my mother had left me in Virginia everyone was only too happy to see the back of me.

'So there you have it. Until I met my dear Lady Disdain, organising and managing everyone's affairs, driving me mad because I could see that beneath her icy exterior there were fires of passion blazing in which I wished to immolate myself, I never felt true affection or love for a woman again. I think that I was afraid to...' There were tears in his eyes as he finished.

For a moment there was silence in the peaceful room. Stacy gently stroked the hand which held hers. 'Oh, Matt, what a terrible story. Poor Camilla, and poor you. I can quite understand that when I began to give birth so incontinently, and in such an isolated situation, it revived all your most painful memories and fears. I am astounded that you found yourself able to help me at all.'

She stopped, and for a moment they were silent again, Matt remembering his lost first love and Stacy seeing a young Matt, quite alone, desolate, and his life lying in ruins about him. It explained so much that had puzzled her. She told him so, adding, 'And will it be too painful for you to stay in England, my love? I know how much you loved your American home.'

Matt shook his head vigorously. 'If I were still the younger son, with no ties, then I would take you back there, but I am not. I am the heir and I have my duty to do, and will do it cheerfully, I hope, with you by my side.'

He leaned over to kiss her cheek. 'And now I'm not afraid to give my heart to you, to risk you having another child, thanks to your bravery while you were bearing Hal. And to some extent I think that I have my father's affection back again. He may never know the whole story of Rollo's treatment of Camilla, but I could not wish him to. Let us leave him with some of his illusions. As to the future— well, I only hope that for our next child there will be a warm, comfortable bedroom, a doctor and nurses standing by, and that I may be allowed to pace outside in the corridor with my shirt safely on!'

Stacy kissed him back with interest. 'Well, I hope that you may have your wish, sir, and that we may soon set about fulfilling it. But, I warn you, I shall also expect Grandam Outhwaite to be present, with both of her blue bottles, for, although you and I birthed the baby, she made sure that we all recovered from it afterwards.'

At that moment there was a series of loud squawks from the nursery next door. Stacy laughed up at her husband, whose face had lightened appreciably since he had at last rid himself of some of the burden which he had carried for so many years.

She said mischievously, 'One day I shall tell you why I call Hal our little lion-cub, but in the meantime you must fetch him to me so that I may feed him, and while I do so we shall discuss buying a wolfhound for you, to replace Prince, for life is about renewal as well as death, my dear.'

Her husband did as he was bid, and sat and watched her feed their 'little cub', as she called him, and thought that on the day on which he had opened the door to the Bank-eress he had opened the door to a new life for them both as well.

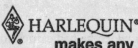

You're not going to believe this offer!

In October and November 2000, buy any two Harlequin or Silhouette books and save $10.00 off future purchases, or buy any three and save $20.00 off future purchases!

Just fill out this form and attach 2 proofs of purchase (cash register receipts) from October and November 2000 books and Harlequin will send you a coupon booklet worth a total savings of $10.00 off future purchases of Harlequin and Silhouette books in 2001. Send us 3 proofs of purchase and we will send you a coupon booklet worth a total savings of $20.00 off future purchases.

Saving money has never been this easy.

I accept your offer! Please send me a coupon booklet:

Name: _____

Address: _____ City: _____

State/Prov.: _____ Zip/Postal Code: _____

Optional Survey!

In a typical month, how many Harlequin or Silhouette books would you buy <u>new</u> at retail stores?

☐ Less than 1   ☐ 1   ☐ 2   ☐ 3 to 4   ☐ 5+

Which of the following statements best describes how you <u>buy</u> Harlequin or Silhouette books? Choose one answer only that <u>best</u> describes you.

☐ I am a regular buyer and reader
☐ I am a regular reader but buy only occasionally
☐ I only buy and read for specific times of the year, e.g. vacations
☐ I subscribe through Reader Service but also buy at retail stores
☐ I mainly borrow and buy only occasionally
☐ I am an occasional buyer and reader

Which of the following statements best describes how you <u>choose</u> the Harlequin and Silhouette series books you buy <u>new</u> at retail stores? By "series," we mean books within a particular line, such as *Harlequin PRESENTS* or *Silhouette SPECIAL EDITION*. Choose one answer only that <u>best</u> describes you.

☐ I only buy books from my favorite series
☐ I generally buy books from my favorite series but also buy books from other series on occasion
☐ I buy some books from my favorite series but also buy from many other series regularly
☐ I buy all types of books depending on my mood and what I find interesting and have no favorite series

Please send this form, along with your cash register receipts as proofs of purchase, to:
In the U.S.: Harlequin Books, P.O. Box 9057, Buffalo, NY 14269
In Canada: Harlequin Books, P.O. Box 622, Fort Erie, Ontario L2A 5X3
(Allow 4-6 weeks for delivery) Offer expires December 31, 2000.   PHQ4002

Presenting...  HARLEQUIN®

REGENCY ROMANCE

Experience the opulence of the era captured
vividly in these novels. Visit elegant country manors,
town houses and the English countryside and explore
the whirlwind of social engagements that London
"Society" revolved around. Embark on captivating
adventures with the feisty heroines who
unintentionally tame the roguish
heroes with their wit, zest
and feminine charm!

Available in October at your favorite retail outlet:

A MOST EXCEPTIONAL QUEST by Sarah Westleigh
DEAR LADY DISDAIN by Paula Marshall
SERENA by Sylvia Andrew
SCANDAL AND MISS SMITH by Julia Byrne

Look for more marriage & mayhem coming in March 2001.

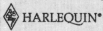

Visit us at www.eHarlequin.com   PHREG1CCAN

Presenting... HARLEQUIN®

REGENCY ROMANCE

Experience the opulence of the era captured vividly in these novels. Visit elegant country manors, town houses and the English countryside and explore the whirlwind of social engagements that London "Society" revolved around. Embark on captivating adventures with the feisty heroines who unintentionally tame the roguish heroes with their wit, zest and feminine charm!

Available in October at your favorite retail outlet:

A MOST EXCEPTIONAL QUEST by Sarah Westleigh
DEAR LADY DISDAIN by Paula Marshall
SERENA by Sylvia Andrew
SCANDAL AND MISS SMITH by Julia Byrne

Look for more marriage & mayhem coming in March 2001.

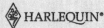

Visit us at www.eHarlequin.com   PHREG1CUS